WAVEBORN

MIKAYLA WHITAKER

Mikayla Whitaker © 2021

All rights reserved. No part of this publication may be reproduced, stored or transmitted in any form or by any means, electronic, mechanical, photocopying, recording, scanning, or otherwise without written permission from the publisher. It is illegal to copy this book, post it to a website, or distribute it by any other means without permission.

This novel is entirely a work of fiction. The names, characters and incidents portrayed in it are the work of the author's imagination. Any resemblance to actual persons, living or dead, events or localities is entirely coincidental.

Hardback ISBN 978-1-0879-4965-9

Paperback ISBN 978-1-0879-5341-0

Edited by Jessica McKellen

Cover design by MiblArt

Published by Mikayla Whitaker

To the dreamers.

TABLE OF CONTENTS

ONE 1
TWO 17
THREE 33
FOUR 47
FIVE 59
SIX 69
SEVEN 85
EIGHT 99
NINE 107
TEN 121
ELEVEN 131
TWELVE 143
THIRTEEN 165
FOURTEEN 179
FIFTEEN 191
SIXTEEN 203
SEVENTEEN 215
EIGHTEEN 227
NINETEEN 239
TWENTY 249
TWENTY-ONE 261

TWENTY-TWO	273
TWENTY-THREE	285
TWENTY-FOUR	297
TWENTY-FIVE	317
TWENTY-SIX	331
TWENTY-SEVEN	345
TWENTY-EIGHT	361
TWENTY-NINE	373
THIRTY	385
THIRTY-ONE	399
THIRTY-TWO	407
THIRTY-THREE	419
EPILOGUE	431
ACKNOWLEDGMENTS	431
ABOUT THE AUTHOR	433

ONE

Ocean boulevard, which ran parallel to the ten miles of ocean-side property along the length of the city, was home to many resorts, restaurants, and the infamous SkyWheel, offering tourists and residents alike a stunning view of the sea from high in the air. But Ocean Boulevard wasn't just home to these sites; it was also home to a three-bedroom beach house hidden between two large skyscrapers. There, at 305 South Ocean Boulevard, sat my grandmother's old cottage, with its blue-green shutters sitting stark against the tan siding of the exterior. This was my home now, complete with half an acre of lush grass and a wooden gate that led straight to the powdery white sand overlooking the sea.

When I entered the beachside cottage, I felt the real mahogany flooring underneath my feet and the wood cabinetry in the kitchen across the room. I had immediately fallen in love with the open floor concept when I visited it years ago when my grandmother was still alive. Smiling to myself, I walked back out to grab my luggage; the moving truck would be here soon, and I was lucky to have convinced them to help move all my furniture and appliances—there was no way I'd be able to do that all on my own. Good thing I didn't have a lot of belongings. I guess it should only take me an afternoon to set up my entire house. Afterward, I planned to organize my guest bedrooms, filling them with comfy blue and white comforters and tons and tons of throw pillows. Not that I planned to have anyone over to sleep in the guest rooms, but who knew? I could always rent out a room to someone in the future.

Once I hung up my clothes in the closet, I heard the loud sound of a horn. Pulling the last shirt onto the hanger, I set it on the hook in my closet and turned around to walk back outside into the sea breeze in order to greet the movers who would help me this afternoon.

As I was locking the front door in its open position, my phone rang, letting out a soft tune before I made a grab for it out of my back pocket. I had texted my mother's best friend, Claire, earlier to let her know I had arrived safely. She had responded immediately, pleased that I had kept my word and gotten in touch with her. She offered to send her son, John, to help unload my furniture if it got to be too much for me. She had moved to South Carolina years ago and I had spent summers up here whenever I could. John had always been a brother to me and didn't mind showing me all the different things we could do on the coast. I guess that was one reason I had fallen in love with the ocean—the peace I felt and the desire to protect it all.

"Hey, Claire," I said, answering the call.

"Hello, dear. I was just wondering how you are getting on. Has the truck arrived yet? Do you need John to come help?" she drawled on the other side of the line, her southern accent hanging on every word.

"Oh, what great timing! The truck has just arrived. If you're sure John won't mind coming over, I can give you the address," I commented, smiling to one of the movers as he waved, walking around to the back of the truck to unlock the door. "I'm sure the guys would love an extra pair of hands."

"One second," she said in her cheery voice before she yelled at her son to get his big butt off the couch and help me move. I couldn't hear John's response from the background, but before I could ask what he said, Claire spoke again. "He'll be right over, dear."

"Alright," I said. "If he's sure, tell him I appreciate the help. He will be able to park in the driveway; there's plenty of room."

"He'll see you soon." She giggled at something I couldn't hear before hanging up.

"Good news, boys," I called to the movers, shaking my head before stuffing my phone back into my pocket. "Not only do you have me, but my friend is on his way to help too. We don't have to wait though; we can start now if y'all want." One of them nodded as he came behind me with a box. "Whatever the box is labeled, please set it in the designated room."

"Alright, ma'am," said one of the men. He wore a black T-shirt and a pair of jeans, and was carrying a box labeled "Dishes" in big black letters.

Just as I was about to grab another box, someone pulled into the driveway next to my blue truck. The white truck seemed to be identical to my own except for the color. The driver got out, messing with the cuff of his shirt before throwing a ball cap on, sunglasses resting on it just like his father always did.

"Hey, Annie!" John greeted as he came toward me, pulling me into a tight bear hug, just as he did every time he saw me. I had to admit, John was attractive with his fiery red hair that emphasized his pale skin that he had inherited from his mother. I had always seen him as a brother, though, even though his mother had always wished we would get together. "How have you been? You know, it's been years, and I was wondering how my baby sister was doing." His blue eyes sparkled when he said this, smiling down at me while he shielded his eyes from the sun.

"I'm older than you, John," I said matter-of-factly, resting my hand on my hip and looking up at him teasingly. "And aw, you missed me?"

"I'm still taller than you, so that makes you my baby sister."

I laughed. "Whatever, Johnny!" I teased. "Alright, are you ready to get to work?"

"I told you I hate that name," he hissed, only half angry. He looked back at me before reaching over to ruffle my hair, but failed when I swatted his hand away. "And yes, *Anna*, I'm as ready as I'll ever be."

"Alright, let's do this," I said, ignoring his comment as I grabbed a box from the trailer while John helped one mover grab the wooden china hutch that had been my grandmother's and then my mother's before they'd passed it on to me.

"Where would you like this?" they asked, passing me.

"Oh, just set it along the wall in the living room," I said, as I set the cardboard box on the kitchen counter.

In a few hours, we had all the furniture and appliances set up in the house. All I had left to do was put away my belongings, then grab groceries at Walmart. Grabbing my wallet from my purse, I handed the movers a twenty, then waved them off as John turned to me.

"Thank you, John, for your help," I said, looking him in the eyes as I smiled appreciatively.

"You're welcome." He smiled. "Do you need help unloading the boxes?"

"Um, if you want to?"

"I'd be happy to help my baby sister with her boxes," John said as we walked back inside and shut the door behind us.

"Oh hush," I called, following him. "I hate it when you tease!"

"You know you love me!" he shot back with a grin, opening one of the many boxes that lined the kitchen counters.

Two hours later, we finished decorating my home, filling the kitchen with all its utensils and dishware, and furnishing each bedroom with its respective dresser, bed, and bedding. Plopping down on the couch, I closed my eyes in contentment as I sighed, enjoying how my home looked and felt with me and my belongings in it. I looked up at John, who was lingering in the front entryway.

"Thank you, again, John."

"You're welcome. If you need nothing else, I think I'm going to head home," he said, walking toward the front door.

Jumping off the couch, I grabbed my wallet and turned to John, throwing a ten into his hand before he could open the door.

"Oh, no, you don't need to pay me," he protested, trying to hand me back the money.

"Are you sure?" I asked. "That was like five hours of work!"

"My mother would kill me if she found out I accepted money from you," he mumbled. "It's fine, really."

"Okay," I replied, sticking the money back in my wallet. "Well, have a safe drive."

"Thanks." He smiled before hugging me quick and opening the front door to leave me alone in my new home. As the silence began to fill the room, I felt my mind begin to wonder to places I wished I would no longer think about: my nightmares of my parent's deaths. Suddenly, without thinking, they filled my vision, holding me captive as I remembered the day of my mother's crash. The devastation coursing through me when she was pronounced dead at the scene and how I had no idea I would lose my father a year later to cancer. I bit back the sob that threatened to escape my trembling lips and breathed in, desperately wishing I wouldn't think about them anymore even though my heart ached to see them again. I wanted to hear their laughter and smell my father's familiar aftershave. I wanted to take our monthly camping trip again. I wanted them here. When I heard John's engine turn over, I grabbed my purse and the grocery list I had made earlier and exited my beach home, locking the door behind me.

    Throwing my purse onto the passenger seat, I quickly crawled into the driver's seat and shut the door. I started the truck, the roar of the engine making me smile before looking behind me at the sea and driving into town. I knew at that moment that this was the start of a new adventure, one that I couldn't wait to see what would happen next.

***

    With a large huff, I dropped the seven sacks onto the dining room table, sweat dripping down my forehead, the weight from the groceries leaving my arms. Man, that was a lot, I didn't realize just how much I actually needed until I got to the store. Filling a kitchen all in one day is rough. Before emptying the sacks, I turned the television on, and the news played through the speakers that John had helped set up. I looked up as the news crew talked about the weather and the swell report for today's surf. I knew one of these days, I would learn how to surf, and I couldn't wait to get started. Maybe after I finished with my groceries, I could take a dip in the cool ocean that my home faced.

Shutting the fridge, I folded all of my cloth sacks and set them near the front door before heading to my bedroom to change into my swimsuit. Peeling off my clothes, I quickly changed and grabbed my beach bag from my closet. Throwing a towel into it, I padded into the kitchen to grab a few water bottles. Suddenly my stomach growled, urging me to eat something before I did anything else. Shaking my head, I made a sandwich, eating it in silence while I looked around the room, admiring the overwhelming amount of beach-themed décor that filled the home after years of collecting them, I could finally use them. I still wanted to go swimming, but knew as soon as the sun was gone, it was dangerous to swim alone.

After I ate, I slid the glass door open, stepping outside. Opening the wooden gate that would lead me to the white sandy beach behind my house, I instantly felt more at home than I ever had before. Pink and orange hues danced across the water, beckoning me closer to the stretch of water behind my home. My feet squished into the partially wet sand, tiny seashells littered the ground below me, leaving their unique print in the sand as I walked around them before my feet touched the water crawling toward me. Laying out my towel, I spun back to the water, grinning as I ran toward it.

Within moments, I was neck deep in the water, swimming happily while the waves rose and broke around me. I felt absolutely free here—that was, until I felt something scaly brush against my leg. I felt my heart stop as panic set in, staring down into the dark water while I tried to see what had just touched my leg.

Within seconds, whatever had touched me before brush against my skin again, making me lose my footing and drop fully into the water. I let out a scream only for it to muffle as the water cascaded over my face. Kicking my legs, I surfaced as quickly as I could, spitting out the saltwater as I drew in quick, panicked breaths. Looking around, I tried to swim away from the spot, feeling a little uneasy. I knew I shouldn't be scared—it was probably just a fish—but in the pit of my stomach, I wasn't exactly sure what this creature was. I knew from experience that sharks didn't have that texture on their bodies.

"Hello!" Someone called near me. I turned toward the low voice, finding myself face to face with a man I had never met. His eyes were silver, nearly white against the white of his eyes, and his long, black hair was wet, sticking to his head. The water seemed to calm around us. "Are you alright?" he asked.

I opened my mouth to speak, but nothing came out.

His brow furrowed, confusion filling his features. "Do you understand me?"

All I could do was nod, knowing that he shouldn't be here. This was a private beach and he was trespassing.

"Can you speak?" he persisted, swimming closer to me.

I felt the scaly creature brush up against my leg again. Panic consumed me as I swam away frantically.

"It's alright. I will not hurt you."

"What—why are you here? You aren't supposed to be here. This is a private beach," I rasped, panic lacing my tone. "Is that a fish? What keeps brushing against me?"

"I think it's just a fish," he replied.

"Okay, well, I would be mindful of where you swim next time," I said, making my way toward shore.

"Wait," he called. "What's your name?"

I turned, the water up to my waist, and smiled, unsure of what to tell him. I didn't want him to know my actual name was Anna, and I gave him my nickname instead. "Annie."

I watched as he mouthed my name back, a hint of a smile on his face. before I turned around and walked onto the shore, feeling the water run down my legs and seep, into the cooling sand. Grabbing my towel off the ground, I dried myself. Glancing back out to sea, I realized instantly that the man who had shown up unexpectedly, who I had just spoken to moments before, was now nowhere to be seen, almost as if he had never been there. All that was left were the waves crashing onto shore.

Confused, I stared at the ocean, my wet hair clinging to my shoulders and face, wondering if something had happened to him or if the creature had pulled him under. But he hadn't called out as if he was in trouble, and I would have been able to hear him if that were the case. As I stared, I wondered if I would ever see the mysterious man again or if he was just a figment of my imagination.

I remembered the feeling of the scaly creature brushing up against me and how quickly the man had arrived straight after it happened. I shook my head. I knew that what I was thinking wasn't likely, was crazy even, but only five percent of the earth's seas had been explored. He couldn't be a merman. It had probably just been a fish. I was being ridiculous. There were no such things as mermaids; they were just stories and nothing else.

When I stared back out to sea, I saw the faintest sign of a fluke breaking the surface, right before it disappeared back into the sea.

TWO

The faucet let out a loud squeak as I turned the shower on. Within seconds, it sprung to life, water pouring out of the shower head, filling the bathroom with steam. Peeling my bathing suit off, I dropped it, letting it fall to the ground with a wet flop before stepping into the tub. I pulled the shower curtain closed and turned toward the water, walking under the waterfall, feeling the sand and salt leave my body, spiraling down the drain.

With a sigh, I felt my muscles relax and I closed my eyes in contentment. As the minutes ticked by, I stood under the water for longer than I probably should have before I made a move to grab my shampoo. Pouring a generous amount into my palm, I kneaded the substance into my natural ginger hair, which was seemed to be darker in the water. Scrubbing until suds covered my hands and arms, I washed the soap away, hoping that I could get all the sand out, although I knew some grains would still stick to my scalp no matter how many times I washed my hair.

    After my shower, I grabbed the large blue towel from its hook and wrapped it around myself, my hair falling in curly ringlets past my shoulders. Padding into my room, I hoped I wouldn't slip and fall, then realized that was probably the least of my problems because I had forgotten to close the curtains before taking my shower. Closing my bedroom door behind me, I sighed, padding over to the large window overlooking the sea, and pulled the curtains closed, accidentally letting the towel fall to the floor.

    "Really?" I exclaimed to no one in particular before reluctantly picking up the towel and drying my body before wrapping my hair up in it. Walking over to my dresser, I pulled out my comfy set of silk cami pajamas and slipped them on.

    The sun was beginning to set by the time I walked into the kitchen to make myself some dinner. The pink and purple hues lit up the sky and reflected across the water as the sun escaped behind the horizon. Smiling to myself, I made myself a quick sandwich, then headed out to the back porch where a lawn chair sat waiting. Easing down into the chair, I stared at the sunset, watching the colors dance across the waves in perfect harmony.

I had a week off before I started my new job at the Marine Life Institute in Myrtle Beach, and I was determined to make tomorrow a worthwhile and fun experience. I would visit every store, learn to surf, maybe even catch my first wave, but I knew I wanted tomorrow to be the most memorable start to my new life. I hoped the weather would stay like today's beautiful eighty degrees.

As I ate, I listened to the calming sound of the waves, relishing the peace I felt in that moment. I enjoyed having the ocean so close to my home. In minutes, I finished eating and walked back inside to wash my plate. After setting it on the drying rack, I walked throughout my house to shut off all the lights, taking my time and admiring my new space. By the time I crawled into bed, I was exhausted. I felt my body relax once more, my eyelids growing heavy as the calming pull of sleep overtook me and I fell into a dreamless sleep.

***

I awoke to the soft sea breeze blowing through my open window, the curtains blowing in the wind while the room filled with the smell of salt and sea. I blinked twice, trying to ease my grogginess as the sun shone through the windows and across my face. Yawning, I sat up in bed, letting the covers fall into a heap on my lap. I crawled out of bed and padded over to the window, opening up the curtains fully so that I could have a better view of the outside world. The sky was as blue as could be, and the water was just as gorgeous. A chime from the bedside table took my attention from the sight of the sea and over to my phone. Grabbing the device off my bedside table, I turned it on, slid my finger across the screen to turn it off, and smiled, knowing that today was going to be a perfect day.

I shimmied out of my pajamas and threw on a pair of denim shorts and a light blue tank top over my purple and pink bikini swimsuit. My favorite thing about being in a beach town was that I could wear my swimsuit into town and no one cared. Making my way into the kitchen, I grabbed a banana off the counter and munched on it while I made a mental list of the things I wanted to do today. Once I finished, I dropped the banana peel into the trashcan and threw a water bottle into my swim bag. I combed my hair with my fingers, grabbed my purse and keys, then threw on a pair of my sandals and was out the door without a second thought. Locking the door behind me, I hopped into my truck, ready to spend time in the city I was now a resident of and planned to live in for the rest of my days.

***

By the time I made it there, the parking lot of Ripley's Aquarium was packed. It was understandable, as it was June and right in the middle of the busiest tourist season the city hosted every year. Shutting my car off, I pulled my purse out, leaving my beach bag on the passenger seat, and slammed the door behind me. Following the wave of tourists, I waited patiently behind a woman with her toddler, silently hoping that I could enter the aquarium in a timely manner. After thirty minutes, I finally made it inside.

The lady behind the register smiled, greeting me as I walked forward. Smiling back, I requested a ticket to the aquarium, knowing that there were several exhibits within this one building. She only nodded before ringing me up and handing me my receipt. "You can just go through those doors," she said, motioning toward a pair of glass doors to my left.

"Thank you!" I exclaimed, before heading through the double doors and making my way into the aquarium.

Soft blue lights illuminated the room, dark as to not disturb the sea creatures inhabiting the surrounding tanks. I watched silently as stingrays swam along the sand, throwing it as they skidded across. A clownfish darted around a sea anemone moving in and out of its tentacles several times before swimming along the coral. I remembered the first time I had ever visited an aquarium. I was twelve, and I had been dying for my parents to take me ever since the aquarium opened. At such a young age, I was entirely captivated by those sea creatures and knew that when I grew up, I would spend my life dedicated to protecting them. That was what I had been trying to do ever since.

An hour passed faster than expected, so I left the aquarium without seeing every exhibit. I had scheduled my first surf lesson with the Surf City Surf Shop across town at one o'clock and had just enough time to drive over there and look around their store before it was time to take my lesson. I made my way back to my truck to begin the eight-minute drive back toward the sea.

As I entered the Surf Shop, the soft sound of the radio greeted me. Rows and rows of swimwear, wetsuits, and surfboards filled the store's interior, along with, of course, ankle leashes, surfboard wax, T-shirts, and several South Carolina knickknacks. Making my way over to the surfboards, I ran my hand along a blue and white five-foot short that matched my five-foot six height perfectly. Smiling to myself, I tiptoed to the longboards, every once in a while looking at my phone to check the time. I suppose if I had been paying attention to my surroundings rather than staring intently at the surfboards in front of me, I would have noticed when the sale associate came over, or that he had been standing behind me for longer than a minute before he spoke.

"Hi, can I help you?" he asked, startling me. I jumped nearly three feet. "Oh, I'm sorry. I didn't mean to startle you."

Turning around to face the shopkeeper, I smiled. "You're fine."

"Can I help you find anything?" he asked again, looking at me with apologetic eyes.

"Oh, no, maybe later. I have a surfing lesson at one, so I just wanted to browse while I waited," I replied, looking down at my phone again. "It's nearly one, so I should probably head over there. It was nice talking to you."

Exiting the shop, I mentally scolded myself for my lack of social skills. It was only a few minutes' drive to the beach, and I was thankful when I parked. I grabbed my beach bag and jumped out of my vehicle. I could hear the waves before I saw them, giddy excitement coursing through my veins as I made my way down the wooden ramp to the sea. Scanning the area for my surf instructor, I continued to walk, hoping I would eventually find them before it was time for the lesson to start. Of course, as I was about to turn around to go back, I spotted a small group several feet away from me, various surfboards scattered around them as they stood in the sand. Picking up my pace, I ran over to them, hoping I wasn't too late.

"Ah, there you are!" a man wearing a pair of swim trunks and a lightweight shirt exclaimed, turning toward me.

"Sorry," I mumbled, dropping my stuff next to me.

"Alright, now that everyone's here, let's begin," the man yelled after introducing himself as Daniel.

Half an hour came and went as we practiced the pop-up position on our boards and how to paddle out to sea. I knew I probably wouldn't catch a wave on my first time out, but I was extremely excited to get out and do it. Excitement filled me with a giddy warmth that spread throughout my body, further intensifying my impatience to begin the lesson in the water.

It seemed like hours passed before we could jump in the water, but of course we couldn't go deep. Daniel had us go in one at a time, instructing us on the best time to pop up on the board, and what we should do when we caught the wave.

I watched as Daniel turned my way, motioning for me to take my turn. I paddled toward the wave, turning at the best possible time. and when I felt the water pick me up, I popped up, placing my feet firmly and steadily on the board as the water pushed me further toward shore. At that moment, I was hooked.

***

By the time I made it home, it was nearly three and I was absolutely exhausted. Pushing my front door open, I wobbled into my living room, sand covering my skin and the smell of salt in my hair. I padded into my bathroom and turned the tub's faucet on, checking the water temperature before putting the plug into the drain. As the tub filled, I threw in a few handfuls of bath salts, the calming smell of lavender filling the bathroom with its aroma.

As I got undressed, I wondered about the man I had met yesterday. I remembered the way his brow had knit together when he thought I didn't understand him, and the beautiful silver color of his eyes. Suddenly, my cheeks burned and I shook my head, trying to think of anything other than that stranger. Stepping into the tub, I sunk down, the water flowing over me. I gently brushed the sand skin and I watched it sink to the bottom of the tub. I took a deep breath, melting into the hot water.

The relaxing feeling disappeared when I heard a loud crash, jolting me out of the bathtub. I grabbed a nearby towel and hastily wrapped it around myself before cautiously running toward the sound. As I rounded the corner, I heard someone yell and curse under their breath. Reaching for the closest thing to me, I pushed my bedroom door open, my heart beating hard against my chest as I walked into the living room.

And there I saw him, scrambling to clean up the broken lamp. I instantly recognized him as the man from yesterday, although he hadn't been stark naked then. He definitely was now. Averting my eyes, I felt a blush creep up my neck. What the hell was he doing in my house?

"Excuse me," I choked out, then cleared my throat and looked at him, trying not to check him out and instead freaking out that there was a naked intruder in my home. "Excuse me, what the hell are you doing in my home?!"

He jumped up, turning around. I could see the panic written across his face. "I, um, I—"

"Why are you naked?" I exclaimed, clutching the lamp more tightly in my hands. "Where are your clothes?!"

"I don't—I'm sorry, I—" He sighed. "This is so not how I wanted this to go."

"How did you want this to go? What's your problem?" I asked, panic lacing my tone as I cautiously walked toward my couch to grab one of the white throw blankets for him. "Here, wrap this around yourself."

"Annie, listen. I'm sorry, I—"

"I'm not mad about the lamp," I said, still clutching the towel against my body. "I'm upset because you just came into my home uninvited. And naked! Why are you here?"

"I had nowhere else to go!" he exclaimed, his silver eyes searching mine. "I'm sorry. I didn't know where else to go. We started off on the wrong foot. Look, my name's Delmare."

"What do you mean you have nowhere else to go?"

"The oceans are dying. I had to flee onto land."

I blinked, searching his face for any sign of lying, but there was none. What did he mean, flee? What was happening?

"You are the only human I know. I figured you wouldn't mind, but if I am too much of a bother, I will leave," he said, turning away from me.

"Human?" I asked. "What do you mean the only *human* you know? You had to flee the ocean?"

He walked cautiously over to me. Without thinking, I tensed and swung the lamp at him in an effort to defend myself from the crazy, half-naked intruder. He caught the shade just in time and pulled it from my grasp just as I kicked up, hitting his crotch with my knee. I spun around and made a dash toward my bedroom to call the police.

"Wait!" he groaned in protest, but I didn't care. I needed to get away from this crazy person and I needed the police. Grasping my phone in my hands, I began to dial, only turning when I heard him run into the room.

"You stay away from me!" I exclaimed, grabbing the closest thing to me, which happened to be a pillow. I lifted it in warning, ready to throw it at him. "Don't come any closer."

"Anna, please. Listen to me. I will not hurt you."

"How do you know my real name? No, don't answer that. I want you out of my house! Get out!" I was beyond angry and distraught by now. I couldn't believe this man had decided to break into my home, let alone buck naked.

"Anna, I'm sorry. Let's start over." He seemed genuinely sorry for what he had done, but I wasn't having any of it.

"If you don't get out of my house right now, I'm calling the police," I warned, still clutching my towel around my body.

"Okay, I'm leaving. Just calm down."

But before I could scream at him that I was perfectly calm, he ran past me and into my bathroom. I ran after him, then watched him casually drop the throw blanket and jump into the tub. Within seconds, his lower half had morphed into a gigantic silver fishtail.

My vision turned black as I fell unconscious next to a being I hadn't known existed until that very moment.

THREE

The darkness slowly disappeared from my vision, but my head still throbbed, sending sparks of pain across my temple. My limbs were numb, giving me no clue as to where I was or what had happened. My memory was a blur of black and white, the figures across my mind's eye foggy and unrecognizable, further frustrating me as I tried to open my eyes again. My senses slowly came back, blood flowing down my arms as the pins and needles sparked across my skin as I came to. My eyes fluttered open. I pushed myself up, trying to register what had happened.

"Oh, good, you're awake!" a man's voice exclaimed from my side. Turning to him, I felt my heart skip a beat as I looked him over, realizing that this man was not only the same man from earlier today, but he was wearing my father's clothes. "I hope you don't mind that I borrowed these." He paused, looking down at the clothes he wore before looking back up at me. "I didn't think you wanted me to walk around naked again."

Without warning, my memories came flooding back like a tidal wave, pulling me down as the information tried to suffocate me. Delmare wasn't human. He had broken into my home while naked. Delmare had fled the ocean and was a merman. I felt the fear then as my hands shook, absentmindedly pushing myself away from him.

"Anna," he said calmly, as he inched toward me. "I'm not here to hurt you."

Closing my eyes, I tried to think of what I could do. There was no way this was real. I was still dreaming; I had to be. But a part of me knew that this was definitely not a dream. This was all too real. We still hadn't investigated the entire ocean floor, and it was entirely possible that there was another intelligent species beneath the depths of the sea. Of course, I wasn't sure how I felt being the one to discover it. He seemed human enough, I mean, in this form, he was entirely too human and incredibly gorgeous. Maybe that was his tactic to pull me in—promising sweet things until he pulled me under the waves to drown me.

"I won't drown you," he said as my eyes shot open. "I mean you no harm, Anna. I know that saying this means nothing right now, but please know that I am being truthful to you."

"Did you just read my mind?" I asked, dumbfounded and a little uneasy. "Why should I believe you or trust you at all?"

He cautiously walked over and sat down at the foot of the bed. "Yes, I can read your mind. I don't believe you will trust me, not now anyway. That's something I must earn, but I guess this isn't the best way to earn that trust."

I nodded as I looked down, realizing I was no longer wrapped in a towel and instead wore my pajamas. "How am I in my pajamas? Did you dress me?" I asked, horrified.

"Yes. I figured you didn't want to be naked in a stranger's presence, so I dressed you in your night clothes. I hope you don't mind." He paused. "This is not what I had in mind when I wished to meet a human for the first time."

With wide eyes, I stood up, completely freaked out that he had seen me naked and had dressed me while I was unconscious. This was not okay! I wanted him out of my house, but where would he go if he couldn't return to the ocean? I cleared my throat. "I mind. You can't go around telling complete strangers that you're a merman, and you definitely can't break in to someone's home naked and then dress them while they're unconscious. That's wrong and disturbing, and it makes me uncomfortable." I began pacing the length of the room, then I stopped abruptly, cautiously looking back up at him.

"I know, and I'm so sorry. I know you have boundaries and I crossed them." He paused, looking back at me sincerely. "I will leave. I am sorry I have made you uncomfortable."

I didn't say anything, just watched him stand and leave me alone in my bedroom. Within minutes, I heard the soft click of the front door as the stranger left wearing my father's clothes. Shutting my eyes, I tried to comprehend everything that had happened and wondered if I was hallucinating.

***

A few days since the break in and I hadn't seen any sight of him. It was nearly a week later, when I pulled into my driveway, that I saw him standing on my doorstep with a bouquet of what looked like coral and shells.

"What—what are you doing here?" I asked, slamming the door to my car.

"I have come to apologize," he said simply, his eyes pleading for me to forgive him.

"Why should I forgive you? You broke in to my home!"

"I'm sorry. I wasn't thinking. Please, can we just start over?"

I looked away, pressing my lips together in a firm line as I thought about what I could do, then I sighed and motioned toward the door. "Go inside. We need to have a chat."

We sat in silence at the dining room table. I watched him, studying him for any sign of lying, but there was only one. I could tell that he hadn't left because the ocean was bad, although there could have definitely been something else. If he had fled his home, it was probably due to something big and I couldn't risk anyone else finding out his secret, otherwise he'd never be able to go back.

"I think it would be best if we start over. You say you have nowhere else to go and I'm afraid that if anyone else finds out about your, um, abilities, you will be in danger, so you can stay here, but I have a few conditions."

He nodded. "Okay, what are your conditions?"

"We need to set boundaries. I don't want us seeing each other naked—I'm not that kind of girl. If you need to change, uh, *forms*, make sure no one is around and that your secret will be safe."

He nodded in understanding. "I can do that. I'm sorry about before," he apologized, guilt written on his face. "Can we forget that ever happened?"

"Yes, let's start over and forget that ever happened." I tried to smile, hoping we could change the subject. I tapped my foot against the hardwood floor as the fact sunk in that I was sitting in front of a being I had thought was a myth until a few days ago. "Anyway, how is your English this good?" I asked. I couldn't help but question him further as my curiosity got the better of me. "Are there more of you out there? Why did you pick me? Why did you want to meet a human? Are there any other abilities I should know about?"

He let out a boisterous laugh. "Hold on. One question at a time."

"Sorry," I mumbled, looking down at the table.

"My mother taught me your language, just as hers taught her," Delmare began, turning to me. "There are many of us within the depths of the sea, different kingdoms and races much like your civilizations. I chose you because you seemed trustworthy and knowledgeable enough about the sea that I felt it wouldn't be as big of a shock. Finding out that there are other intelligent beings not too far away can be stressful, I suppose, but I believe you are handling it well."

"I'm kind of surprised I'm handling the idea of mer-people existing so well, but I know we haven't searched the entire ocean. The existence of other intelligent beings was possible. I'm still trying to figure out if I'm dreaming. You're intending on staying with me, aren't you?"

"If you don't think I will be a burden."

I shook my head, knowing that he had nowhere else to go and I had to take him in, "You can stay. Just remember: boundaries."

We spent the rest of the afternoon getting to know each other. Soon, what felt like an interrogation turned into a vibrant conversation and I hadn't realized the sun had already set until Delmare looked back at me.

"It's nearly high tide. You should probably get some sleep."

I nodded as a yawn tore through me, echoing throughout the room. Delmare chuckled, a sound I wanted to hear again and again. What the hell was wrong with me?

"I should probably show you where you're going to sleep. We'll have to go to the store in the morning and get you some clothes. I only have a few of my dad's things left, and I don't think you'll feel comfortable wearing the same raggedy T-shirt and jeans every day. I have work tomorrow, so we will have to go after. Can you entertain yourself until I get back at four?"

"I should be fine, Anna," he assured me before I stood, leading him into one of the guest bedrooms across the hall from mine.

The room was spacious, sporting a queen-sized bed furnished with a comfortable quilt, a dresser, and a door leading to a bathroom. I watched as Delmare smiled to himself, sitting down on the bed. "Um, I have a toothbrush in there," I continued, "a few towels if you want to take a shower. Er, I suppose you can't take a shower because of your tail, but there's a full tub so you should be fine." I was rambling, not realizing that he had gotten up and was walking toward me. "What?"

"I'll be fine. You don't have to worry."

I let out a breath I hadn't realized I was holding. Nodding to him, I turned around and was heading to my room when I heard him call, "Thank you."

Glancing back, I smiled. "You're welcome. Good night, Delmare."

"Good night, Anna."

Shutting the door behind me, I tiptoed back into my bedroom, crawling into bed after shutting off the lights. Instantly. I felt my limbs grow heavy as sleep overtook me, pulling me into my dream.

Within moments, I was dreaming, the night of Mom's crash filling my vision. memories all around me. I watched as the paramedics rushed toward her Jeep, which was now crushed against the side of a semi. I knew this wasn't real, but still. A scream tore through me just as it had years before when my Mom had passed. And just as I was about to run up and hug my mother one last time, I realized that the parent I expected to be there wasn't lying on the street. My father's body was almost unrecognizable, but as soon as I realized it was him, the dream vanished, filling the void with an endless sea. I was drowning in the sea, and just when I was about to succumb, I awoke, a terrifying scream echoing from my lips, my sobs overtaking me. Mom had died in the crash, not Dad. Why were their deaths mixed in my nightmares? How long would I have to endure these nightmares until I healed?

Someone burst through my bedroom door, panic and concern etched across his face. He looked at me, taking in the fact that I was drenched in sweat and clutching my bed sheets for dear life. "Are you alright?"

"Sorry," I rasped. "I just had a nightmare."

I watched as Delmare took a few steps toward me, silently debating whether he should come closer or just leave me be. Thankfully, he came toward me, sitting on the side of my bed and looking at me with watchful eyes. "Do you want to talk about it?"

I shook my head, pushing the covers off me as I tried to calm my racing heartbeat.

"Will you be alright if I go back to bed?"

I nodded, taking a deep breath before closing my eyes. Before I could tell if I was asleep or awake, my body reacted on its own, grabbing hold of his hand. I spoke without thinking, asking the question I knew would change everything. "Will you stay with me? Just until I fall asleep. You don't have to if you don't want to. I mean, I don't know why I'm asking you this. We barely know each other—"

"Yes," Delmare whispered, turning back to me. His surprise was replaced with understanding. "I'll stay with you until you fall asleep."

"Thank you."

He only nodded before letting go of my hand and crawling over to the left side of the bed while I took the right. As we got comfortable, I thought I would feel awkward sharing a bed with a man I didn't know, let alone a being who wasn't even human, but I didn't. I felt entirely comfortable. His presence felt familiar in a way that I couldn't quite explain.

As my body relaxed, I turned on my side, feeling sleep overtake me once more. And this time, no nightmares of my parent's deaths plagued my dreams, only a peaceful darkness.

FOUR

My eyes fluttered open as the sun shone bright against my face, spreading its warmth across my features and awakening me from my peaceful escape from reality. I heard the soft sounds of someone breathing near my ear and feel his chest rise and fall against my back. Delmare's arms were wrapped around me in a protective and comfortable hold. I felt my body relax further as he pulled me closer to him in his sleep, my body wishing it could go back to its peaceful state of rest while I leaned into Delmare's embrace. Part of me knew I couldn't stay in this bed, wrapped in his embrace forever. I knew I had a job to do and I couldn't just not show up, especially on my first day.

"Delmare," I whispered, unsure of what I should say or whether I should wake him.

He mumbled in his sleep for me to go back to sleep and he nestled his face into my neck, closing the distance between us as if we weren't inches from each other already.

"Delmare, please. I have to get up. I have work to do," I pleaded halfheartedly, finding myself nestling deeper against him. I felt something hard press up against my butt, causing a blush to spread across my face and neck. God, what was I getting myself into? Why was I acting like this?

"Just five more minutes," he groaned sleepily as I tried unsuccessfully to peel his arms off me so I could escape his comfortable embrace.

"Seriously, I can't stay here all day," I huffed, slightly annoyed when he tightened his hold on me, the embrace no longer as comfortable as it had been.

He mumbled unhappily as I unraveled myself from his arms and crawled out of bed, my feet hitting the cold hardwood floor. As quickly as I could, I got dressed, hoping he wasn't watching me as I pulled my shirt over my head. Once I was dressed, I grabbed my purse and keys, glancing at the time on my phone. I felt the panic rise in me as I saw the time. I grabbed a banana off the counter and scarfed it down. I was just about to walk out the door when I saw Delmare come around the corner, rubbing his eyes as he tried to wake himself up.

"What time is it?" he asked.

"It's early. Go back to bed," I replied, opening the front door. "I'll be home around four."

With that said, I exited my home, leaving behind a man who wasn't human to fend for himself. A merman whose arms I had just spent the night embraced in. I knew we had had a rocky start and I just met him, but I couldn't help but be drawn to him. I hoped he stayed put and didn't cause any trouble. I must be insane to think it was a good idea to leave a stranger in my home or spend the night in bed with him.

During the drive to the Institute, I was a nervous wreck. I knew I had nothing to be nervous about, but the feeling never ceased. I would just be filing paperwork and overlooking charts today. Nothing insanely strenuous. So why did I feel like something bad was about to happen?

As I parked in the employee parking, I could still feel the nervousness churn in the pit of my stomach. Taking a deep breath, I exited my truck, locking the doors securely behind me. Swinging my purse over my shoulder, I made my way inside, the humidity not yet clinging to my skin this early in the morning. As I entered, I felt my nervousness wash away as I watched the fish swimming in the surrounding tanks, the water swishing slightly on the other side of the frosted glass. Smiling to myself, I made my way over to the front desk, hoping I could find my way to the HR department so I could start my shift.

"Hi, my name's Anna Lisle. Today is my first day working with this company and I was wondering if you can let your human resources manager know I'm here," I said in the most professional manner I could muster.

"Right, okay. Give me one second and I'll call them," the short brunette replied from the other side of the desk, quickly picking up the phone and dialing.

As the phone rang, I stared into one tank along the wall. Coral rested in the middle of the tank as fish darted in and around it. I wondered what it would be like to breathe underwater. Would it be as easy and light as air, or would the water be tougher to draw into one's lungs? Did Delmare have gills that helped him breathe? How was he able to change forms so easily? I was so consumed in my thoughts that I was startled when the receptionist let me know that the HR manager would come down to greet me. Moments later, I felt a tap on my shoulder and turned to for her standing right behind me.

"Oh, I'm sorry," I said. "My mind just ran away from me."

"It's alright, dear," the woman in her forties said, her kind eyes looking back at me. "My name is Diana, shall we get started?"

I nodded before following her further into the building. She pointed to different rooms, mentioning names as we passed. When we finally made it to her office, my mind was swirling with all the newfound information I hoped I would still remember by the end of the day. She flicked on the light to her office, motioning for me to take a seat. I did so, thanking her. She sat across from me at her desk. I noticed an enormous number of Post-it notes stuck to every available space around her computer screen, the colors striking against the gray paint of the walls.

"Alright, now if I could have you sign these documents for me, we can get your profile completed and take a photo for your ID. I believe James has a few things he'd like you to get done today. I'm so glad you've accepted the position as one of our marine biologists and I hope you enjoy your time here." She beamed as I took the forms from her outstretched hand and signed them.

After everything was signed, Diana took my signed documents and led me to the back of the facility where they held injured marine life. One room caught my eye, although I wasn't sure why. It held a large tank, empty of any contents. However, what *was* strikingly unusual was the amount of monitoring equipment across from it and the eerie sense that this room held secrets. Secrets that I wanted to find out.

"Ah, you must be Miss Lisle. My name is Dr. Jones but everyone here calls me James, It's great to finally meet you," a man said as he walked toward us wearing a button down and slacks. How he could stand to wear all that in this humidity was beyond my understanding. Giving my hand a firm shake, he let me know about the water levels and got me up to speed on the Atlantic's current marine life. One thing was certain—I knew about a species of marine life that he didn't.

Once we made our introductions, I followed him into another room filled with filing cabinets and a desk stacked high with paperwork. To anyone else this would seem boring, but to me I couldn't hide the excitement. Without another word, James left me to the piles of paperwork and without a second thought, I took my seat at one of the desks. Not wasting any time, I grabbed a few of the files, looking over the data as the silence willed the room, the only sound being the rustling of paper but then, in silence your mind can wonder. And mine did just that as I thought of Delmare and the feeling of his arms around me. I could get used to waking up to him. I still wasn't sure why he had such an effect on me. With a sigh, I tried to focus on my work, knowing that if I continued to dwell on this morning my mind would run away to thoughts I shouldn't be thinking about.

After work, I drove home while listening to the radio, almost forgetting that I had left Delmare at my home just a few hours ago. As I pulled up the drive, I noticed that the property was still in one piece and hoped that the inside looked just as good as the exterior. Shutting the door, my keys jingled in my hands as I nervously walked up to my front door and stuck the key into the lock. I held my breath, readying myself for whatever may lie on the other side.

"Delmare?" I called, setting my purse and keys down on the table near the door. "I'm home."

"Hey," he greeted from the couch as the sound of the TV came through the speakers. "Did you have fun at work?"

He was spread out on the couch, the remote resting on his chest. He seemed almost human as he lay there, peacefully watching whatever film he had picked, and I almost forgot he had asked me a question.

"Um, yeah. I had a good day," I replied, walking over to the couch where Delmare was stretched out. He moved his legs so I could sit down. "How was your day?"

"It was good," he said, laying his legs on my lap. "I ate that red stuff in the fridge, but I haven't gotten to cleaning my dishes yet."

"Do you mean spaghetti?" I asked, fighting back laughter.

"Is that what that's called?" he asked, his eyes filled with amazement.

"Yes, that's what that's called, and that's okay, I'll do them later," I commented, brushing him off before turning to him. "Are you ready to go to the store?"

"Sure," he said, jumping off the couch and turning the television off.

I unlocked the truck, pulling my hair up in a ponytail as the humidity clung to my skin. I watched as Delmare stared at my vehicle for a minute before fumbling with the handle and successfully pulling the door open. I hopped into the truck and watched as he followed my movements exactly, tentatively making sure he was doing everything right. I clicked my seatbelt into place and heard him do the same. "Ready?"

"Yeah." He nodded as I started the truck and backed out of the drive.

We were quiet as we drove to Walmart, even quieter when we got out and I grabbed a cart. I felt my nervousness spark again as Delmare walked beside me, smiling at everyone who passed us by. When we entered the men's section, I grabbed a shirt off of the rack and pressed it against his torso, checking the size before throwing five shirts and a five-pack of white T-shirts into the cart. After we threw in a package of boxers that I hoped fit him, estimating the size he needed based on his jeans size, we walked over to the beauty section to grab his toiletries. I eyed the Old Spice shampoo and conditioner. I took a sniff. My grandpa had always used Old Spice, and memories from my past seemed to flood around me. I smiled to myself.

"What's that?" Delmare asked as he looked over at me.

"Oh, it's just shampoo, it helps you clean your hair," I replied, moving to set it back on the shelf.

"I see. Does it smell good?" I only nodded as Delmare grabbed it and gave it a good sniff before smiling and setting it into the basket. "Do we need anything else?"

"No, I think we're good," I replied.

And as we made our way up to the registers, I wondered what I had gotten myself into and what it would be like to have a merman for a roommate.

FIVE

By the time we arrived home, it was nearly five, and the back of the truck was filled with several cloth bags with various clothing items and toiletries. I grabbed a few bags and Delmare grabbed the rest so I could unlock the door. I watched as he held the door for me with his back, still holding the bags in his hands. I walked past him and quickly set the bags down on the dining room table, looking over at Delmare as he followed in my footsteps.

"We should probably wash your clothes before we put them away," I said, unwrapping the packages with the white undershirts. "It'll take a few loads, I think. You don't mind staying in those clothes for a few hours while they're in the wash, do you?"

He looked up, his eyebrows furrowed, "Um, no, I don't mind staying in these clothes. How do you wash your clothes on land?"

"Oh, sorry." I gathered the clothes into my arms before making my way to the laundry room. "Come on, I'll show you how I do it."

I felt his presence at my side as I opened the washer. "Okay, first, stuff the clothes into the washer, then close the door." I let the door shut with a click before grabbing the laundry detergent from the shelf. "Then you pour about half of the liquid into this container then close it. Then you'll change your settings and then hit start," I finished, pushing the button. I told him what the additional settings meant.

"Interesting piece of equipment," Delmare commented, staring at it for a moment before turning back to me. "And the machine above it dries them?"

I nodded. "Yes, you'll want to add a dryer sheet in there. Shut the door and then hit start. The machines will go off once they're done." I walked back into the kitchen. "You can set your toiletries in the bathroom. I think I'm going to get started on those dishes and make some dinner."

"Okay," he agreed.

I started working on the dishes that lay waiting in the sink. As I cleaned, I found my mind wandering to this morning, the way his arms had wrapped around me in a comfortable embrace, how I had leaned into him without even thinking. I knew what he was, and that he was a stranger to me, but why did I feel so comfortable around him? Why was it so easy to talk to him? What made him different from anyone else I had ever spoken to?

I hadn't realized he'd walked back into the kitchen until he spoke behind me, making me jump. I accidentally dropped the plate I'd been scrubbing into the sink. Thankfully, the plate didn't break and laid there, undisturbed, under the rushing water.

"Are you alright?"

"Yeah," I gasped, placing my hand on my chest, trying desperately to calm my now-racing heartbeat, "I'm fine. You just spooked me."

"I'm sorry."

"You're fine. Did you finish putting your stuff away?" I asked.

He nodded, then turned toward the unwashed dishes in the sink. "Do you need help with those?" He took a step toward me, his hand grazing my forearm.

I looked up, unable to speak, my heart stopping completely. His eyes that were once a striking silver were now gold, glowing against his black hair that fell into his eyes. I wanted to push the stray hair out of his eyes, to feel his hair in between my fingers as I caressed the back of his neck. Before I did something I would regret, I looked away, feeling a blush creep up my neck and along my cheeks. I cleared my throat, remembering that he had asked me a question. "No, I'm fine. I—I think I need some air."

Before I could register what was happening, I was running out the back door toward the gate that led to the ocean. The beaches weren't closed yet, but still people weren't swimming this late. My bare feet squished into the sand, sinking slightly with each step I took. I wasn't sure what I was doing or what I thought I could gain, but this was no time to catch feelings for someone, let alone a merman! Why did his eyes change colors? What if someone found out what he was? Did mer-people have laws against intermixing between species? What was the underwater world like? Why was he staying on land? A million questions swirled in my mind as I walked closer and closer to the water. The lull of the sea seemed to lure me to it as I tried to process everything that had happened in the last two days. Before I knew it, I was walking into the surf, the water spraying over my toes and calves. Taking a deep breath, I tried to concentrate on the salty sea air filling my lungs and not the merman I had taken in as a roommate.

"Anna!" a familiar voice called my name, sounding gruff yet kind and filled with concern.

I looked back and saw him walking toward me.

"Annie, I'm sorry I sprang the existence of my kind on you, and now you have to keep me here. I will leave if I must, if this is too much of a burden for you." he paused, pain clear in his tone as he stood next to me.

"Why are you running from the ocean? Do you have to stay on land? Why is it so easy to talk to you? Why am I comfortable with you if I know nothing about you? You're a complete stranger and you broke in to my home naked!" I blurted the questions out in a rush, my mind swirling with unanswered questions.

"Let's go back inside and I will answer your questions," he said, glancing back at the sea uneasily before turning back to me. His eyes pleaded for me to follow him. I only nodded, walking back into the house as Delmare followed me. As I slid the sliding door closed behind us, I turned back to Delmare, motioning toward one of the dining chairs, then I took my seat. I watched as he sat down, the sound of the washer running in the background while my mind rambled with more questions.

Another second passed before he looked back at me, worry evident on his face as if he was concerned about how I would react to the information he was about to give me, "Let's begin, with why I am here. I am arranged to marry a Symari I do not love. I've always wanted to visit the land, so I decided if I was going to be miserable in a loveless marriage, that I will spend some of my remaining freedom on land. But then, I met you. And you opened your arms to me, you purchased me new clothes, and have kept my kind a secret. I am eternally grateful to you, and I believe the only way I can repay you is by giving you information." he paused, his eyes flickering back to their gold color as he looked down, trying to decide whether he should tell me more. "My name is Delmare Triton Stormborn and I am the heir to the throne of Arcania. I am to be king one day."

I just stared, unable to comprehend what he had just told me. I was sitting across from not only a merman, but royalty! *What the hell did you get yourself into, Anna?* I thought. There were kingdoms under the sea? Were there civilizations? A working economy? What was a Symari? Is that what they call themselves? How are the reproductive systems of these Symari supposed to work? I felt my cheeks heat at this thought, trying not to think about what it would be like for Delmare to sleep with someone. Why was I so horny lately? Could he purposefully read my mind, or did he do it accidentally? If he listened in on purpose, did he know I had these inappropriate thoughts about him? *God, I hope not.*

"Are you okay?"

I looked up, unsure of how to respond to his question. Was I okay? No, I wasn't. I was trying to absorb all of this newfound information, and I didn't know what to do with any of it. I wanted to ask him all kinds of questions because I found him fascinating. I wanted to see what made him tick, what made him unique. And to make matters worse, I wasn't sure why I was so drawn to him. Never in my wildest dreams would I ever share a bed with a man I had just met. Did he put some kind of spell on me to make me like him and more apt to help him?

"Annie?"

"Um." I pinched the bridge of my nose as a headache formed at the back of my head. "I'm fine, it's just a lot to process."

He only nodded, not saying anything.

"I think I'm going to go to bed early. Help yourself to whatever's in the fridge. I'm no longer hungry."

And with one last glance back at him, I made my way into my bedroom. Peeling my clothes off until I was naked, my mind raced with hundreds of thoughts. *God, I really hope he isn't listening in on my thoughts right now.*

For the third time that day, I felt my skin warm as redness crept up my face. As I was about to crawl into bed buck naked, I turned around to see my door slowly open. I froze, turning to him, knowing exactly who it was that was coming into my bedroom without knocking.

Golden eyes met my blue ones as he came toward me. I completely forgot I was standing stark naked in my bedroom when Delmare moved toward me, his eyes never leaving mine as he closed the distance between us.

Only a second passed before his hands were on my hips, pulling me against him as our lips locked in sheer need and desire. I wasn't thinking. All I could think about was the feeling of my fingers through his hair, how my legs wrapped around his hips, and the way he placed soft kisses down my neck. Part of me felt like this was real, but my rational mind knew that this couldn't possibly be real at all. I couldn't remember falling asleep. Was I hallucinating this? Pulling his shirt over his head, I had no other thoughts other than how badly I wanted him. I hoped this was a dream. I wouldn't sleep with a man I'd only known for two days. If this was a dream, I really hoped Delmare wasn't listening in. Otherwise, I had so much explaining to do.

SIX

When I awoke, I turned onto my side, expecting Delmare to be there, sleeping soundly beside me, but he wasn't. Sitting up in bed, I tried to remember the events of the night. Looking down, I realized I was still naked and could feel a blush creeping up my skin again. Did we…? No, that wouldn't make sense. Why would I sleep with him if I knew nothing about him?

Swinging my feet over the side of the bed, I noticed my hips weren't sore like they would be if we'd really had sex. I sighed, relieved, and stood, changing into my clothes for the day before I exited my bedroom. Delmare was casually sitting on the couch. It was the weekend, so I had a couple days off before I went back to work on Monday. I was determined to learn everything I could about the underwater world that Delmare was from.

"Hey," I greeted, sitting on the couch next to him. "What are you watching?"

"This picture film—um, TV Show—*Siren*." He paused, looking over at me, his eyes filled with laughter. "It is interesting what humans believe to be true about my kind."

"That's a good show," I agreed, shifting in my seat so I could fold my feet underneath my butt. "I've been meaning to talk to you about that, about your kind."

"What do you want to know?" he asked.

I twirled my hair nervously, trying to think of where I should start. "What is a Symari? Is that what you call yourselves?" I inquire. "Are there other kingdoms? What is your economy like? How are you able to change forms so easily? You say you can read minds, but do you do it purposefully or is it by accident?" I paused, staring back at him as the next question tumbled from my mouth. "Your kind can have children, right? Are your pregnancies different from ours?"

He softly chuckled before he spoke, his eyes shining their unusual gold color, reminding me fiercely of the sexy dream I'd had. "Well, first off,

Symari is indeed what we call ourselves, just as you call us mer-people. There are different kingdoms and rulers that rule over each ocean. I will rule over the Arctic Ocean, just as my parents did, and my grandmother, Sedna, did all those years ago. Although, I suppose I wouldn't turn my people into monsters." He laughed, but I was thoroughly confused. "We have a goddess, Keilani. She is the mother of all sea life and the biological mother of the five rulers of the sea. From what I have seen of your world, we run our economy the same as yours. We trade with other kingdoms, farm food, and have our own militia, although there hasn't been a war since my grandmother's reign in 1770." he paused, looking back at me expectantly.

"Okay, so, how do you change forms?" I asked, my mind still racing.

"We have evolved so that changing forms comes naturally and hurts less than it did thousands of years ago. To answer your question about my ability, I do it purposefully, and for the record, we did not have sex last night." His eyes burned gold as the slightest sign of intrigue spread across his features.

"So," I interrupted, "what you're saying is that your great-grandmother is a goddess, your grandmother turned her people into monsters, and you're related to everyone in the sea? What do you do about children? You're just going to marry your cousin? And what do you mean, 1770? How old *are* you?" I asked, "I can't believe you purposefully listen in to my thoughts! That's not right!"

"Annie, calm down. Listen, I don't do it *that* often. Now, where was I? Ah, you wanted to know how we have children. Well, we don't have, um, our intimacies," he paused as a blush swept across his skin, "in our sea form. We do it in our human form. The pregnancy lasts around four months, but we age much slower than humans. At least, back in the day we did; now we age as fast as humans do. Although we can intermix between species, we usually don't because it might be too much of a burden for the human."

"Why would it be a burden?" I asked just as someone knocked on the door, pulling our attention away from our conversation. "Hold that thought." I got up to see who visited me.

When I opened the door, I was surprised to see Claire. She grinned at me, holding a pan filled with lasagna in her arms.

"Hi sweetie, I just thought I'd stop by. I brought some lasagna." She walked past me and I shut the door behind her. "Oh, I didn't realized you had company."

Delmare stood and turned around just as Claire gasped. Looking over at Claire, I saw the shock written on her face as she stared at Delmare. "Claire, is something wrong?" I asked.

"What are you doing here, your—" She paused, cutting herself off as she glanced at me and then back to Delmare.

"I am taking a quick vacation, Mrs. Saltheir," Delmare replied, not missing a beat. "And you do not need to worry. Anna knows about the Symari world, or at least some of it. I was just explaining about how our young come to be when you arrived."

"Why would you tell a human this information? I'm sorry, your highness, but you could have jeopardized the entire Symari race!" Claire exclaimed, her eyes fierce and face red, clearly disappointed.

"I'm right here," I mumbled, grabbing the lasagna Claire held and setting it gently in the fridge. I tried to not listen as they bickered back and forth.

"Why would you choose Anna to share the existence of your kind? Why would you risk all the Symari lives like that, Delmare? What would —"

Claire was cut off as Delmare yelled, his eyes burning a bright gold. "Because she is my Mate!"

The room was silent then. No one said a word as I made my way into the living room. I looked between Claire and Delmare as they stared at each other, Claire's disappointment seeming to fade away as her features softened to understanding.

"What do you mean, your Mate?" I asked, my eyebrow furrowed.

Delmare looked at me, his eyes shining their familiar golden color.

"What's going on? How do you two know each other?"

Delmare walked toward me, his eyes searching mine before reaching out for my hand. "Anna, I have to tell you something, I wanted to wait, but now that I've made a fool of myself, I suppose now is as good of a time as any." he paused, leading me over to the couch. We sat down and Claire gave him a pointed look as he looked back at me, worry clear on his face. "How do I put this?"

"Just be honest with me," I said, feeling the concern radiating off him in waves, adding to my anxiety.

"When a Symari is born, they're born with only half a soul. When they meet their soulmate—their Mate as we call them—their souls are complete. Their Mate is their life partner. This Mate is usually a Symari, but in some circumstances, they are humans." He gestured to Claire, who was standing to the side, anxiously looking between us. "Claire is the human Mate of the second in command of the Stowryn kingdom. For mates, it's usually an instant connection— they realize it immediately— but other times, it takes a few days for them to realize it." He looked up, his eyes flickering blue, a color I had yet to see. "I knew instantly."

"You knew I was your Mate back when we first met?" I asked, still trying to process everything. My head was spinning as I stared back at Delmare. "Is that why I have this insane sense of familiarity? Why I'm so comfortable around you when we barely know each other?"

He only nodded.

If Delmare was a prince does that mean I'm expected to help rule his kingdom? He can't stay here if he has a responsibility to the ocean and his people. What if his guards come to take him back? What would they say when his people find out he has a human for a Mate?

Clearing her throat, Claire turned to me. "I think I'm going to head home. You call me if you need anything, alright, Anna?"

"Okay," I said, not looking at her. I stared at Delmare, unsure of what he was thinking, but I had a feeling he knew exactly what was on my mind. "Are you going to say something, or are we going to just stare at each other all day?"

"I'm not sure what you want me to say," he admitted as the sound of the front door clicked shut. "I know that this is a lot for you. I'm trying to ease you into this, but I know you have a right to know about your future and what it means to be my Mate."

I opened my mouth to speak, but I wasn't sure what to say. My life was an utter mess. Not only had I just found out mer-people exist, but I'm fated to be with one forever as if I had no choice in the matter at all. And to make matters worse, Claire, her husband, Adam, and John have been lying to me for years.

I closed my eyes, trying to make sense of everything, knowing that I didn't like the idea of someone choosing my future for me. Even if I was okay with the fact that I just met my soulmate, he was a prince and he was expecting to rule a kingdom soon and if I married him, I would have to rule beside him. This was all too much. I needed space to think.

"Anna, are you okay?" Delmare asked as I opened my eyes to meet his gaze.

I shook my head, a laugh poured from my lips, anger suddenly filling me at his question, "No Delmare, I'm not okay! You're a merman. I just found out that you are my soulmate and I have no choice in my future. To top it off, Claire, Adam, and John, have been lying to me for years." I paused, rubbing my temple as a headache began to spread throughout my mind, "I'm sorry, I just, I need some time to think."

Standing, I made my way into my bedroom, my mind racing when I sat on the bed. With a huff, I fell backwards, falling onto the mattress. Staring at the ceiling, I laid there in silence as I tried to process everything. Why is this happening to me? Why can't I have a moment of peace where I'm not bombarded with new information like I'm attracted to a merman who is actually my soulmate? Why can't I have a normal life? What am I going to do? It seemed like hours had past before I heard a knock on my door, I hadn't realized that I closed it until I turned to look in the direction of the noise.

"Anna, can we talk?" I heard Delmare ask from the other side of it, "Please, we need to talk." I bit the inside of my cheek, not wanting to get up before I heard him again, "Are you hungry?"

Sighing, I stood, my bare feet touching the cold floor and made my way toward the door where Delmare waited on the other side and yanked it open. "Delmare, what is it?" I asked, staring at him as he ran his fingers through his hair nervously.

"Anna, please don't be mad at me." he replied, his eyes filled with worry.

"Delmare…" I sighed, "I'm overwhelmed. I'm trying to be okay with everything but honestly, I'm not okay. You expect me to be your soulmate and eventually, I would assume, rule a kingdom and have an heir. It's too much and to top it off, I barely know you! I don't want anyone dictating what I can and cannot do in *my* future. I just want to do my job in peace and not have to worry about the fact that I'm living with a merman who happens to be my soulmate and royalty. I just, I need some time to think."

Delmare only nodded as I stared at him, wanting him to say something, anything, that will tell me I have a choice.

"Then let's start small," he suggested, reaching for my hand and cautiously holding it as if he wasn't sure if he should be. "Let's get to know each other and then we can discuss our future."

I nodded, "Okay."

"Are you hungry?" he inquired.

"I'm fine." I lied, just as my stomach roared.

"Your stomach says otherwise." he chuckled, "Would you like to go for lunch with me, Anna?"

"Like on a date?" I asked, my heartrate beginning to quicken at the thought.

"What is a date? Do you mean a courtship?"

"Um, kind of. On a date we would do something together that we both enjoy. On a first date, we might go out to dinner so we can get to know each other," I replied, giving him a soft smile. "I'd love to take a walk on the beach, but seeing as you were so hesitant to go near the sea, we probably shouldn't if you still intend on staying hidden."

Delmare looked away, deep in thought. I found my mind wandering to my dream from last night. Part of me knew it was insanely too soon to do any of that, but another part of me did not want to wait. This bond or whatever was a serious pain in my ass.

"So, would that be something you would be interested in?" I asked, instinctively taking a step toward him.

"I would love nothing more," he said, smiling at me. "And don't feel bad that you are being drawn to me. It is the bond taking hold. Your soul knows it has found its other half and cannot wait for it to be complete."

"How do our souls become complete?" I asked.

Delmare gave me a pointed look, as if to say I knew exactly what he meant.

I swallowed nervously. Would we just have to kiss or would it be something much more intimate? I couldn't remember the last time I had slept with a man. It wasn't something I just did with anyone, or spur of the moment. When was the last time I had taken my birth control? Would birth control pills even work with a Symari? God, this was so overwhelming.

"I think I'm going to take a shower and get ready," I mumbled, feeling my cheeks burn as my mind wandered to more intimate matters.

"Okay," he said as I turned. "What should I wear?"

"A nice button down and jeans should be good." I replied, taking in a sharp breath as I imagined how cute he would look in it. I couldn't stop myself when I added, "I think you'd look cute in them."

As I stepped into the shower, I found my mind racing. All this information was just too much, and I only hoped that the rest of my afternoon wouldn't be as eventful. But I knew, as the water ran over my face and down my body, that this day was just the beginning of my adventure with Delmare Stormborn, the future king of an underwater kingdom I apparently would rule as well.

SEVEN

I tried not to think about all the events of the past week. After blow-drying my hair, I made my way into my bedroom, towel wrapped securely around my body. Fumbling through my closet, I pulled out a cute, but comfortable, sundress. The navy-blue stripes ran parallel across the white fabric, bringing out the red in my hair. I pulled the dress on over my head, then grabbed a pair of my favorite sandals and slipped them onto my feet. I didn't bother to put on makeup as I didn't own any. I made my way into the living room to wait for Delmare.

A few minutes later, I turned around to see Delmare walking toward me, his hair falling into his unique eyes, which were their normal silver color. He wore a light blue button down and a nice pair of denim jeans. I swallowed hard as my stomach began to flutter at the sight of him. I was breathless. Never had I ever seen a man as gorgeous as the merman before me. I couldn't help but take a step toward him.. He smiled at me as he came closer, automatically making me smile back at him.

"You look great," I said, finally able to speak before placing my purse strap on my arm.

"So do you." He grinned. "Are you ready to go?"

"Yeah, I am." I moved to open the front door but Delmare beat me to it, opening the door and waving for me to go ahead of him. "You eat sea food, right? And thanks for opening the front door. That was sweet of you."

"You're welcome," he said, grinning proudly.

I walked past him and climbed into my truck just as he hopped in beside me.

"And yes, we eat seafood."

"Good, because there's some good seafood places around here." I smiled almost shyly as I started up the vehicle, ready to get on the road.

The five-minute drive to the restaurant seemed to go by too fast. I parked at the side of the building. I hadn't been nervous earlier, but now I could distinctly remember how the butterflies felt yesterday because they were back, filling my stomach with a storm of anxiety.

"Are you okay?" Delmare asked as he unbuckled his seatbelt, concern lacing his tone.

"I'm just nervous," I admitted, escaping from the driver's seat and stepping onto the pavement.

"You're nervous." He laughed, his tone as nervous as mine. "This is the first time I will be in public with a room full of humans."

I couldn't help but giggle at the predicament we were in. "Yeah, I guess you have more reason to be nervous than I do." I paused, shutting the door. "Let's just go in and have lunch together. Don't worry about anyone else, let's just try to have a good time."

He smiled at me, the nervousness still evident across his features, but I could tell he was feeling better about our lunch date. "Okay, let's do this."

I grinned, exiting my vehicle, then walking together into the restaurant, our arms touching slightly as we greeted the woman standing at the podium. She grabbed our silverware and menus and we followed her to a table overlooking the sea.

"Your server will be right with you. Can I interest you in anything to drink?" she asked. Delmare sat across from me.

"Water is fine, thank you." I replied.

Delmare said the same and then we were left alone, staring at each other, not saying a word. His eyes flickered gold, shining bright against the dark color of his hair. I realized with a start that someone might see the mystical change of his irises. "Delmare, can you control your eye color? Someone might see you!"

I watched him smile at my panic, his eyes not changing back. "I can't believe you agreed to this." He paused, fumbling with his napkin. "I can't believe that you are so calm about all that you have been told these last few days. I find it interesting how you are okay with it all, how you just go with the flow, and that you haven't freaked out yet."

"I mean, I wouldn't say I've taken it *insanely* well," I replied, absentmindedly scratching the back of my head. "I *did* faint when you changed." I whispered the last word so no one would hear, entirely in tune with the fact that we were surrounded by people who might not take too kindly to another intelligent being in their world.

"Yeah," he said, taking a drink from his glass. "That's true. I'm sorry about that, and your lamp, and you know, showing up in your home not entirely clothed."

A blush made its way across my skin when he mentioned being naked, and I couldn't help but picture it. "It's alright. Let's just put it behind us and start over." I cleared my throat as I tried not to think about his nakedness or the fact that he had dressed me later that night. I wondered if he had tried to shield my assets when he dressed me or if he had admired me. I knew that if we *did* do anything more than just talk, we would probably regret it, and it was in our own best interest that we wait. This "bond," on the other hand, wanted me to rip the clothes off his handsome body.

I watched his eyes spark in amusement as he stared back at me, calculating what he should say. A terrible realization hit me.

"Are you reading my mind?" To anyone else, the horrified tone in my voice would tell them I was thinking some thoughts I probably shouldn't. Embarrassment took hold.

He nodded, his face as red as mine.

I gasped and playfully hit his hand. "Quit that!"

"I couldn't help it!" He grinned cheekily at me. "I always want to know what's on your mind."

We were so engrossed in each other that we hadn't realized our server had arrived until she spoke beside us. "Hi, my name is Beth and I'll be your server this afternoon. Are we wanting to start with some appetizers today?"

Immediately, I looked over, trying to process what she had said. My mind still swirled with my previous thoughts. "Um, I'm sorry, I think we're good," I replied, "We're going to need a few minutes to decide what we want. Sorry!"

"That's fine. Take all the time you need!" She grinned before turning away to help another table.

I picked up my menu, pursing my lips as I tried not to think about the man sitting across the table from me, focusing entirely on what I wanted to eat. I fumbled through the menu, finally deciding. As I was considering over my options for my salad, I looked up, feeling eyes on me.

Delmare's eyes were back to their silver color, as he stared at me. "What are you having?"

"Oh, snow crab legs, asparagus, and mashed potatoes. It also comes with a salad; I think I might go with a Caesar." I folded my menu just as our server came back to take our orders.

Delmare requested what I was having, and I realized that he'd probably never tried mashed potatoes or asparagus before. "It's good to try something new," he said.

I smiled as I handed Beth our menus. "Just don't puke in my truck," I teased, winking at him as I took another sip from my glass.

He shook his head, grinning at me as if I'd told the funniest joke on the planet. "I'll try not to."

"Do you like it on land?" I asked, not sure where to start the conversation as my leg began to bounce.

"I do. You have more technological advances than our world but I like it all the same." He smiled, reaching across the table where my hand rested and held my hand in his. The warmth beginning to spread up my arms at his touch while my heart hammered against my chest.

"Um, uh, great. I'm glad you enjoy it." I said, almost breathless as I let go of his hand.

"So, um, tell me about yourself." I paused as our salads were brought out and placed in front of us, "What does the heir to the Arcanian throne like to do for fun?"

"Well, I enjoy reading, although, I do like that device along your wall in your living room."

"The television?" I offered, stabbing lettuce onto my fork.

I watched as his eyes lit up in amazement. "Is that what that's called?"

I nodded, my mouth full of food.

Delmare cautiously put a forkful into his mouth before taking another bite and then another. Pleasure was written all over his face. "This is amazing!" he practically moaned.

"Glad you like it." I smiled at him as I finished my salad.

"So, what do you like to do for fun?" he asked "Also, I never asked you what you do for work."

"If I'm not working, I'm usually swimming, I just moved here, so I'm still not used to being so close to the ocean. I also like music and reading." I paused, smiling at the server who was approaching with our food. "And I am a marine biologist at the Marine Life Institute here in town. I study marine life, the ocean, and pollution levels to see if we can help protect the creatures that inhabit our waterways."

I smiled as I broke open one of the crab legs, pulling the meat off and sticking it in my mouth. The meat seemed to melt in my mouth as I closed my eyes, enjoying the taste of the seafood, and I couldn't help but let out a soft moan. I heard Delmare chuckle and I immediately opened my eyes.

"I'm going to guess it's good?"

I only nodded, grabbing another piece, and popping it into my mouth.

"Marine biology seems like an honorable profession." Delmare commented as he eyed his asparagus on his fork.

"I guess it is." I shrugged, "You can find a lot of them on the coast but there aren't very many jobs inland."

"That would make sense as it is a profession involving the ocean." he said, nibbling on his asparagus before his nose scrunched up in disgust.

"Is it good?" I asked, laughter filling my tone.

Delmare shook his head as he discarded his fork, "I don't care much for it."

"Oh, don't be so formal! It's gross you can say it's gross."

He laughed and nodded, "Yeah, it is gross."

After we finished our food, I paid the server and walked with Delmare to my truck. We were barely inches away from each other, my arm brushing against his as we walked side by side and as we entered the truck and shut our doors, I turned to Delmare, grinning ear to ear. That date had possibly the best I'd ever had.

"I had a good time," I said, starting up the truck.

"I did as well," he replied.

I backed out of my parking spot. "What did you think of our food?" I asked, turning onto the street that would take us back home.

"It was good. I especially liked how you were moaning," he teased.

I scoffed, shaking my head. "I'm sure you did." I laughed despite my embarrassment. I tried to focus on the road as I pulled up onto Ocean Boulevard. "What do you want to do when we get home?"

"I'm not sure," he admitted. "I wouldn't mind continuing that *Siren* TV show."

"That sounds good. You can tell me the differences between their version of mer-people and your kind," I said just as we pulled into the driveway.

"I'm sure there will be a lot to tell." He chuckled, opening the truck door. Salty sea air blew inside the vehicle, sweeping my hair into my face as I followed close behind him and into my home. As I closed the front door, I immediately kicked off my sandals, my feet aching as if I had just walked a five-mile trek. I followed Delmare over to the couch and plopped down next to him as he reached for the remote. He seemed so mundane that a part of me completely forgot he wasn't human at all. I stared, admiring how his eyebrows knit together as he concentrated. I wondered if what I was feeling was the bond already forming between us, or if it was how I truly felt.

He turned toward me then, his eyes flashing the golden color that I loved so much. "What's wrong?" he asked.

"Nothing," I replied, looking away as I tried to figure out what was happening to me. Why had I been drawn to him so quickly? Why did I want to speed things up rather than slow things down? "I'm going to lie down," I announced, before maneuvering until my head laid on the armrest and my feet on Delmare's lap. "You don't mind, do you?"

"No," he said, pushing play on the remote. "You don't mind if I lay with you, do you?"

I shook my head, scooting over so that he would have enough room. I held my breath as he carefully arranged himself behind me, his leg finding its way around my own as I felt every part of him against me. Immediately my body tensed as the nervousness set in. I wasn't sure what I should be doing or if he was comfortable as I inhaled sharply, hoping I could calm down.

After a few minutes, I felt my body relax as his arm fell over my waist so he could hold my hand, our fingers entwined a moment after. I could feel his slow and steady breathing against my hair while I closed my eyes, as he shifted, the feeling of his lips against my neck making my heart thunder against my chest. While he held me, I felt as comfortable as I had when we were in bed, but this time, I felt entirely safe as if this was where I was meant to be, here with him, my other half, as crazy as that sounded.

EIGHT

The water in the large tub was still warm as I lay in it, my hair floating around me, each individual strand distinctive underneath the clear water. I tried not to move, fearing that if I did, the water would shift and splash onto the hardwood floor. Closing my eyes, I felt my body relax, letting the warmth of the water calm my nerves. It had been a month since I met Delmare, and nearly the same amount of time that I had spent dating him.

We hadn't kissed yet, despite the bond begging us to—amongst other unmentionable things. My rational brain knew that a month was too soon, but the mystical and frustratingly enticing Mate bond between the two of us did not care for what was rational.

Only that morning, he had said that he had a surprise for me, his eyes sparking their golden color that I knew meant he was *in the mood*, not that I couldn't tell from the boner he had every time I touched him. I smiled cheekily at the thought, knowing he had amazing self-control if his bond was as intense as mine. I wanted to rip his clothes off every time I saw him, but I was sure that if we did it, we would regret it soon after. Were we ready to take things up a notch or was what we were feeling for each other the bond?

Sitting up, my mind raced with possibilities as water droplets made their way down my body. I had been so consumed with my thoughts that I hadn't realized that the once-warm water was now freezing cold. Goosebumps spread across my skin. I stood and pulled the plug, letting the water drain as I stepped out onto the hardwood floor, water pooling where my feet rested. Wrapping a towel around my body, I tried to dry my hair as best I could with another towel, hoping that the water would be absorbed soon. I padded into my bedroom—I guess I should say *our* bedroom, as we had started sleeping together in the same bed not three weeks ago. I fumbled through my drawer, trying to find the cute bra I had found at the mall the other day.

"Ah-ha!" I exclaimed, pulling it out. I let the towel drop to the floor and pulled my underwear and bra on, then dressed in a sundress. I unwrapped my hair from the towel before letting my damp hair fall around my face. Picking up my discarded towels off the floor, I quickly threw them in the hamper and made my way into the living room where music was softly playing through the speakers.

As I turned the corner and walked into the kitchen, I saw Delmare busy cooking, intensely staring at the pot that was boiling before he glanced back at the box of what looked like macaroni and cheese. I had been teaching him things about the world above for the past month, much to his excitement. He caught on quickly for someone who had spent their entire existence underwater. Cautiously and quietly, I made my way toward him, hoping he wouldn't turn around or that the floors wouldn't squeak. Smiling to myself, I closed the distance between us, wrapping my arms around him as I hugged him tight. I felt his muscles tense, then instantly relax when he realized who I was. Breathing in his familiar scent, I pressed my cheek against his back, holding him in place while he chuckled. "I'm trying to cook. You aren't helping."

"Fine, I won't touch you anymore," I teased, letting go of him and backing away.

"Wait, no," he said, turning around to face me. His bottom lip stuck out in a pout as his eyes pleaded for me to take it back. "That's not fair."

"Hmm, true, but if you turn the burner off and catch me, maybe I'll let you touch me some more." I grinned as I watched the excitement spread across his face,

He shouted "Deal!" and flicked the burner off.

I made a dash for the living room, squealing in delight, fully knowing he would catch me as I made a dash toward our bedroom. Jumping onto the bed, I felt it squeak under the pressure. Delmare followed right after, happily wrapping his arms around me as if to say he had caught me. I looked at him, his eyes a mix of gold and orange as they flickered back and forth between mine.

"I caught you!" he exclaimed, a huge grin on his face.

Giggling, I shifted my weight on the bed while he inched closer to me. This time, I stayed in the middle of the bed and without any hesitation, I reached up and kissed him, my lips brushing against his in a soft, almost needy embrace. My hands moved on their own accord, running my fingers through his hair. He grabbed my waist, pulling me closer to him as we pressed our bodies against the bed underneath us. I felt his emotions like a freight train, hitting me so hard I could barely focus on anything else. I felt his need mixed with my own, our desire to continue, to complete the bond that had been growing and maturing but was not yet complete.

I gasped then, letting out a breathy moan I hadn't realized I was holding back while he kissed my neck, pulling aside the strap of my dress to touch the soft skin at the base of my collarbone. "Can I?" he whispered, his words brushing against my skin. I shivered, goosebumps spreading across my skin.

"Can you what?" I asked, but I knew what he wanted without asking. It was what we both wanted, what we had been waiting for for the past month.

"Can I take your dress off?" His eyes flashed gold.

"Yes," I said without hesitation. My desire overwhelmed me and I sat up, watching as he did the same. I bit my lip and I looked away. "Can we ease into it?"

He nodded. "Of course. If you are uncomfortable, let me know and we can stop."

I nodded. "Okay," I said, entirely breathless. "If you are as well, let me know."

He only nodded before watching as I peeled my dress off, throwing it to the ground. His gaze ran the length of my body, his eyes maintaining their gold color. He bit his lip, looking me in the eye as we stared at each other. I moved closer and ripped his shirt off, a few buttons popping off like I had imagined so many times before. The haunting need that had plagued my dreams overwhelmed me in that moment and I kissed him again. I trailed soft kisses along his neck and collarbone, relishing the sound of the moan that escaped his lips while he caressed my waist, pulling me closer to him instinctively.

We pulled the covers over our bodies, arms and legs intertwined, our faces inches apart. I felt his hand move, making light circular motions along my back and shoulder as I shifted positions, laying on my left side as he spooned me from behind, his arm draped over my stomach. I felt his lips brush against my shoulder, kissing the spot a few times before he played with my bra strap, caressing the soft skin that wasn't covered in fabric. My body shivered involuntarily, goosebumps prickling my skin despite the heat radiating off it. I felt him reach for the clasp of my bra, unhooking it effortlessly so that I could untangle myself from it and throw it across the room.

Turning onto my back, I looked at Delmare, smiling slightly at him as he smiled back at me, his pupils entirely dilated, and I knew mine were as well. I closed my eyes, resting my head on the pillow. Opening them again, I turned to him, my hands reaching over to unbuckle his pants, entirely consumed with the need for release, but he was already doing it, pulling his jeans from under the blankets along with his boxers, and I watched as he threw them, letting them join the rest of our discarded clothing.

"Do you want to?" I asked, entirely breathless as he moved the covers away and sat in front of me, his knees pressing against the bed, towering over me. He peeled my underwear off. "I don't think this is easing into it." I giggled and wrapped my leg around his, playing with his hair.

"We can stop," he said, concern lacing his tone.

I shook my head. "No, I'm okay," I said, giving him an innocent kiss on his cheek before catching his mouth with mine.

He kissed me back before he bent down to kiss my neck. He moved down my body and my breathing hitched. His gold eyes glowed against his ebony hair. "Delmare," I said, barely above a whisper, meeting his eyes as he gently pressed his hand against my thigh. "I—" I tried, before being cut off by my moan.

"I know, Anna." His tone as breathy as mine was. "I want you too."

He moved closer to me, kissing me one last time before fully entering me, a gasp escaping my lips before I wrapped my legs around him, pulling him closer to me. My back arched from the pleasure. I finally knew what it meant for our bond to be complete. Something like a soul connection would never be as intimate if we stopped at just kissing each other. Even though we had waited, I knew it was well worth it. I would never want to be with anyone else on this entire Earth. There was no one I'd rather spend the rest of my life with, even if they weren't entirely human.

NINE

The soreness in my hips reminded me of the afternoon I had spent with Delmare. It was uncomfortable, yet amazing at the same time. We lay together in bed, our arms and legs wrapped together in a tangled mess while the sun shone through the window, dancing across the waves. I stifled a yawn as Delmare nestled closer to me in his sleep. He mumbled something I couldn't understand, his nose brushing against the exposed skin of my neck. Trying not to disturb him, I shifted onto my back. His arm instinctively wrapped around my waist and he rested his head on my chest. The sudden movement though made my bladder hate me and I groaned slightly. "Delmare," I whispered, touching his shoulder softly shaking him. "I need to get out of bed."

I did not get any words in response, only groans as he wrapped his leg around me, further keeping me cuddled up to him. I shook my head. "If you don't let me get out of bed, I will pee myself," I proclaimed.

He immediately let go of me, moving over before sitting up in bed. Jumping out of bed, I ran to the bathroom, throwing the door closed so I could empty my bladder.

After washing my hands, I got dressed for work and then I made my way into the kitchen, grabbing the box of Corn Flakes from the cabinet and pouring myself a bowl of cereal. As I did, I felt strong arms wrap around my waist. He kissed the back of my head, sending butterflies to my stomach immediately at his touch.

"Good morning," Delmare murmured in my ear, still hugging me close while I poured the milk.

"Good morning," I said, taking a step backwards.

Delmare moved with me.

"I have to grab a spoon."

He sighed, letting me go so he could walk to the coffeemaker to make himself a cup of coffee. Not that he needed it—he was always a ball of energy. Grabbing a spoon from the drawer, I scooped the cereal and took a bite, watching Delmare pour the coffee grounds into the coffeemaker, the smell of coffee filling the kitchen.

"So, what do you want to do today?" Delmare asked, turning to me before reaching up to grab a mug from the cabinet.

"Hmm," I hummed. "It's supposed to be a nice day today. You could probably go swimming if you wanted to. You can't keep avoiding it, you haven't spoken to your family in over a month. They are bound to wonder where you went. And besides, it's only a few hour swim right? You'll be back before you know it." I commented, turning to him as I set my bowl down on the counter, wanting him to know he had my full attention.

His eyes were light blue and he frowned, sadness filled his face. "I haven't talked to them since I met you, but you are probably right, they might be worried about me. If I'm being honest, I'm not sure if I want to go back. I don't want to leave you here."

I shook my head. "I'll be fine. Besides, you handle my nine-hour shifts at work just fine. This will be nothing," I replied, walking toward him. I cupped his cheek in my hand while he looked down at me. "Go see your family, Delmare. They have every right to know you're safe and well. Cherish them, because they won't always be there."

I fought back the sadness in my voice as I hugged him, remembering I had yet to find closure with my parents' deaths. I didn't want his parents to feel the pain of thinking their child was dead. "Besides, you can tell them you won't be able to marry that other Symari because you have a hot ass human in South Carolina." I grinned, letting him go.

He chuckled slightly. "Yeah, that's true," he said, hesitation still evident in his tone.

"Delmare, if I have to drag you into the sea so you'll see your family, I will. Don't worry about me. I'll be fine. Besides, I think your day might be a lot more interesting than my boring day doing lab work."

"It's not boring," he responded defensively. "You're protecting the marine life. I think it is an honorable profession."

"I'm joking, Del."

"Oh," he said. "Should I leave now so you can see me off, or would you like me to wait?"

"Don't drag this out, Delmare," I replied, giving him a knowing look. "Your family has waited long enough. You can't make them wait any longer. Now kiss me before you leave. I'm not sure when—"

He cut me off, practically running toward me. His arms lifted me up onto the counter, kissing me passionately as if he wouldn't see me for a long time. We knew that we would make this a proper temporary goodbye, one we would play in our minds over and over until we saw each other again and could do it again, again, and again. Even though I wasn't quite sure when or if I would ever see him again.

***

The drive to work was deathly silent, except for the soft sobs that escaped from my lips. As much as I tried to stop my emotions from getting the better of me, it was no use. I was at war with myself, knowing that it was the right thing to do to let him see his family, but also wanting him here, with me. I parked, but didn't get out. I knew my eyes would now be puffy and red and everyone would know I had just spent the last ten minutes crying.

Grabbing a tissue from my glove box, I dried my face, then grabbed another to blow my nose before checking my face in the mirror. My eyes were still a little swollen, and my face was blotchy from crying, but a little cold water would help. As I exited the truck, I had an odd feeling come over me, like something wasn't right. Once inside, I made a beeline for the bathroom, turning the faucet on and cupping water in my hands before splashing the cool substance over my warm cheeks. I dabbed my face dry, hoping that would help calm me down so that I could do my work in peace and not to think about Delmare leaving. I could think about how we had made love the night before, but I supposed that would just make me miss him more. Checking my reflection in the mirror again, I grabbed my purse and headed towards the back of the building, swiping my keycard. It flashed green, clocking me in for the day, I stuffed my purse into my locker, then stood and walked back out into the hall. Before I passed through the doors leading to the lab, I heard someone shout for help.

"What's going on?" I asked, not expecting an answer. I walked toward the sound, toward the eerie room that held the empty tank I had noticed one month before. "Do you need any help?" I asked from the doorway, staring at the five men that were carrying a large net.

I saw the fin press against the netting, causing a large gash, a silver liquid oozing from the wound. My heart skipped a beat as I followed the familiar silver fishtail up the creature's torso. I saw human-like flesh and eyes that shone a bright red. In an instant, I knew they were holding Delmare. *My* Delmare.

I instinctively took a step forward, wanting to free him from the netting, but knew that if I did, they would wonder why. Why was I helping him?

What was I after? Instead, I stood still, turning to my colleagues in the most professional manner I could muster, "What is that? What are you doing with this creature?"

"We found this bloody thing on our radar. Dr. Jones wanted to take a look, and we brought it up on the ship. James wants to do some further testing; we need to get him in the tank," one of the men replied, his accent thick, bewilderment and excitement filling his tone as if he couldn't believe he was holding a creature who was thought to be a myth.

This is bad. This is so bad! What can I do, what should I do? I needed to get him out of here, but I needed to do it when everyone wasn't here.

"Here, you boys get him in the tank, and I'll start up the machines," I said, turning to the monitors and turning them on, the machines humming to life. With a loud splash, I heard them drop Delmare into the tank. Looking up, I watched through the frosted glass his silver blood floated in the water for a few seconds before stopping as his wound healed over. I didn't know he could do that. God, I hoped he would forgive me for what I would have to do while he was here.

"Ah, Ms. Lisle!" I heard James call as he came toward me, grinning from ear to ear. "Isn't this an extraordinary day? I have actually found the existence of another intelligent being!"

"Yes, it is," was all I said, my mind preoccupied as I tried to think of what I could do. "It's hard to believe that this is real."

"I assure you, Ms. Lisle, this *being* is entirely real." He grinned, his eyes bright.

"*He*," I corrected, unable to stop myself. "*He* is not a being. *He* is a *he*, and he probably has a family and people who care about him and you have ripped him from them. Do you expect to keep him here? You don't know what he needs to continue living, and I don't approve of this." I sounded upset, and I was, I had full reason to be, but I knew I probably shouldn't have made an outburst like that. I needed to stay close to Delmare, so I needed James to agree to let me help with testing of Delmare. If he didn't keep me around, I wouldn't be able to know what they were doing to him or help get him out.

"Ms. Lisle, I don't need your approval on this. I am your superior. We are going to study him and find out what his needs are so that he will live a happy and healthy life here."

I bit my tongue, looking away. That bastard, who did he think he was? *He can't just keep him here!*

"I'm going to take your silence as an okay. Now, can you get started on the data sheets?" he asked.

I nodded, leaving the room as quickly as I could while I tried to control my emotions. I made a dash to the bathroom, falling to the floor as I retched up the breakfast from this morning into the toilet.

I cried, unable to control myself as my emotions overwhelmed me. They were going to test him, poke him with needles, find out information about him by any means necessary, and I had the sinking feeling that if it came to it, they would keep him until he died.

"Are you alright in there?" I heard someone call from the other side of the stall, but I didn't answer.

I didn't want to talk to anyone, I just wanted Delmare safe. I sniffed, grabbing some toilet paper, I wiped my face clean. I fumbled with the lock and swung the door open.

Diana was on the other side, her eyes filled with concern. "Oh, honey, are you alright, dear?"

I shook my head, walking past her to the sink to wash my mouth out. "I'm—" I paused, trying to think of a suitable answer to her question. "I'm just not feeling well."

"Oh dear, why don't you take the day off if you aren't feeling well?" she suggested. "There's obviously something going on in the lab today. Maybe it will be good for you to take a day off."

I shook my head, "No, I can't." I couldn't leave Delmare here alone. I couldn't bear it.

"Oh, nonsense, we'll be fine. You run along home and feel better soon, alright?" she cooed, practically leading me out the bathroom door and to my locker. I looked at her and then back to my locker, unsure if I should take the day off. "I'll see you in a few days, dear. Call me when you're feeling better," she called, leaving me to grab my stuff from my locker.

I stood and left the locker room, passing by the room with Delmare in it. Concern consumed me. The metal door was shut securely, but a small window gave me just enough view to see one man stick him with a needle. He didn't even flinch, as he gave me a knowing look before grabbing one of my coworkers and headbutting him hard causing the man to cry out in pain. I watched as they all struggled to hold him down before more men rushed past me and into the lab, hoping to contain Delmare. I wanted to go in there. I wanted to yell at them to stop, to let him go. But I couldn't.

So instead, I thought hard. I thought that I would be back soon. I thought about how much I cared about him. I thought about the fact that I would do anything to save him.

Knowing that that was everything I could do right then, I turned and walked to the entrance of the Institution. I just hoped that he had been listening in to my thoughts.

***

The house was quiet as I entered. I immediately dropped my purse, then walked into our bedroom and undressed until I was only wearing my underwear. I felt numb, empty, as if I was missing something—or someone. Shuffling through his drawer, I threw on one of his T-shirts and a pair of his sweats that he had insisted on buying. I curled up in the bed, breathing in Delmare's scent, holding on to his pillow, willing the tears to stay away. I stayed still, staring out the window, past my fence and out to sea.

As I listened to the waves, I fell asleep, my mind and heart heavy, hoping that some sleep would do me good. I knew I would do anything in my power to get him out of there, even if it killed me. All I wanted was for Delmare to be safe, away from prying eyes and those who wanted to use him for their own personal gain.

TEN

I woke up a few hours later, drenched in sweat, my hair wet and clinging to my forehead. I was cold despite my phone telling me it was eighty degrees outside. I sat up in bed, fumbling with the hem of Delmare's shirt, my heart heavy as I remembered the events of this morning. Rubbing my eyes, I tried to ease the grogginess that plagued me as I stood, padding slowly into the kitchen and rubbing my arms while I walked. I was sore everywhere, each step aching.

I poured a glass of water and drank, gulping the glass down in seconds before filling it again. I did this a few times, unable to quench my thirst. Setting the cup back down, I made my way into my bathroom, opening the medicine cabinet to find the thermometer so I could take my temperature. I stuck it in my mouth, taking a seat on the toilet lid as I waited. Suddenly it let out a long beep, and I took it out to read my results. 101 degrees Fahrenheit blinked back at me.

"Well, that explains a lot." I sighed, rubbing my temple. "Now I'm sick *and* worried about Delmare."

Turning around, I started the tub, putting it on a lukewarm temperature as I let it fill. I needed to get over this sickness soon. I wasn't sure what my coworkers were doing with Delmare and I needed to find out. I needed to save him at all costs. As the tub filled, I grabbed a handful of bath salts and threw them in, hoping they would help me get better sooner. Peeling Delmare's clothes off me, I couldn't help but take a deep breath of the clothing, remembering his scent and desperately wishing he was here. Suddenly, I felt a sharp pain in my stomach, as if I were being stabbed with a knife. Clutching my stomach, I gasped, unsure what was happening to me. I fell to my knees. I moaned, trying to concentrate on anything other than the pain. Something was wrong.

I crawled to the tub and turned the water off, wincing when the water touched my skin, the liquid feeling like ice even though I knew it wasn't that cold. Easing into the tub, I tried to relax, but my muscles still tensed as the cramps persisted. I took a deep breath and dunked my head, then let out a loud scream as I tried to cope with everything that had happened. What could I do? I was sick and couldn't go back to work until I was better, and every day I spent away was a day they spent studying Delmare. Every day I was away from Delmare, the more danger he was in, and I couldn't protect him.

Sitting up, I clutched my legs to my chest, my breasts sensitive as I hugged my legs. What was wrong with me? I had never had these symptoms before unless I was on my period, and that wasn't for another two weeks.

"Oh, God," I whispered. As the realization sunk in, I jumped out of the tub and grabbed a towel, quickly drying myself before throwing on the clothes that were laying in a pile on the floor.

Grabbing my purse from the floor in the foyer, I quickly threw on a pair of sandals and practically ran out the door, not caring about the heat outside as I drove away from my home and toward the drugstore a block away.

***

I peed on both tests, knowing that it would probably be too early to tell for a normal pregnancy, but I wasn't sure how pregnancy with a mer-child would work. I didn't want to wait until I got home to take them and made a bee line for the bathroom. But now, I wished I had waited until I was home as the questions overwhelmed me. Would the baby come out with a fin or with legs? I had been fine until this morning. Why had I started feeling sick after I left Delmare this morning? Was it because we weren't around each other anymore? No, I was never sick when I left for work each day. It had only started after we had sex this morning.

Staring at the test, I held my breath and picked one of them up. Usually, it would have a pink plus sign if you were pregnant, or a pink minus if you weren't. Where the pink line should have been, was a blue line. What the hell did that mean? Setting it down, I picked up the next one. It matched the other perfectly, I closed my eyes. What in the world was I going to do?

It's okay, I thought. *I'll wait a few days and see what happens.* I would get better, get Delmare out of there, and we could figure out what to do next. My stomach churned at the thought of Delmare, alone in a tank, surrounded by scientists as they ran tests on him. I needed to stop worrying, but I couldn't help it.

I stood and threw the tests in the sack, flushing the toilet as I exited the stall. Washing my hands, I looked up, staring at my reflection in the mirror. My hair was a mess, my skin was pale and blotchy, and my eyes had dark crescents underneath them as if I hadn't slept at all. Shaking my head, I made my way out of the bathroom, quietly walking past the cashier who gave me a sympathetic look as I exited the store. Making my way to my truck, I tossed the bag into the passenger seat, hopping into the driver's seat just as my phone vibrated in my pocket.

 Starting my truck, I began the drive back home, letting whoever had called me leave a message on my voicemail. I didn't feel like talking to anyone right now. I arrived home, staying in my car for a few minutes until I jumped out, taking the bag with me and walked into my home. What should I do? Grabbing my phone from my pocket, I pressed the phone to my ear, letting it ring until I heard Claire speak on the other line.

 "Hi Anna. What's wrong, dear?" she asked, her tone filled with concern.

 "Are you busy?" I asked as I fought back a sob. "I need to talk to you."

 "I'll be right over," she said before the call ended and I sat down on the couch, setting the tests on the coffee table.

I fumbled with the hem of Delmare's shirt again as I waited for what seemed like hours before Claire arrived. Turning around, I gave her a small smile as I looked at her with tired eyes.

"Oh, honey, what happened? Are you alright?" she asked as she came toward me, sitting beside me on the couch. She grabbed my hand, patting it slightly as I turned to look at her. "Where's Delmare?"

"He's at the research center." I paused, taking a deep breath as I recounted the past few days, blushing as I told her how Delmare and I had slept together the night before. "Delmare was on his way to see his family, but he must have been caught by my coworkers because they had him at the institute this morning. And then I threw up, so they let me go home. But now I have a fever and I'm sore everywhere, and my boobs hurt, and I just drank a gallon of water." I looked over at her. "Then I remembered that I'm near ovulation so I took a pregnancy test, but the lines are blue. What's happening to me? Is this normal?"

"Everything's going to be fine," Claire said. "This is normal, but usually we try to avoid this. Your baby can tell you're worried and that Delmare isn't here. So your body is reacting. Once Delmare is here, your symptoms will mellow down."

"So I'm really pregnant?"

"Symari pregnancies are different," Claire explained. "They last only four months, so the baby grows faster than a normal human child. After a week or so, it will be as if you're six weeks along. That's what happened when I was pregnant with John."

I took a deep breath, biting my lip as I tried to process everything that had happened in the last twenty-four hours. This was all too much. Suddenly, my stomach growled, begging me to eat something. I wanted—no, *needed*—seafood!

"I'll have my husband gather some guards and get Delmare out of there. You don't need to worry. Do you want me to pick you up something to eat? Have you started craving yet?"

"Can you get me some seafood?" I asked, hopeful.

She smiled and nodded.

"Make sure he's safe."

"He will be, dear. For now, how about you take a nap?" she suggested as she stood. "I'll be back soon."

"Thank you!" I called, feeling the heaviness of my heart lift.

Laying down on the couch, I felt my body relax, a feeling I hadn't felt all day. I just hoped that they would get Delmare out of there safely. I closed my eyes, falling into a deep sleep, no longer overwhelmed with concern about Delmare's safety.

I wondered if our baby's eyes would change colors like their father's did, or if they would be a mix of our own.

ELEVEN

I was standing barefoot in the sand, the warmth from the sun no longer burning my skin. The sound of the waves crashed around me as I gazed out to sea. Smiling to myself, I admired the blue water as it crept onto shore, the waves breaking along the horizon. For once, I wasn't dreaming about my parents.

As if on cue, I heard a familiar voice call my name, a woman's voice I hadn't heard in years. "Anna," she called from behind me, her tone calm and reassuring. "Baby."

"Mom," I whispered as I turned around, wishing to see my mother's smiling face again after all these years.

To my surprise, she stood before me, wearing a flowing white gown, her red hair falling around her face in waves, blowing in the soft sea breeze. "Hi, baby girl," she greeted as I ran toward her. I wrapped my arms around her and cried, overwhelmed to see her, even if this wasn't real.

"I can't believe I'm seeing you again after all this time," I mumbled as she brushed my hair back, kissing me softly on my head.

"I know, honey, I know," she cooed. "I'm glad I get to see you again too. Your father would have come, too, but only one of us could see you."

"What do you mean?" I asked, pulling away. "This isn't real, right?"

"This is a special place. You are visiting it through your dreams, yes, but I am real. I am really talking to you right now."

"But Mom, you're—" I started, before my mother cupped my cheek with her hand, her eyes looking over at me knowingly. "How is this possible?"

"We never truly die, Anna. We are with you always." She smiled. "Also, you got yourself a looker," she teased, playfully winking at me as a blush crept up my skin. "You're going to be a great mom, baby girl. You've grown into an amazing young woman. I'm so proud of you." She smiled thoughtfully. "Do you remember when you had to take care of that robot baby for your home economics class?"

"Yeah, no matter what I did, it wouldn't stop crying." I shook my head, remembering that Dad had wanted to throw it out the window because of the noise. "He wanted to murder his robot grandbaby."

Mom laughed, a sound I had thought I'd never hear again. She smiled before her expression turned serious. "Don't let your past haunt you any longer. You couldn't have prevented our deaths, nor could you have prevented my future son-in-law from being captured. Be happy, Anna. Focus on your future and live your life helping and serving others as you always have, but still remember to think of yourself and your family's wellbeing." She paused. "I must go now. I was told to give you this," she said as she pulled out a necklace out of thin air.

"What is it?" I asked, as she clasped the necklace around my neck. It hummed and glowed to life.

"It will help you when you take your true place as queen," she said, her voice barely above a whisper. "You will breathe underwater, see clearly under the darkest of depths, and the sea's harsh temperatures will no longer bother you as they once did. When you awaken, go home to Arcania."

"But—" I replied, turning around to see that my mother was no longer there. I was all alone. Nothing but the sea greeted me before I awoke, staring up at the ceiling of our bedroom.

My senses came back to me all at once, the feeling of someone's arms around me as I laid there, the familiar feeling making me think of Delmare. Turning over, I realized with sadness that Delmare was not beside me and I was entirely alone in my bedroom, the sound of the water in the distance filling the silence. With a heavy sigh, I crawled out of bed, my body aching and my skin burning with each step I took toward the bathroom. Stepping into the shower, I closed the curtains, turning the shower on so that I could try to enjoy the lukewarm water escaping the shower head. My stomach growled as I carefully cleaned my body, hissing as my body screamed every time I moved a certain way. With a long sigh, I washed the soap from my body, the spray hitting my face with such force it began to ease the fever burning my skin. I stood there for a few minutes, letting the water run and not caring that it may raise my water bill or that I had already been in there for twenty minutes at least.

Shutting the water off, I let the water pool near my feet before I stepped out of the shower, pulling a towel off of the hook and drying myself. I padded into my bedroom and threw some clothes on, not bothering to pay attention to what they looked like as my stomach growled from hunger. I wasn't sure how long I had been asleep, or how long it had been since Delmare was captured. Everything was starting to blur together.

As I entered the living room, I noticed the familiar short, ginger hair of a man I had known for years sitting on my couch.

I couldn't help but smile. "Hi," I greeted, my voice breaking when I rounded the corner.

John turned to look behind him, a worried look across his features. "Hey, Anna. How are you feeling?" He stood, then took a few steps toward me. The somewhat boyish grin he always sported was gone, and his beard had grown since I last saw him. There were dark crescents under his eyes.

"How do you think I feel?" I inquired, aiming for a sarcastic remark, but it sounded as if I was upset. "I have a fever, everything hurts, I've gotten myself pregnant, and the man I love has been captured by my coworkers." I paused, walking over to the kitchen to grab an apple from the fruit bowl on the counter, before looking back at one of my childhood friends and taking a sloppy bite of the crisp green apple in my hand. I chewed and swallowed before I spoke again. "I'm absolutely *perfect*, John, thank you for asking."

He didn't say anything, a knowing look spreading across his face as if he wanted to lecture me about using the proper protection before sleeping with someone, but he didn't and looked away.

"I know," I said with a sigh, finishing off the apple and throwing the core in the compost bin.

"What?" John asked, his brow furrowed.

"I know we should have used protection, but we weren't thinking. At least, we weren't thinking about the fact that I was ovulating or that I haven't taken my birth control in a few months because I've been so busy I haven't gotten around to the pharmacy. I know what you must be thinking, John, that we—that *I'm*—stupid for letting this happen. I should have gotten a refill of my prescription sooner, but honestly, I didn't think I was going to sleep with anyone. It's been years! And now Delmare is captured and he's being studied, and I feel awful and I'm worried about him and my emotions are everywhere and now I have to deal with it all. I—" I stopped, feeling my stomach lurch. I jumped toward the sink, the contents on my stomach stinging my throat as I threw it up. I groaned, turning the faucet on. I heard John's footsteps as he came behind me, his fingers brushing my hair back as I puked again.

Annoyed, I rinsed my mouth out before rinsing the sink and turning back around to stare up at my childhood friend. Without a second thought, he wrapped his around me, hugging me tight. I hugged him back, smelling the familiar scent of his shampoo. "It's going to be okay," he whispered and I nodded as he pulled away. "Dad's getting a group together to get Delmare out and Mom wanted me to watch you while she was at work."

I hadn't noticed the sunshine streaming through the windows until I looked past him and then back into his eyes. "John?"

"Yes?"

"How long have I been asleep? I dreamed about my mom. She said I can breathe underwater now. Is that possible?"

"I—I'm not sure. You should drink something and go back to bed. It will be good for you." He paused, glancing down at my stomach then back into my eyes. "And the baby."

I nodded, filling a glass and gulping the contents until my stomach was full, then let my best friend lead me back to my room and help me under the covers. "I'm going to grab you a wet cloth for your forehead. One second."

"Thank you," I called.

"No problem, sis!" he shot back.

I closed my eyes, trying to ignore the soreness that filled my body and the nausea that threatened to make me puke again, instead focusing on the sound of the ocean outside my window. Within seconds, John was back, carrying a damp cloth in his hand. Grabbing it, I set it on my forehead, the water desperately trying to soothe the warmth of my skin. The bed squeaked as John crawled onto the bed beside me. He sighed and I imagined him leaning his head up against Delmare's pillow.

"Hey, Johnny?"

"Yes, Annie?" I could tell from the tone of his voice that he was grinning cheekily.

I opened my eyes and looked over at him. "When were you going to tell me you weren't human?"

"We're doing this now?" John asked.

"Yes. We're doing it now." I replied without missing a beat, "Why didn't you trust me?"

John let out a long sigh before looking over at me, "I wanted to trust you, to tell you what I was but I wasn't sure how you would react."

"I probably wouldn't have reacted well. That doesn't mean I wouldn't see you any different John. I just wish you would have told me." I admitted, "I understand that you were protecting your species and that information can be dangerous in the wrong hands."

He nodded, worry evident in his tone, "So, you aren't mad at me?"

I shook my head, a yawn escaping from my lips as we sat in silence.

"Thank you," I finally said, "for watching over me and telling me the truth. I love you, you know that?"

"I love you too. Now get some sleep," he said, smiling over at me as I curled onto my side, feeling my exhaustion overtake me despite the blinding sunlight pouring through the open window.

I had two thoughts before I lost consciousness: how much I missed and worried about Delmare, and how strange it was to dream about my mother as if she were alive and well. I hoped someone would have answers to what that was or if it had just been a crazy dream.

TWELVE

I sat cuddled on the couch in Delmare's clothes while John sat beside me, skimming through my movie library on the television. I leaned my head against the back of the couch, my mind racing as I listened to the pinging of the options as he scrolled through them. I took a deep breath, my skin still burning as it had been for four days now—or was it five? I couldn't remember now. The days had all blurred together.

"What do you want to watch?" John asked, turning to me as he tried desperately to act like everything was normal, but I knew he was worried about me. I was getting worse as the days dragged on.

"Um," I hummed, looking up at the screen. "What about something with Tom Hanks?"

"Let's see," he said. "Uh, what about *Forrest Gump?*"

"Sure," I replied, honestly not caring what we watched, and desperately wishing that my pain would cease so I no longer had this awful fever that filled my entire body.

When he pushed play, I stood, padding to the kitchen to grab some water. I had been drinking gallons upon gallons of water, but it wasn't enough. I still felt thirsty and it wasn't regulating my temperature as I hoped it would. Cold compresses didn't help, they just melted. I wondered if I should be going to the emergency room, but Claire and John acted as if this was normal. Walking back with my cup, I set it on the side table before easing down onto the furniture, wincing as the pain stung my muscles.

"This sucks, John." I sighed, resting my bare feet against the coffee table. "I feel like my body is angry with me."

John chuckled beside me. "Well, your body is more angry with Delmare for impregnating you and leaving. You'll feel better once he comes back."

"You better not do this to anyone," I said, looking him dead in the eyes. "If you manage to be stupid like me and not use protection, you will be present for their entire life."

He gave me a look that said he already knew what I was going to say. "I know, Anna. If I manage to knock a girl up, I won't let her go through it alone. If course, I always use condoms, unlike some people." He grinned before I playfully swatted his shoulder. "Ow!"

"Don't scold the sick, pregnant lady!"

He laughed before looking back at the movie that was playing. "I don't know any of those."

I grumbled, trying to ignore his teasing comment as I stood, my bladder screaming at me to use the bathroom. I relieved myself and washed my hands, looking at my reflection in the mirror. I looked awful. My hair was a rat's nest, my skin an ashen color despite the red tint on my cheeks. I barely recognized myself.

Turning away, I joined John back on the couch, trying to concentrate on the movie playing ahead of us.

"So, John, do you have any lady friend I need to know about?" I asked as I looked over at him. As I mentioned him with a woman, his face burned bright scarlet. "Oh, so there *is* someone! Do tell!"

"I don't know what you're talking about," he said, his tone and body language absolutely betraying him. "Why are you bringing my love life up?"

"Oh, no reason. So, how is it?" I grinned, leaning toward him as his blush deepened.

He looked away.

"Why haven't I met her yet?"

"I was planning for you to meet her today, but seeing as you're…" he paused, searching for the right words, "going through something, I figured it wasn't the right time."

"I see. So, what is she like? What's her name?"

"Her name is Asherah Trench, and she has this beautiful head of blonde hair that I can just dig my fingers through." He paused, his face blushing even darker. "She's really nice and sweet. You would love her. I—I love her."

"Did you just meet?" I paused. "You love her?"

"Yeah," he grinned. "We met a few weeks ago. Mom and Dad haven't met her yet, but I'm planning for them to meet her soon."

"I'm happy for you, I really am." I smiled, and he sheepishly looked back toward the television. "I can't wait to meet her, John. I'm glad you found happiness. I just wish you had told me sooner."

"Yeah, like how you told me you'd fallen in love with royalty. Now I have to call you my princess."

"Oh, hush." I waved him off. "Are you hungry?"

"I mean, I could eat," he said, stretching on the couch. "What are you and that little rascal hungry for?"

"Mmm," I hummed. "Pizza."

"Hawaiian?" John asked with a knowing look as he grabbed his phone out of his pocket.

"Of course." I grinned cheekily.

He shook his head. "Pineapple does not belong on pizza," he said, grimacing before dialing the number and pressing the phone to his ear.

As he ordered me my favorite type of pizza and his supreme, I guzzled down my glass of water and used the restroom for the fifth time today. Suddenly my head began to throb as I stood and washed my hands. Rummaging in the medicine cabinet, I finally found the bottle I was looking for, and popped the required dosage into my mouth, screwing the lid back on, and setting it back into the cabinet.

I plopped back onto the couch and rested my head back against the back, closing my eyes, my head still throbbing while my stomach growled.

"Alright, thanks!" John exclaimed. He walked into the living room, easing back into his spot beside me. "Our food should be here in twenty minutes."

"Great." I mumbled, wishing my medicine would kick in soon, before looking over at John as he plopped back down next to me, "Have we heard anything back from the group who will get Delmare out?"

He only nodded. "They're planning to get him out soon. The problem is they need to get clearance cards in order to unlock the doors. Then they have to figure out how to get him out of the facility without them noticing that he's gone. But he is under surveillance all the time."

"Why don't they just take out the cameras?" I suggested. "I still have my key card. They could use that."

"But you're on sick leave," he replied with a pointed look. "I've had to talk to your HR manager a few times because she was worried about you."

"Poor Diana. I'm sorry I'm worrying her."

Someone knocked on the door and I stood to answer the door. The man handed me the pizzas and I paid him before slamming the door shut. I set the food on the counter and pulled out two plates from the cabinet, greedily setting two slices of pizza, licking my fingers afterward. I sat down in the dining room, John joining me at the table a moment later. We had just started eating when someone burst through the front door.

"Mom, is that you?" John asked, his mouth full.

A woman spoke, whose voice I hadn't heard before. "No, John. It's Asherah."

Immediately John stood, running over to the woman who had just arrived in my home without knocking. He kissed her quickly on the mouth, the amount of love and adoration coming off of them making my heart swell with want and hurt all at the same time. I missed Delmare, and I wished he was here with me. Taking a sip from my glass, I stood and walked toward the couple, smiling even though my body was screaming at me to stop moving. When I saw Delmare again, he was going to get an earful from me.

"It's nice to meet you, Asherah," I greeted, offering my hand. She tentatively shook it. "John mentioned you earlier."

"Did he now?" She grinned, her scarlet red eyes burning bright against her sun-kissed skin, "He has mentioned you several times, Anna. I'm glad I've finally gotten to meet you."

"Me too. We have some pizza if you're hungry," I offered, motioning behind me.

"If you don't mind. I'd hate to impose."

"Oh nonsense, there's plenty of food," I replied, padding back into the kitchen to grab her a plate.

All three of us ate in silence, the only sound was our chewing and the sound of the ocean. Midway through dinner, though, my soreness and fever got the better of me and I escaped into my bedroom. By then, Asherah had to go home and John went with her, leaving me alone. Not that I minded, I was glad I no longer felt like I was being watched as if I would fall apart at any moment.

I crawled into bed and hugged my pillow, sleep overtaking me, claiming me and pulling me into its sweet darkness.

***

When I awoke, I immediately recognized the person lying beside me, his black hair a mess, falling over his face.

"Delmare!" I exclaimed.

His eyes shot open, ready for any danger. He sat up, his arm falling over me, shielding me as if he would protect me from anything that might hurt me. "What—what is it?" he asked, his voice filled with concern.

I wrapped my arms around him, pulling him closer to me. I felt his body relax as he realized there was no danger. "I'm so glad you're safe," I mumbled. He reached up to cup my cheek in his hand, rubbing his thumb along my skin as tears made their way down my face. "I was so worried about you."

"I know, but there is no reason to be worried now," he reassured me, kissing me softly on my forehead, sparking a warm feeling that spread throughout my body as I felt the comfort in his arms as he lovingly touched my stomach. "I'm here and I'm safe."

"Okay," I breathed, leaning against him. My stomach growled ferociously.

"Oh, Claire brought food. Do you want me to heat it up for you?" he asked.

"If you want to. If not, I can get out of bed and get it," I said, standing.

He shook his head in protest. "No, it's fine. Besides, you need your rest. You are carrying our child after all." He grinned, his eyes flashing a mix of orange and purple, colors I had yet to see, and I loved them. I looked down then, touching my stomach without even thinking. I smiled at him, feeling a rush of joy when he looked at me, the love and care clear on his face. "I'll be right back," he called as he left me to grab my food.

I smiled to myself, absentmindedly rubbing my stomach as I stared out the window at the sea. I watched as the waves broke, reminding me of the dream I just had and what my mother had said. Could I really breathe underwater now? I was curious if what she said was true, but wasn't sure I was willing to risk my unborn child's death because

I wanted to test a theory. A moment later, Delmare came back with a plate filled with food, steam rising above it. As he handed it to me, he cautioned me to be careful.

"I know it's hot," I teased, setting the plate on my lap. I stabbed a piece of shrimp with my fork and blew on it a few times before sticking it in my mouth.

"I just don't want you to get hurt," he said, as he sat cross-legged next to me.

"I'll be okay," I reassured him, then blurted, "I saw my mother."

"What?" he asked as I swallowed.

"She was in my dream." I recounted all of what had happened in my dream as Delmare listened intently. "She says I should be able to breathe underwater. Could that be possible? I don't want to risk hurting the baby, but I kinda want to test it out."

"Did she say *any* water or just seawater?" he asked, standing and taking my plate.

I followed him and watched as he rinsed my dish in the sink. "She said underwater. She didn't specify what type." I paused. "I'm assuming any kind of water."

"I think we should wait till you're feeling better before we test that theory." he said, turning back around. "How are you feeling?"

How was I feeling? I was feeling great, my fever was gone, and I wasn't as sore as I was before. "I feel great, better than I was. I had this awful fever, and everything hurt."

"I'm sorry. I should have been there for you."

I shook my head. "Don't be sorry. It's not your fault. You're here now. That's all that matters."

He hugged me, pulling me closer to him. I closed my eyes, not realizing how much I had missed him until he was gone. We stood there for a few minutes, just holding each other, before we made our way back into the bedroom, cuddling up to each other as we laid in silence. Every once in a while, we gave each other passionate kisses before going back to cuddling. I was exhausted. As much as I wanted to stay awake and spend my evening with Delmare, my body refused, my eyelids growing heavy for the third time that day. I suppose that was normal, as the child was growing at an exceptionally fast rate. I wondered what that would do to my body.

"Go to sleep," Delmare whispered in my ear. "I'm not going anywhere."

"Delmare?" I asked suddenly, refusing to fall asleep.

"Yes?"

"How did you get captured? What did my co-workers do to you? How were they able to get you out? They didn't hurt you, right?" I inquired, the questions spilling out of me.

He sighed, "Anna, I don't want you to worry."

"I just want to know what happened."

"Fine, I was captured a few miles off the coast and they brought me to your work. They did a few tests, that's all. I don't remember escaping the facility. When I awoke, I was in the living room and saw your pregnancy tests before Claire explained the situation you were in." he finished, looking over at me, "Now go to sleep, you need to rest."

A second later, I felt the comforter being pulled over me as sleep took me, pulling me into a dark abyss with no dream in sight. As I fell asleep, I felt Delmare's lips brush against my cheek before I lost consciousness.

***

The next morning, I took a shower, not bothering to look in the mirror as I stripped off my clothes and turned the faucet on. Glancing down, I noticed the bulge in my stomach that hadn't been there before. That would be normal had I been ten weeks along. But I wasn't.

"There is no way I'll be able to get used to you growing like that," I said, talking directly to my baby—our baby. "You're just stubborn, aren't you? That's okay, your grandma was stubborn too." I smiled to myself as I stepped into the shower, the warm water relaxing me as I cleaned myself.

When I was done, I walked into the bedroom. Delmare wasn't asleep on the bed anymore, and the smell of bacon on the skillet informed me he was most likely in the kitchen. Getting dressed in a comfortable pair of sweats and Delmare's hoodie instead of my usual sundress, I unraveled my hair from the towel and threw it into the hamper. Padding into the kitchen, I watched as Delmare stood in front of the stove, casually cooking away, unaware that I was near him.

"What are you making?" I asked.

Delmare jumped, cursing under his breath as the bacon grease popped and splattered onto his skin.

"Are you okay? I didn't mean to scare you."

"Yeah, I'm fine," he said, turning to look at me before placing the lid on the pan. "Good morning."

"Good morning." I grinned, walking over to him and interlacing my fingers in his and resting my head on his shoulder. "That smells good."

"Thanks. I was going to make some eggs and toast, as well, but I was going to use the same pan so we don't have as many dishes. Do you want some?"

"Yeah. I'll probably get some strawberries too."

"That sounds good," he replied as I let go of his hand so he could place the bacon onto the plate. "Do you want scrambled eggs or fried?"

"Scrambled, please," I said, walking over to the fridge to grab the container of strawberries as Delmare cracked the eggs into a bowl. Taking a seat at the dining table, I took a bite from a strawberry, the sweet and tangy juice spreading along my taste buds before I swallowed, but immediately my gag reflex fought back. I ran to the sink, puking up the strawberry and everything else in my stomach.

"Why?" I mumbled, turning the faucet on to rinse the sink and my mouth.

"Are you okay?" Delmare asked as I wiped my mouth with a towel.

I nodded. "Yeah. I don't think the baby likes strawberries."

He chuckled. "Probably not. We usually eat seafood, not things like vegetables and fruits like you have on land." He paused, dishing the food out onto two plates as the toast popped out of the toaster. "We can see if the little pup likes what it's father made."

"Thank you for making breakfast," I said, grabbing the strawberries and setting them back into the fridge. I looked back at him, amusement in my tone. "*Pup*? Like a baby shark?"

"You're welcome, and yes, pup." He grinned, handing me my plate and a fork. "I enjoy cooking. It's relaxing. Especially if I get to serve the woman I love."

I looked up as he sat down, the eggs that I had scooped onto my fork falling back onto my plate. His eyes flashed purple and gold, further confirming what he said was true.

"You love me?" I asked, setting my fork down. I stared back at him, smiling at the thought.

"Yes, Anna, I love you," he stated firmly, his smile growing bigger by the second.

"I love you too." I beamed, smiling like an idiot while my heart leaped with joy.

We ate in silence, listening to the sound of the waves crashing softly in the background until I looked up. "Delmare?"

"Yes?"

"I think it would be in the best interest of our family if we go to Arcania. You have been gone for a long time and you have a duty to your family and to your kingdom." I paused. "And I'd love to meet your family."

"Are you sure? What about your life on land? You can't just leave. You have a job, your coworkers will wonder what has happened to you."

"We could fake my death," I answered instantly.

"What?"

"Yeah, we could do that! We lose people at sea all the time. When's the next storm? I could go out on a boat right before a storm and then jump into the water and we could start our trip to Arcania. Then the boat will wash up on shore and police will assume I've drowned during the storm."

"Do you think that could work?" he asked as he grabbed my empty plate and set it in the sink.

- "Possibly, or we could just leave. I don't think I'm planning to come back, so there should be no reason to worry about my current life on land."

"But did you make friends while you were here?" he asked.

I shook my head. "No, most of my friends are from my high school years and are in Kansas. I haven't spoken to them in years. I hadn't made many friends here, except for John, but he knows about the underwater world. The police would come to my house and investigate my disappearance for a while and then I'll end up in a file somewhere and they'll forget about me." I paused, standing and walking toward him. I wrapped my arms around him. "I just want to spend the rest of my days with you and raise our children together. I'm not sure how to rule a kingdom, but I'm sure I can learn."

"When do you want to leave?" he asked, grabbing a towel and drying his hands with it.

"I think we should leave tomorrow, and I want to spend some time on the beach and with you today,"

I replied. I let go just as Delmare turned around, his eyes sparking gold.

"I swear, you're horny all the time." I giggled, watching as he smiled mischievously at me before closing the distance between us with a kiss.

"I don't think that's a bad thing. Do you?" he grinned cheekily as his hands played with the bottom of my dress, touching the outside of my thigh in the process. He kissed me again, leaving trails of kisses across my cheek, along my jaw, and down my neck.

My heart fluttered at the feeling. I pulled at his shirt as he led me to our bedroom. I wasn't sure if having sex while I was already pregnant would harm the baby, but the overwhelming need for him consumed me.

"It won't," he replied, almost breathless, as we crawled onto the bed. "It won't hurt the baby."

"I told you to quit reading my thoughts!" I exclaimed, but my tone lost its sense of authority as he pulled my dress off.

I kissed him back, peeling his shirt off as he leaned into me, his hand brushing across my skin, making goosebumps sprout everywhere he touched. In an instant, we were all over each other, and I knew that this would be a day I would remember for the rest of my life.

THIRTEEN

As I played with Delmare's hair, he rested his head on my breasts despite the soreness that filled them. His eyes were closed as we laid there peacefully, holding on to each other. It was nearly one in the afternoon and I knew by now the sun would be high in the sky, the water warm and ready to greet the beach lovers.

He mumbled in his sleep, wrapping his arm around my waist tighter, protectively pulling me closer to him. I sighed as my bladder set off alarms. I discretely tried to escape his hold on me without waking Delmare.

"Mmm, no, don't go," he mumbled, reaching for me as I sat up, resting his head against my back.

"I have to pee," I insisted, the bed squeaking as I stood. "I'll be gone for just a moment."

I heard him let out a loud sigh as I used the restroom. I wasn't sure if he was being so protective or clingy because of the baby or what, but it was getting annoying. I wasn't helpless; I could take care of myself. As I washed my hands, I looked up and stared at myself in the mirror, realizing the dark crescents under my eyes had disappeared and the worried look I had had a few days before had quickly vanished. Smiling a bit at my reflection, I made my way back to bed, wrapping my arms around Delmare before squeezing him tight.

"You know, we can't stay in bed all day," I mumbled, gaining a groan of protest from the merman cuddling with me. "I thought it would be good for us to get some sun."

"What if I say no?" he protested, turning to me with a mischievous look in his eyes.

"Then I'll go by myself and you can stay here alone," I replied, hopping out of bed. I shimmied out of my clothes to pull on my swimsuit. My bump was noticeable now. It no longer looked like I was bloated; it was obvious I was pregnant. Pulling a cover up over my body, I tied the string around my waist before grabbing my beach bag and swinging it onto my shoulder. "Are you coming?"

"Hang on, let me get my trunks on."

I left our bedroom and made my way into the kitchen to stuff a few water bottles into my bag.

As I shut the fridge door, Delmare came behind me wearing nothing but his swim trunks and a smile. Grabbing his hand, we walked outside, toward the white sandy beaches of Myrtle Beach. Our feet touched the hot, powdery sand as the water crashed ahead of us. I set the bag down when we were about halfway between home and the water, then grinned at him mischievously and made a dash for the water, letting go of his hand as my feet dug into the sand. Within seconds, my feet were greeted by the warm water of the Atlantic. Normally it would feel good, but not as good as it currently felt against my skin. It felt absolutely perfect.

"Anna, what are you doing?!" I heard Delmare yell from behind me as I squished my toes into the wet sand.

"I'm taking a walk!" I called back, as I heard him jog toward me.

"Just be careful," he said beside me.

"You act as if I'll fall apart at any moment," I teased, walking further into the water so the waves sprayed over my calves. "A little water hurt no one."

He shook his head before lacing his fingers with mine as we walked along the surf. Delmare could decide whether he had a tail, so he could still dip his legs in the water with me as we trailed along the wet sand, the water flowing around our feet. Leaning my head on his shoulder as we walked, I breathed in the salt-filled air, feeling entirely at peace as we walked together.

"I want to go for a swim. Do you want to come with me?" I asked, turning to him.

"Sure, but I get to carry you." He grinned mischievously before hoisting me up in his arms. He walked into the sea until the water reached his chest, then he gently set me into the sea.

As I surfaced, I brushed my hair out of my face and kicked my legs to keep myself afloat. Delmare wrapped his arms around my waist, holding me up. My legs brushed up against something scaly and I realized he must have changed forms. I wrapped my legs around him, kissing him quick on the lips. His eyes shifted from their normal silver to purple.

"I love you too." I grinned as I realized what purple meant. He kissed me back, this time harder and with more passion than I had intended.

He left trails of kisses down my neck and a whisper of a moan escaped my lips.

Someone cleared their throat near us.

Startled, I jumped away from Delmare, and I felt his hold on me tense. I shifted, turning toward the sound. Four men rose from the water beside us. They carried spears, war paint spread across their bodies in intricate lines.

"Your Highness," one of them greeted as they all bowed in unison. "We have come to escort you and your lady back to Arcania."

I fell back into the water as Delmare let go. The water cascaded over me as I gasped, but instead of filling my lungs with pure saltwater, it felt as if I was breathing in pure oxygen. It was lighter than I thought. I was breathing in water! Quickly surfacing, I turned to Delmare, who looked over at me apologetically.

"Are you alright?"

"I can breathe underwater!" I exclaimed, my voice filled with shock even though I knew my mother had told me I could.

"Great," the merman said. "We must leave now. I don't want any other humans seeing us. Your Highness, my lady, follow me, please." He and his men dove underwater, their multicolored tails shining bright against the water before disappearing under the surface.

"Did he just call me a lady?" I asked, turning to Delmare.

"I believe that will be your title until we are married. You will be known as the Princess Consort until I take the throne, which is when you will be sworn in as queen. But I don't think that will be for a while. You will need to learn more about the kingdoms and their people before then," he informed me, taking my hand. "Shall we?"

I nodded as he dove underwater, pulling me along gently under the surface as I clutched his hand for dear life. The dark water was now crystal clear, exposing me to an underwater world I could never explore before. Marine life of all shapes and colors darted along the sea floor as we swam, following the group of guards throughout the water.

"Where is Arcania?" I asked, after we were swimming for what felt like an hour, hoping I could break the silence that filled the group.

"It is nestled deep in the Arctic ocean, just off the coast of the North Pole. The water is cold there, and the ocean is the shallowest of all Earth's oceans," Delmare replied, turning to me with a smile. "You aren't cold now, right?"

I shook my head. "No, I'm perfectly fine. But I think it's going to be awhile before I get used to being able to breathe underwater and live down here."

Delmare only nodded, deep in thought as the guards suddenly stopped in front of a blue and white carriage carried by two beluga whales. One guard turned to me, his hair as white as snow, wrinkles around his eyes. "The queen has requested the lady take this carriage, as she wasn't sure you would be too keen on meeting the people just yet."

"Are you sure?" I asked. "Why don't we take turns?"

The guard shook his head. "I am sure you are tired by now as you aren't used to swimming for this long. It will not be bothersome. Go ahead."

Looking back at Delmare, he nodded toward the carriage. I protested when one man tried to open the door for me, saying I had two hands, and could do it myself. Pulling the door open, I swam in just as Delmare made a dash to swim in beside me before locking the carriage door.

"I don't want to hear any lovemaking in there!" the guard from before said, chuckling as the carriage halted for a second, then moved forward.

I felt my cheeks flush for a moment before Delmare moved to sit next to me, his tail brushing against my skin. He felt warm as he wrapped his arms around me, pulling me closer as the moving carriage lulled me asleep. I wasn't sure how long this trip was going to last, but I hoped I wouldn't make a fool of myself once we arrive.

I woke up to someone lightly shaking my shoulder, pulling me from my dreamless sleep. The carriage had stopped and Delmare still had his arms around me, never letting go as I had fallen asleep.

"Are we here?" I asked as a yawn escaped my lips.

Delmare nodded, his eyes flashing orange as excitement filled his features. "Are you ready to go?"

"Am I supposed to curtsy? Is what I'm wearing okay? What if your parents don't like me?" I asked, worry filling my voice.

Delmare shook his head. "You'll be fine. What you're wearing is fine, and you can curtsey if you want, but I'm sure my parents will understand if you don't." He stood, pulling me to my feet. "Do you need a second?"

I shook my head, "No. I'm still nervous, but as long as you're with me, hopefully I won't make a fool of myself."

"I think you'll be just fine," he said as he unlocked the carriage and swung the door open, exiting the carriage before offering me his hand and helping me out. Immediately, I laced my fingers with his as the guards bowed to us and Delmare led me toward the enormous castle that sat before us. It looked like it was made entirely out of sea glass, the colors a range of blues and greens, sparkling around us. The guards on either side of the door bowed their heads slightly before opening the double doors for us. I felt my heart flutter as I followed Delmare inside. Warmth surrounded my skin, feeling as if I was soaking in a warm bath. Immediately, a plump woman with a bright yellow tail swam toward us.

"Ah, your highness, my lady! Welcome to your new home," the woman greeted, her violet eyes sparkling with excitement at the sight of me. "I hope you don't mind, but what is your name, dear?"

"Um, do you want my full name?" I asked, feeling a little overwhelmed. She nodded before I answered, "Anna Jane Lisle and I'm not a lady."

"You are now, dearie. That's a lovely name you have there, Lady Anna." She smiled before turning to Delmare. "Now, I hope you don't mind, but I will have to take your Mate away from you, your Highness. I must get her ready to meet the king and queen."

"But wait—" I protested, but the woman grabbed my hand and pulled me away.

"My name is Mrs. Berkeley. My grandmother was in Queen Sedna's service when she became queen and my family has been in the service of the Royals of Arcania ever since." She pulled me along the hallway before stopping at a door that looked the same as any of the others around us. "This is where you will stay." As she swung the door open, I was amazed at the enormity of the room. A queen-sized bed sat along one wall while a balcony overlooking the city was across from it. A fire burned in the hearth even though we were completely submerged in water.

"How…" I started, turning to Mrs. Berkeley. "How long have you known I would come?"

"Only a few weeks. Mr. Saltheir alerted us that Prince Delmare had found his Mate, and that you were human. We weren't sure if you could visit us, but our Mother Ocean assured us you could take your place as queen."

"Mother Ocean?" I asked. She led me inside, closing the door and opening the wardrobe.

"Yes, she is the creator of all the Symari and the great-grandmother of your Mate," she responded as she pulled out a blue dress, one that reminded me of those Edwardian dresses women wore in the early 1900s. "Now, get undressed and I'll help you into your gown."

"Do you mean Keilani? Would she be the one who gave me the ability to breathe underwater?" I asked as I untied my cover up.

"Yes, the goddess Keilani. We also know her for bestowing gifts on humans who are mated to her creations. So it is likely that she gave you the ability to live here," she explained. I saw her stare at the slight bump that had formed on my stomach before looking back at me, a blush creeping over my skin.

"It is nothing to be ashamed of, dearie. You will be a member of the Royal Court, so you must get used to women helping you get dressed," she said, not commenting on the evident largeness of my stomach. I peeled my swimsuit off before she grabbed something that looked like clams and clasped them onto me. "This will help hold your breasts up, unlike that scrap of clothing you insisted on wearing." As she pulled the dress over my form, it flowed over my body, showing off my best features and not insinuating my baby bump. "Now, we'll just pin your hair back here and be good to see your future in-laws."

Letting out a nervous breath, I let Mrs. Berkeley do my hair as I felt the nervousness spark in my stomach. What if they didn't like me? When she was done, Mrs. Berkeley led me outside where Delmare was waiting for me, his eyes sparkling with gold as he smiled at me. I knew that if he was by my side, I would not fail.

FOURTEEN

I grabbed hold of Delmare's hand and he smiled over at me, his eyes burning gold. I let out a nervous laugh as he pulled me to his side, kissing me softly on my cheek. I laid my head on his shoulder and breathed. *I just need a moment. This is a lot to take in.*

"I know," he whispered. "Take all the time you need."

"It's just... I *just* found out I'm pregnant and now I have to meet your parents and I'll eventually rule a kingdom I know nothing about. It's a lot to take in and I'm worried that I'll make a fool of myself or that your parents won't like me. What if they hate me? What if—"

I was cut off as Delmare let go of my waist, moving in front of me, placing both of his hands on my face, his expression entirely sincere. "I know it is a lot and we will work through it together. I'm sure my parents will love you. I understand you are nervous and worried, but you won't be alone in any of this. I will help you, and I know my parents will as well," he said, his tone sincere.

"Okay," I breathed out. "I'm ready now."

He nodded before offering his arm. I took it, holding on to him as he led me to wherever his parents were. We rounded a few corridors, and I was sure we were lost until two guards opened a pair of double doors not too far from where we were swimming. As we entered, someone said our names and a couple stood. I nervously tugged on my dress, unsure of what I should do.

"Oh, Delmare, you're back!" a woman exclaimed, her voice filling the room with an angelic sound.

The Symari standing before us wore her violet hair up in several braids, her crown resting atop her head, her silver eyes and tail flashing against her pale skin. Delmare let go, swimming over to hug his mother, who kissed him quickly on the cheek before turning to me. Her expression was entirely warm as she looked at me fondly before swimming over to me. I immediately stopped fidgeting, frozen in place as she came toward me and placed her warm hand on my cheek before quickly hugging me. The comfort I felt immediately consuming me as I relaxed, almost certain that there was no reason to be worried at all. I wrapped my arms around her as well.

"It's good to finally meet you, Anna." She smiled, her eyes shining bright. "I was hoping we could have tea tomorrow, so we can get to know each other better." She turned to the merman who hadn't moved, who I assumed was the king. His hair was as black as Delmare's and I could see where Delmare got his looks from. He was definitely a mix of both of his parents. "Honey, say hello."

"I'm trying to decide why a human is an excellent choice as the wife to our son and the mother of our grandchildren, as I can see that they have already sired children," he said, before turning to Delmare. "You've only known this human for a month and you're sleeping with her?" I clenched my jaw while the king and Delmare's father stared at me with a look of pure distrust. "If you had married Emilia like you were told to, none of this would have happened!"

"Father, do not talk about Anna that way!" Delmare bellowed beside me, making me jump at the loudness of his voice. "I will not have you hate her because you hate her race. She is kind, thoughtful, and cares about the ocean and its citizens. She is my Mate, and an amazing woman, and I can think of no one better to rule beside me as my wife and help raise our children, which we will do *together*. You will no longer control my life, and if being with Anna means I will give up my right as heir, so be it."

I held my breath as the room went silent, no one speaking a word. I looked at Delmare, his eyes flashing red as I reached for his hand, hoping to comfort him. I laced his fingers with mine, giving them a quick squeeze as I looked over at Delmare's mother. She looked at me apologetically, glaring at her husband for a moment before looking back at her son. Someone in the crowd began a slow clap.

As we turned toward the sound, we watched as Delmare's father clapped slowly and smiled, his expression entirely happy. "I thought you'd never tell me what for, and here you are, months before your coronation, to tell me how it is. I'm glad you will put your family before your own personal gain, especially with the throne, but I caution you to do what is best not only for your children and Anna, but for the citizens you serve," he said before turning to me. "Now, what exactly do you do on land?"

"I—" I paused, a little shocked at his words. "You mean, what did I do for a living?"

"Yes, what is your employment?"

"Oh, I'm a marine biologist," I explained. "I usually took samples of the water, checked the ocean population, and helped rehabilitate marine life that needed saving."

The king just smiled, nodding slightly. "Interesting." He paused. "So how did you take the news of our son being a merman, not a human?"

I laughed. "Well, first off, he showed up at my home naked."

"I didn't have any clothes!" he exclaimed, trying to defend himself.

Shaking my head, I turned back to Delmare's dad. "Anyway, I fainted. Well, after I threw a blanket at him and he jumped in the tub to show me his tail." I smiled, looking at Delmare again. He wrapped his arms around my waist. "But I think everything turned out okay."

The king chuckled before turning to his wife. "I'm sure finding his Mate after all this time might have clouded his judgment, but I am glad everything turned out okay. And that you both found each other."

"Are you hungry?" Delmare's mother asked, turning to me. "You must be starving after your long journey."

"I am a little, your Majesty," I replied, grimacing as I wasn't sure if I had addressed her properly.

"Oh hush, no need for formalities. Call me Theodosia or Mom. My husband has yet to introduce himself, but his name is Ronan, named after his father Ronan Alexander Stormborn."

"So, you're a junior?" I asked, turning to the king. He nodded. "That's cool."

"Well, dinner should be served by now. Shall we head to the dining room?" Theodosia suggested. Delmare reached for my hand, squeezing it reassuringly as we followed the king and queen through the halls and into the dining room.

As soon as we entered, several maids filed out, standing along the wall patiently as we took our seats. Ronan sat at the head of the table while his wife sat to his right. She motioned for me to sit beside her. As I took my seat, Delmare sat across from me, smiling as if this was the best day of his life. The table was set with several plates, two glasses, and five different pieces of silverware. Looking up nervously, I wondered what all of this silverware was for and why on Earth I couldn't just use one fork and one knife.

Immediately, a group of people set food in front of us and I turned to thank whoever did it next to me. They smiled sweetly at me before escaping through another set of doors. I looked down at my plate, feeling my anxiety rise as I wondered what on Earth I had gotten myself into. Glancing at Theodosia's plate, I noticed she had grabbed the fork at the end. Reaching for it, I took a bite of what looked like lobster. Immediately, I closed my eyes, enjoying the taste of the seafood as I swallowed and took another bite.

"Good, isn't it?" Theodosia chuckled beside me as I nodded enthusiastically. "After dinner, it might be good for you to retire to bed. Delmare, would you take her to her room?"

"Sure, I'd love to," he said as I looked up at him, his eyes a mix of purple and gold, a combination I had learned to love.

After dinner, our plates were cleared quickly, and I stood, completely full to the brim. Delmare offered me his arm and I linked my arm in his. Resting my head on his shoulder as we swam, we were at my bedroom in minutes. I was exhausted by the time we made it there. Delmare swung open the bedroom door. I was glad I wouldn't be greeted by strange maids who would insist on running my bath or dressing me.

"Would it be bad if I asked you to stay with me tonight?" I asked, turning to Delmare who led us into the bedroom. "I'm kind of feeling homesick."

"Not at all. I'd love to. And besides, our rooms are joined until we are married, so it's not like I'm at the end of the hall," he replied, his eyes still gold and purple. "I wouldn't mind breaking the rules so that you feel comfortable."

I couldn't help but smile as I turned to him. "Can you help me out of my dress? I don't want to ruin it."

I felt him gently pull my dress off, unclasping the clam shell bra, which floated off of me. I turned around, staring up at Delmare as I placed my hand on his cheek. He grabbed my waist and I smiled at him as he placed a quick kiss on my forehead before rummaging through my wardrobe to find something for me to wear to bed. Turning around, he handed me a nearly translucent nightdress that seemed to end at my knees.

"You look so hot right now," he blurted, his eyes sparkling gold.

I laughed, shaking my head as I hugged him, just as his scales were replaced with flesh. "I don't think I can tonight," I said, knowing exactly what he was thinking. "It's been a long day."

"That's okay." He grinned, leading me to the bed so I could crawl into it.

My body relaxed as Delmare cuddled close to me, his hand making circular motions along my bump while he kissed my shoulder a few times. Turning around to face him, I opened my eyes to see his eyes shut. He looked so peaceful, as if he was exactly where he needed to be. Shuffling closer to him, I kissed him softly on his forehead as he pulled me closer to the hardness at his waist. I felt a blush creep up my neck. You would think I would be used to it by now, but the rush I felt now was unmistakable even though I knew I was exhausted.

Playing with his hair, I watched as he inched closer to me, resting his head on my chest as I felt my eyelids grow heavy, sleep overtaking me.

FIFTEEN

I awoke in the middle of the night as the need to pee overtook me. How would I pee underwater? Was there a bathroom I could use? Delmare was entangled around me, his arms wrapped protectively across my body as he nestled closer to me in his sleep.

"Delmare," I said, slightly above a whisper as I shook his shoulder. "Delmare, wake up."

He mumbled in his sleep, his voice sleepy when he sat up. "What, what's wrong?"

"I have to pee."

"You always have to pee," he teased, rubbing his eyes as he tried to wake himself up.

"Well, I *am* peeing for two people," I replied pointedly as I stood, unraveling myself from the covers, Delmare following me.

"That's true," he replied as he led me into another room where a bathtub, toilet, and sink sat, looking completely new. "Close the door, please."

"Um, okay," I said, doing as I was told. Suddenly, the water around us drained away and we both fell to the floor, breathing in oxygen. "What just happened?"

"My mother just drained the castle of water. She does it every once in a while, but lately she had been talking about making it permanent," Delmare explained. He motioned toward the toilet and I immediately sat on it.

I was still trying to figure out how they could drain the castle in mere seconds. I stood and I walked to the sink, surprised to see water gushing out of the faucet. Looking up at Delmare inquisitively, he only smiled as I washed my hands.

"How do you guys have plumbing? Wouldn't the water pressure be too much for it?" I asked as I went to wring the water out of my hair, only noticing as I touched it that my hair was entirely dry. "What the—? Why am I not wet?"

"You are asking a lot of questions right now, Annie." He yawned. "Can I answer them in the morning?"

I pursed my lips, looking away as I realized it was still in the middle of the night, but now I didn't think I could go back to sleep now that my mind was abuzz with hundreds of questions. I nodded my head, watching Delmare escape the bathroom and make his way back under the covers.

Sighing, I followed him, the blanket still warm as I lay on my back, staring at the ceiling. In mere seconds, Delmare was asleep beside me, his arms wrapped around me as if begging me to follow in his footsteps back into the calming abyss of sleep. But, I couldn't. My mind was busy, overwhelmed with the events of the past few days and months that had filled my life and controlled my future. I needed to think, to process everything, but I couldn't while Delmare slept peacefully beside me.

Carefully exiting the bed, I casually unhooked a robe from the wardrobe, wrapping it securely around myself as I opened the door that led into the hallway. Wincing as it let out a loud squeak, I looked over at Delmare, who still slept soundly on the bed. Holding my breath, I made my way into the hallway, shutting the bedroom door, careful not to make a lot of noise. I turned around, immediately facing a guard.

"My lady, what are you doing up this late?" He paused on his route, turning toward me with a concerned look. "You should be in bed."

"I'm sorry, sir, but I can't sleep." I paused. "Can you escort me to the library? I don't want to be a bother, but I don't know where it is."

"My lady, I don't think it will be a wise idea to escort you without a chaperone," he said again, this time in a more professional manner.

"I'm not going to sleep with you!" I exclaimed. "Can you give me directions? I'll just go by myself."

He sighed before reluctantly informing me that the library was down the hallway and to the left. After thanking him, I made my way that direction, my feet padding against the somewhat warm floor, making a slight echo throughout the hall. Lit sconces glowed along the walls, lighting up part of the hallway as I pulled open the library door, the creaking sound of the door echoing throughout the halls. A few sconces filled the room, and a candle lay unlit on a table next to a stack of books.

Lighting a match, I lit the wick, the candle burning brightly as the fire took hold. I picked the candle up and walked along a shelf of books, starring at the wording along the bindings. Most of the languages I didn't recognize, but one I did. Pulling the book out from the shelf, I walked over to the table, setting the book down along with the candle and took a seat. Just as I was about to open the book to read, someone barged into the library, closing the door quietly behind them before making their way toward me.

"My lady!" His voice was filled with panic as if something or someone was after him, "Thank goodness you're safe."

"What's wrong?" I asked as I stood, concern in my tone as I wondered why the guard before me was panicking. "What's going on?"

"There is no time to explain, we must get you to the safe room at once." He walked toward me, the candle lighting his features.

"The safe room? Are we under attack? Is Delmare alright? And the king and queen?" I asked as the guard led me to the back of the library before he pressed a stone. The wall opened up to reveal a hidden corridor.

"We are under attack, my lady. Now please, follow me for the safety of both you and the heir." He glanced down at my stomach before looking into my eyes, a knowing look written across his features as he ushered me further into the corridor. The wall closed behind us, filling the area with darkness.

We walked in silence, and the guard grabbed a sconce from along the wall and quickly set it ablaze, the light filling the hall as we made our way forward. He let me walk beside him, scanning the area before us, his left hand on the hilt of his sword, ready to attack at any moment. My mind was racing by the time we stopped in front of a dead end, wondering whether Delmare and his parents were safe. Quickly, the guard placed his hand along the wall, feeling along until he found the button that opened the wall door. Slowly, the wall slid open, more light billowing through and the loud sound of someone pulling out their sword filled the room.

"Identify yourself!" they called as the guard beside me put his sword back.

"Captain Eugene Wentworth, soldier. I am with Lady Anna Lisle. I am charged to make sure she is safely here until the castle is clear of all traitors," he said, motioning for me to follow him, which I did, watching as the group of soldiers put their swords away.

I heard a woman gasp and move toward me. Theodosia's face was filled with worry as she hugged me, squeezing me close before taking my hand and ushering me to sit beside her. "Thank goodness you're safe."

"What's happening? Is Delmare alright? Where's your husband?" I paused, correcting myself. "Where's the king? Captain Wentworth said we've been attacked. Attacked by what?" I felt the questions flowing out of me like a waterfall, concern and worry filling my tone.

"Syrens attacked us. They are creatures Ronan's mother created before she died. She did not know that they had offspring, so when she lifted her curse, the children remained, even more filled with hatred and more animal than Symari." She paused, squeezing my hand. "They attacked a few hours ago, infiltrating the castle. I was asleep when they attacked, but my husband was in his study. The guards took me here while we waited for news about you. You weren't in your room and the guard stationed there did not know where you had gone."

"That doesn't make sense. I literally asked him for directions. I was only gone for a few minutes." I paused. "Where's Delmare and the king?"

She shook her head, confirming my worries. "We must wait here until the coast is clear. If you would like to sleep, you can."

"No, I don't think I can go to sleep, not with monsters roaming around the castle and not without knowing where Delmare or your husband are. Will they be alright?"

"I'm sure they will be fine," she said, trying to reassure me. "They can handle themselves."

I bit my lip, fumbling with the fabric of the robe around my body as I tried not to think about Delmare getting hurt or the monstrous Syren creatures I hadn't seen before. I tried to calm down, knowing that stress and worry wasn't good for the baby. Leaning my head up against the wall, I waited in silence as the seconds ticked by, hoping to hear from Delmare soon. Mentally begging whoever might listen that he wouldn't be killed.

It seemed like hours before we looked up. The sound of rocks scraping filled the room as one of the rock wall doors opened. The guards in front of us unsheathed their swords immediately, their stances widening, ready for anything on the other side.

"Who's there?" one guard called as Theodosia squeezed my hand.

I heard coughing then, and what sounded like Delmare wheezing. "It's me."

I immediately tried to stand before Theodosia stopped me, shaking her head at me as I stayed silent. One of the guards walked forward, into the abyss. Suddenly the guard screamed, making me jump as two of the men stiffened their stances just as whoever was in the hallway ran into the safe room. He looked exactly like Delmare, but their eyes were a black abyss as he snarled at us. I froze, fear taking hold as the creature stared at me with a devilish grin.

"I'm coming for you, *darling*."

Instantly the guards jumped on the creature. He attacked, blocking their attacks all at once just before someone jumped from behind the creature, digging their sword into its back. It screeched, black blood flowing from its wound as it fell to the floor. I felt my heart beat against my chest, my eyes wide as I stared at the lifeless creature. Looking back up at whoever had attacked it, I felt my heart burst with joy as I saw Delmare—the real Delmare—panting as he stood. He was covered in a black substance that I could have guessed was other Syrens' blood. Standing, I made a move toward him, stopping as Theodosia grabbed my arm.

"Delmare?" I asked.

He looked up, the anger in his eyes replaced with violet as relief washed over his features. "Annie!" he exclaimed, running to me as the guards separated. Quickly, he placed a kiss on my lips, holding me close to him as if he would never see me again. "I'm so glad you're safe. Where did you go?"

"I was in the library because I couldn't sleep," I explained, hugging him back as I felt the relief wash over me. "Where's your dad?"

I watched as his eyes changed colors and he frowned, sadness written all over his face. He moved to kneel in front of his mother. Her face changed and she let out a shriek, covering her mouth before tears could fall from her eyes while Delmare hugged her tight. My heart ached. The man I had just met, Delmare's father, was dead.

I covered my mouth, shutting my eyes as I felt for Theodosia and Delmare, for their loss. Delmare looked up, still holding on to his mother as he looked at me, tears falling down his face, his eyes shining light blue. I knew exactly what it felt like to lose a parent and I knew I would be there for him and for my future mother-in-law no matter what. This would be a hard time for them, and I hoped I could comfort them.

Standing, I wrapped my arms around them, my emotions overtaking me as they hugged me back just as the guards informed us the coast was clear.

SIXTEEN

The walk back to my room was a silent one. Delmare's mother was quiet, unable to breathe a word while the captain walked her back to her room. Her eyes, which had once been happy and filled with so much raw emotion, were now dark and cold, filled with a raging storm of hurt, sorrow, and shock while she walked, completely numb. The group of guards split up, some walking with Delmare's mother to her room while others walked with us, making sure we were safe. I held on to Delmare as he tried to process all that had happened, never speaking a word. I opened the door to my room, guiding him to my bed after I thanked the guards, dismissing them to go back to their posts. I didn't care that Delmare was covered in the black blood from those horrible creatures, all I cared about was comforting him, easing him of the pain and hurt that clutched hard against his heart. As I tucked him in, I watched the shock and sadness spread across his face, a feeling I knew too well.

Caressing his cheek, I kissed him softly on his forehead before turning to hang my robe back on its hook. I felt a hand gently touch my forearm and I turned to look behind me.

"Please," Delmare said, his voice cracking, barely above a whisper. "Don't."

"I'm not going anywhere," I said calmly, hoping to ease his worry. "I'm just going to put my robe up and then I can join you, alright?"

I turned around and untied my robe, setting it on the hook where it belonged before I padded across the room to lie down beside him. Curling under the covers, I immediately felt his body relax against mine, the worries of the night drifting away as I fell asleep, hoping I wouldn't dream about those awful Syren creatures.

I awoke to a terrified scream from the person who had, just moments before, been asleep beside me. Turning over, I tried to soothe him, waving away the guards that ran through the bedroom door, dismissing them as I knew there was no danger.

"It's okay, it was only a dream," I cooed as he held on to me, burying his face in my neck as his sobs consumed him. "Do you want to talk about it?" I asked, rubbing his back, hoping I could ease his pain.

"I don't want to burden you with it," he mumbled, holding me close as I comforted him, his sobs calming down as we spoke to one another.

"You can never be a burden to me," I replied. "Talking about your dream and how you're feeling will help. Trust me. I know how it feels to lose someone you love, especially a parent." I could hear the sadness in my voice, and I knew bringing up my parents' deaths just after Delmare had lost his dad probably wasn't the best idea.

"What were they like?" he asked, looking over at me in the dark of night, wrapped in each other's embrace.

"They were kind, the type of people you strive to become someday. My parents didn't have any siblings, so it was just us, and then my granny Anna Jane McAdams stayed with us until she passed. I'm named after her. She was as stubborn as they come, and her daughter, my mom, was as well. We used to live on a farm in the country, acres and acres of land filled with wildlife. My mother refused to let my father go hunting as she didn't believe in killing an animal that was innocent." I smiled thoughtfully. "One time, we were on our way home from the bowling alley in town. It was dark and my dad couldn't see very well and he had accidentally hit a deer. My mom was so distraught, she was more concerned for the animal than us. Of course, she knew we were fine. She was so caring, so compassionate about the world and its citizens."

"Like you," he commented, his eyes back to their violet color, no longer showing the fear and heartbreak I had seen before.

"Yeah," I breathed. "I guess I am a little like my mother."

"A little?" he asked with an eyebrow raised, amusement in his eyes.

"Okay, a lot. But I can definitely be okay with killing an animal as long as you use the meat for food and the pelt for warmth. I don't believe in killing for sport. I'm like my father in that aspect."

Delmare simply nodded. "What were their names?"

"Paul Eugene Lisle and Alana Rose McAdams." I smiled, remembering their faces as clearly as if they were standing in front of me. I remembered visiting with my mother during my dream. "My mom said we never truly die, that our loved ones are with us always. Maybe… maybe your dad is with you now."

"Maybe," he said. "We should probably go back to sleep."

I watched as he closed his eyes, which were red and puffy from crying, trying to fall back asleep. I kissed him softly on his forehead and whispered to him as he fell asleep, wishing him sweet dreams as I too fell into the dreamscape of my mind, finding much needed rest.

***

The next morning, a maid arrived to ask us if we would like to take our breakfast in our room. We agreed, not wanting to leave the bedroom. I made a mental note to visit Theodosia today to see how she was and if she needed any help with her husband's funeral. However, before I could tell Delmare of my plans, someone came through the door, informing us that the queen, who would be referred to as the queen mother now that her husband had passed, requested our presence in one of the many entertainment rooms that the castle held.

Delmare had his arms around me, resting his hand across my stomach. I felt as if I had grown three inches since yesterday and knew that that statement was probably true. I could tell Delmare was grinning like a fool, even though I couldn't see his face.

"We're going to have to set up an appointment with our physician. I want to make sure our child is healthy and happy," he said just as my stomach growled.

"That would probably be good. I'd like to know if our child is healthy. I have a feeling they're just fine. Right now, though, I would like to get dressed and get something to eat."

I crawled out of bed and quickly got dressed in one of the many dresses from my wardrobe. The fabric was gray and fell to the floor. I knew I should probably pick a more neutral color, and I hoped I wouldn't offend with my dress choice.

Delmare left the comfort of my bed, then walked into his room that adjoined my own. The room was large and inviting despite its intimidating size. A fire burned in the marble-looking fireplace and sat stark against the stone castle walls. Along one wall sat a large mahogany wardrobe of which sat a large piled high with paperwork. As he got dressed, I waited patiently on his bed, admiring the items on his bedside table.

"Are you ready to go?" he asked as he turned to me, dressed for the day, his eyes still puffy from last night and still showing a hint of sadness that I knew he was trying to control. He could only control his emotions for so long before he cracked. He needed time to grieve, and I would help him and his mother in this troubling time.

"Yeah." I smiled, and he walked me out of his bedroom, leading the way to where we would meet Theodosia.

With our hands entwined and our stomachs grumbling, we walked silently together. As we rounded the corner, the guards stationed at their posts opened the large double doors so we could enter. Once inside, I was immediately hit with the smell of something foreign, but absolutely amazing. Queen Theodosia sat in a large chair near the fireplace which burned a fiery blue, lighting up her features when she turned toward us.

I noticed dark circles under her eyes and the defeated look she was trying to hide. Her husband had just passed away. I could only imagine what she was going through. I wasn't sure what I would've done if Delmare had died yesterday. With that thought, Delmare squeezed my hand, and I knew he was reading my thoughts. I looked over at him and thought hard that I wished he would stop reading my mind, which only received a smirk from him, annoying me further.

"Good morning," Theodosia greeted, her voice hoarse. "Please sit and eat. I would like to have a word with the both of you."

We did as we were told, Delmare handing a plates full of food to me and his mother, who refused the plate, saying she wasn't hungry. We ate silently as Theodosia stared at us and we wondered what she was hoping to talk to us about.

"As you know, our king, your father is..." She trailed off, unable to say the words as tears pooled in her eyes. Instinctively, I reached over, placing my hand on hers which rested on her lap. She placed her other hand over mine, a sign she was thankful for my concern and comfort. "As you know, Delmare, once this happens, you are to be crowned king immediately. Your father's funeral is tomorrow. The country will have a few days to morn for his loss, and then we will have your coronation the following week. Have you discussed what that will mean for Anna?"

"I mean, we have discussed that I am the heir and that she will be queen, but—" He paused, realization hitting him.

"But what?" I asked, turning to him, pushing my plate away.

"Well," he said, "I never really asked you."

"Asked me if I want to be queen?" I offered, as I saw the conflicting colors run across his irises.

"He scratched the back of his head and looked directly at his mother before looking back at me, his eyes shining a dark purple. "That, and, if you will marry me."

"Are you asking me right now?"

"Um, well, I mean. I *can* if you want me to, but don't you want me to get down on one knee with a ring and everything?" He paused. "I can understand if you need more time. We've only known each other for a few months, and I know I have put your life on hold and changed it into something you could never have imagined, but I—"

"Delmare," I said, watching his eyes change and his mind race. He continued as if I had said nothing at all.

"I really want you to be happy and I know your emotions and your hormones are everywhere because of the baby, and I'm sorry I got you pregnant—well, I'm kind of *not* sorry because I love you and I want you to be my wife and I'm glad you're my Mate and I—"

"Delmare." I stood to walk in front of him, my mind racing as I watched his eyes flicker to their purple hue. "I will marry you. I am the mother of your child and will be the mother of your future children if we have more. I will stand by your side through the bad times and the good." I took a deep breath as Delmare touched my cheek, brushing a stray hair that had escaped and fallen into my eyes. "I will learn how to run a kingdom and help you rule successfully. I want to grow old with you. I want to live the rest of my life happy, full of contentment, and helping other people, but most of all, I want *you* to be happy. So, Delmare, you don't need to get down on one knee or have a diamond ring in your hand to profess your love to me, because I already know how much you love me."

"Okay," he said, closing the distance between us, sealing our promise with a kiss. I watched out of the corner of my eye as Theodosia began to tear up at the sight of us.

SEVENTEEN

After breakfast, Theodosia insisted that I ask for the help of the maids as they were getting paid and they should be able to do their job. As much as I hated having things done for me, I agreed, knowing that I probably would never get used to it. This was a part of what meant to be in the Royal Court. When we arrived back in my room, two ladies curtsied as they greeted us.

"Good morning, my lady, your Highness," one of them greeted, her hair dark and striking against the blue sea glass of the castle walls. Her skin was a dark chocolate brown and, like magic, had no blemishes across her skin. She turned to Delmare, her eyes sad. "I'm so sorry for your loss. The late king will be missed."

"Thank you," Delmare said. "What are your names?"

"My name is Consuela, and this is Ondina," she replied, not looking Delmare in the eyes.

"It is nice to meet you both," he said before turning to me and kissing me quickly on the cheek. "I have some things I need to do but I will come by to see you later."

"Where are you going?" I asked, turning around as he walked toward the door.

"I need to start the preparations for my father's funeral."

"Do you want help? You don't need to go alone," I replied, worry clear in my voice.

"No, Annie, it's fine."

I shook my head, reaching for his arm as he grabbed the door handle. "No, let me come with you. I will not let you do this alone."

He looked at me, smiling a little, but worry and concern was still there. "Okay. We'll do this together. But afterward, we're seeing the physician, alright? I don't want you getting stressed out and risk hurting the baby."

"You're with child?" one of the maids asked. We both turned around. It was Ondina who had spoken, her violet eyes burning with excitement against her aqua-colored hair.

Delmare cursed under his breath as he mumbled something I couldn't hear.

"Yes, I am," I said, turning to Delmare. "I thought everyone knew."

"No, we haven't even announced that you exist."

"Oh," I replied, turning back to the women standing excitedly in front of us. "Can we keep this between us? The kingdom will know in time, but we would like to stick to *our* timeline."

"Of course, my lady," Consuela said, giddy with excitement.

I nodded, but still knew they might tell everyone they knew regardless of us asking it to stay quiet. At least they didn't know about our engagement, but I suppose it was implied if I was pregnant with the soon-to-be king's heir.

Walking with Delmare through the halls, I held on to his arm, my shoes not making a sound as we walked. I followed him into a room with another pair of double doors where Theodosia and the captain who had escorted me last night stood behind a table covered with several sheets of paper. They both looked up, Theodosia looking worse than she had this morning, but the captain was calm besides the hint of sadness in his eyes. Ronan must have been a good man if his death had this much effect on his people. I wish I had known him longer.

"Good morning, Prince Delmare, Lady Anna," the captain greeted as I moved to stand beside Theodosia, grasping her hand and squeezing it, a choked sob escaping her lips. At the sound, I couldn't help but hug her, feeling for her as both of our emotions fell around us.

"Anna," Delmare said from behind me. "Anna, why don't you take my mother outside? It would be good for both of you to get to know each other."

"What about you?" I asked, turning around. "I can't leave you here to do this by yourself."

He shook his head. "I'll be fine."

Reluctantly, I nodded before turning my attention to my future mother-in-law, guiding her out of the room and into the hallway where I saw a maid walk by. "Miss," I called. "I would like to take the queen back to her room. Can you show me where it is?"

"Of course, my lady," she responded, curtsying before showing me the way. Theodosia clutched my hand, her sobs consuming her while we retreated to her room.

Leading her to bed, I pulled the covers off, motioning for her to get into bed, which she did, tears flowing from her eyes. I turned back to the maid. "Would you mind bringing us some tea?"

"Of course, my lady." She smiled, curtsying quickly before leaving Theodosia and I alone.

"Thank you," Theodosia said, her voice cracking while I pulled the covers over her thin frame. I knew she probably hadn't eaten, knowing that even if she wanted to eat, she couldn't. Losing her husband was too much for her, and her body was reacting.

"You're welcome," I said, taking off my shoes. "Do you mind if I join you?"

She shook her head, letting me crawl into the enormous bed beside her, leaning against the headboard, absent-mindedly making circular motions around my stomach. We were silent when the maid came back with our tea, setting the tray on the side table. The maid handed Theodosia her cup, and she sat up in bed, resting her back against the headboard as I was. We sipped our tea silently. I could tell her mind was a raging storm, one I wanted to distract.

"Delmare wants to go to the physician today," I said, turning to Theodosia. Her straight hair was no longer as perfect as it had been yesterday. "He wants to see how the baby is doing."

"You might find out what you are having in the next couple of days. I found out we were pregnant with a boy, Delmare, around this time," she commented, a slight smile on her lips as I saw a hint of joy spark in her eyes. "A few years later, I got pregnant with my daughter Sedna. She should be here any moment. She was visiting the Waverly kingdom."

"Delmare has a sister?" I asked.

Delmare had a sister and he never told me! What is she like? Would she be as open to the idea of having me here as the rest of his family has?

"Oh, yes. She's as stubborn as they come, but has a big heart. You remind me of her, from what I have seen. I am glad you and Delmare have found each other, honestly. It isn't ideal to be pregnant before the wedding, but I am happy I will have a grandbaby running around here." She smiled, placing her hand on my leg. "Can I touch your baby bump? I know it may be uncomfortable for you, but—" She trailed off, looking over at me with a hint of excitement.

"Sure," I said, smiling slightly.

I tried to relax as I waited for Theodosia to feel my rapidly growing baby bump and felt as if she was a strong motherly figure. I couldn't help but admire her and was glad I was giving her a grandchild. I just hoped I wouldn't disappoint her.

Theodosia carefully placed her hands on my stomach. I watched as her expression changed to complete awe as she looked at me. "Do you have twins in your family?"

"Um, I think my granny was a twin? What does that have to do with anything?" I ask as she looked at my stomach knowingly. "Are you saying I could have twins?"

"I'm saying that I feel there is a potential for you to be carrying twins. You are farther along than I was with Delmare around this time, and he was quite large."

"How big was he when he was born?" I asked.

"He was about nine pounds. His sister was seven pounds," she replied thoughtfully. She crawled out of bed and rummaged through some boxes. "I have some pictures around here somewhere." Suddenly she turned around, holding a large photo album.

She settled in beside me once more, flipping the album open. Several pictures were scattered across the pages, most of them in black and white. One of them caught my eye. It was a couple who I knew instantly to be Ronan and Theodosia. They looked younger in this picture, but both wore clothing from the 1880s. Looking back at Theodosia, she simply smiled, knowing exactly what was on my mind.

"I am much older than I look, yes." She paused. "Ronan was born in 1770, and I was born in 1772. And don't worry, dear, Delmare isn't as old as his parents. He was only born twenty-six years ago. We wanted to travel the world before bringing children into this world. Sedna was born just four years after him, but I had complications while I was pregnant with Sedna so I cannot have any more children."

"That's good. I mean, I'm sorry you weren't able to have any more children, but secretly I was concerned I'd fallen in love with a three hundred-year-old," I replied.

Theodosia laughed, a sound I was glad to hear. "Oh dear, you have no idea. With the royals, you never know how old any of them are. I believe Sedna, Ronan's mother, was born in the 1300s. She passed away just after Ronan was born. She sacrificed herself to correct the wrongs she had inflicted upon her people and her family. I wish I could have met her before she was consumed with her hatred. I am told she was a kind woman. That's why I am glad you can meet me." She paused, turning to me. "I've always wanted to meet the woman my son would fall in love with, and I am overjoyed at what an extraordinary woman you are. You will be a great queen one day. But, of course, before that happens, we will need to start etiquette and history classes so you can learn about the kingdoms of the ocean soon."

"Hopefully I won't disappoint you," I said, slightly nervous as I looked back down at the photo album.

"Just be yourself and try your best and you will be fine," she replied, smiling over at me as she sipped her tea. This reminded me of the conversation I had had with her son earlier and I began to realize just home much Delmare was like his mother: a compassionate and positive soul that could rival any other. "I'm feeling better. Thank you, Anna."

"You're welcome. I just wish I could help you and Delmare at the same time. I may not know what it's like to lose the love of my life, but I know what it's like to lose a parent," I said with sadness.

I had found some closure in seeing my mother in that dream, but seeing her again had reopened some feelings I had tried to keep hidden. I wanted to be strong for them, and for my newfound family.

"How did they pass?" she asked, folding the photo album closed and setting it to the side before looking over at me, her eyes filled with so much sympathy.

"My mom died in a car accident when I was twenty in 2017, and my father passed a little over two years ago. They're buried under an old oak tree in the graveyard near my hometown in Kansas. I would always lay flowers on their anniversary. It was just us. I don't have any cousins, and my parents were only children." I paused, not wanting to talk anymore about my family's death. "I moved to the coast a few months ago after I graduated. I was fully intending on spending the rest of my life there, but I guess fate had different plans."

She looked over at me. I could tell she wanted to say something, but didn't. She just pulled me into a hug, a motherly one, the type that I missed and had longed for for years. Hugging her back, we held each other for a while longer before breaking apart.

She got out of bed, seemingly renewed after our conversation. "Why don't we go see our physician? On the way, we can grab Delmare. I'm sure he needs a distraction right now."

I crawled out of bed, my feet hitting the cold floor. "I think that would be a good idea," I replied, smiling at her.

"Alright, then. Let's go find my son and find out if my new grandbaby is as healthy as I believe it is." She smiled, hooking my arm with hers as we exited her bedroom, leaving the empty cups and photo album by the bed.

EIGHTEEN

By the time we made it back to the room, Delmare and the captain were discussing the funeral and nearly an hour had gone by. Both men looked up, quizzical looks written all over their faces.

"Are you at a stopping point?" I asked.

The men looked at each other and then back to us.

"Why? Do you need me?" Delmare inquired as the captain scribbled something down.

"We were going to go to the physician for a checkup and I was wondering if you wanted to come," I replied, taking a step toward him. "That is, if you are close to a stopping point or nearly finished with the preparations."

"I can take a break," he said.

The captain waved him off. "It's alright. I can take everything from here. It will be good for you to spend time with Lady Anna."

"Okay," Delmare said, grinning as he came toward me, instantly entwining his hand in mine. "I'm ready to go."

Theodosia grinned, spinning on her heels as she led us out of the large room and into the hallway. Delmare's presence seemed to calm me while we walked. I wasn't sure why I was so nervous about seeing the physician, and I hoped he wouldn't ask me why.

"So, what did you and my mom talk about?"

I shrugged. "We talked about how your mother is nearly 250 years old and how you aren't an old man in disguise. She showed me some family photos, and we talked about my parents." I paused. "She suspects I might be carrying twins. Also, when were you going to tell me you have a sister?"

"I haven't told you about Sedna?" he asked, thoroughly confused until a cocky grin spread across his face. "You thought you were sleeping with a three hundred-year-old?"

I heard a gasp and Theodosia stopped walking, turning back around to give Delmare an angry glare.

"Delmare, what have I told you about using such horrid language!?"

I saw the guilt written all over his face. I couldn't help but stifle a laugh as Delmare swiftly apologized.

"Is that all you got out of what I just said? We could have twins, Delmare. Twins!"

"If we end up having twins, they'll be loved just as much, if not more than just having one child. We will get through it together," he said, turning to me, a hint of excitement in his voice. "Besides, I can't wait to see the cute head of red hair our child will have, just like their mother."

I couldn't help but blush while looking away. "Yeah, and they'll have your gorgeous eyes that always seem to be gold, or are you just horny all the time?" I teased as Theodosia protested in front of us.

"Will you two cut it out?" She sighed as she rounded the corner. "Kids today."

I knew she was teasing us like most mothers did, and I couldn't help but feel a little pride as she opened another door and led us into a room furnished with several beds, cabinets filled with jars of ointments and herbs, and a large desk on the other side of the room where a man sat. He looked up as we arrived, surprise written on his face. He quickly stood and bowed to us.

"George, it is wonderful to see you," Theodosia greeted. "How are you?"

"I am doing well, my queen. I am sorry for your loss. If there is anything I can do to help, let me know." He looked over at us. "Ah, my prince, I see you have brought Lady Anna with you."

"Thank you for your kind words, George," Theodosia said. "There is something you can help me with today. Anna, here, hasn't seen a doctor since she found out she is with child, and I would like you to check and see how the baby is developing." She paused before looking over her shoulder at me and smiling before turning back to the doctor who looked me up and down. "I know that rumors might have spread throughout the castle about Anna's arrival, about who she is and why she is here. All will be revealed in time. I don't want to overwhelm the country after everything that has happened. We will make an announcement soon. We just need to prepare Anna for her future here. She is not from Arcania."

"I can understand that. You have my word that anything that is discussed and any information I find out this afternoon will remain confidential between the four of us," he said confidently, nodding to us.

"Good." Theodosia smiled before turning around to look at Delmare and I, giddy excitement falling off of her in waves. I knew that this was a wonderful distraction for the both of them, but I hoped they weren't just forcing their emotions down. If they were, they would never heal. Delmare squeezed my hand and I looked over at him. I knew he was reading my mind, but I didn't care.

I took a step forward, my nervousness filling me as George looked me in the eye.

"It's alright, Lady Anna. There is no reason to be nervous." He paused, giving me a knowing look as he smiled sweetly. "Lay down on one of the beds and we'll get started."

"It's just Anna," I said, looking back at him, realizing I was tired of being called a lady as if I was someone of importance when it wasn't true.

"I'm sorry?" he asked, his eyebrow raised.

"I'm not a lady. I'm a human who just happens to be Mated to a merman who's supposed to be king soon. I studied for four years to do something I loved and now I am expected to raise an heir and help rule a kingdom and I don't know how to do that. Yes, I will do both things because I care about Delmare and the ocean, and I will raise this child, but… I'm terrified I—" I paused, realizing I was ranting in front of the queen and my fiancé. "I'm sorry. I know I should be okay right now and I know you're both hurting and I want to help, I really do. But I know nothing about your customs. I don't know about the kingdoms, what to do at balls or social events. I'm just a woman who loves the sea and wanted to learn everything about it, but I haven't even done that." I hadn't realized I was crying until I felt Delmare hug me, his arms wrapping around me, holding me close.

We stood there for what felt like hours. I knew I was being emotional because of the rise in hormones, and I hated that I'd made an outburst like that. I was being selfish. They had just lost their king—their husband and their father—and here I was complaining and ranting and crying. My problems were not as big as those around me, and I needed to suck it up.

"No," Delmare said near my ear as he held me tight. "You have full reason to be upset. I know that this is a big change for you. I did not expect for you to be okay with everything instantly, and you may never get used to it." He let me go, resting his head against my forehead, his eyes back to their normal silver color. "You will learn about the kingdoms and our customs. I want you to feel included, not miserable. If you would like to learn about the sea and discover its mysteries, I would love to show you its secrets."

I sighed, looking back at him, relieved. I smiled. "Okay. Thank you for understanding."

"Now, let's see how the little guppy is doing." He grinned, his eyes flashing purple.

"Well, I don't think the little guppy enjoys being referred to as just a simple aquarium fish," I said, teasing as I sat down on the edge of the bed, easing myself down.

"Oh," Delmare said as the doctor came around my side, smiling over at us as he rolled up his sleeves. "And what do you think our child wishes to be called?"

"I'd say a pearl. They are precious and rare. Oh, but pearl isn't quite so gender-neutral, I suppose."

"You are far enough along that you might be able to find out what you are having," George said, excitement in his voice. "Unless you don't want to find out until your child is born."

"We can find out now? But it's only been a few days. I knew that it was going fast, but that seems insanely too quick."

"I said you might be able to find out. Nothing is set in stone," he said. "Now, my hands will be warm. Don't worry about your dress. I don't need to touch your skin."

Thee doctor hovered his hands above my baby bump, warmth radiating off of him. I tried to take in deep, calming breaths. Quietly, I waited, enthralled as I watched his face contort, not in fear, but in amazement.

"Congratulations." He smiled. "You have two healthy pups on your hands."

"Pups? Like what shark babies are called?" I asked, suddenly worried that I could be giving birth to a finned baby rather than entirely human, "Wait, did you just say *two*? We're having twins?"

"Yes, pups are what we call our children, but it is a somewhat outdated term. And yes, you are pregnant with twins. In the next two weeks, I should be able to tell what gender." He smiled, taking a step away from us.

I turned to Delmare. I couldn't describe the amount of sheer amazement, love, and excitement written all over his face. It swirled around him, enveloping me in his mix of emotions. His eyes were a rainbow of colors as he leaned in, kissing me long and hard.

"You shouldn't be surprised," Theodosia gushed, her mood completely different from earlier. "Sedna's niece, Louisa, gave birth to twins. They do run in both sides of the family, it seems. I'm so happy for you two! Now we can decorate the nursery."

I couldn't help but smile as I sat up, carefully cupping Delmare's cheek while I stared at him. I didn't want to distract him from his healing process. It was healthy to grieve, but I also didn't want to distance myself from him. I wanted to do everything with him.

"We can start on the nursery, but I think it would be good if you give me a quick summary of your kingdoms and your family tree. I know some of your family will arrive tomorrow for the funeral and I don't want to offend anyone by not knowing anything about the kingdoms and the members who rule them," I said, standing before turning to the doctor. "Thank you."

"You are welcome, Anna," George replied. "Come back again in a few weeks."

I nodded before turning back to Delmare and Theodosia. "We can get started right now," she said.

I followed her out the door and into the hallway, making our way back into the library I had been in just last night.

Looking around at the shelves filled with books, I admired the calm sense of surety in this room. This room filled with so much knowledge and history, and I couldn't help but think about teaching our children how to read here and what their first words would be. I wondered which of our features they would have. Would they have Delmare's ability to read minds or my grandmother's stubborn attitude? Smiling to myself, I looked over at Delmare, realizing he had been staring at me this entire time.

"What?"

"I love you so damn much," he said, grinning proudly at me while his mother scolded him once again for his awful language.

NINETEEN

Delmare spread out a map and several pictures in front of us, and he and Theodosia began to explain their family history and the kingdoms in great detail.

Theodosia started, her eyes sparking as she recounted the history of her people. "The goddess Keilani married a human named Marcellus in the early 1340s and they had five children together: Delmare, the king of Terenia in the Atlantic Ocean; Oshun, the king of Stowryn in the Indian Ocean; Triton, the king of Waverly, which is nestled deep in the Pacific Ocean." She paused, taking out a portrait of a woman with light blue skin, dark midnight blue hair, and striking golden eyes—eyes I recognized on Delmare. "Sedna was born next and reigned in Arcania until her death in 1770 just after giving birth to Ronan, Jr. And finally, Avisa, the queen of Thaiba, or the Southern Ocean. She died before having any heirs, so

Triton's daughter, Louisa, took over responsibilities as queen while her elder sister, Theodosia, ruled over their father's kingdom."

"None of my aunts and uncles are alive today, but many of my cousins are," Delmare said as he turned to me, giving me time to absorb all the information I had been given.

"Wow, you have an enormous family," I breathed, looking at the family tree that lay before me. "How many cousins do you have?"

"Only fourteen," he replied with a shrug. "Eight of them are still alive. You will meet them all tomorrow when we have the uh—" He paused, his tone turning quiet and sad as he looked away. "The funeral."

I bit my lip, feeling for him as the room went silent. Cautiously, I placed my hand on his arm, leaning against him, hoping I could comfort him. "I think I'm going to take a walk," I announced, standing and turning to Delmare. "Would you like to go with me?"

"A walk sounds nice," he replied, but I could tell he wasn't entirely here, his mind occupied by something else as he looked at me.

I knew he needed time to deal with his grief, but it seemed like he was trying hard to be strong for everyone around him, like he refused to let it all out. Like he feared that if he showed any emotion he would be seen as weak. I wanted him to know that wasn't the case, and that he had no reason to feel like that. I said nothing, taking his hand in mine as we walked out of the library. I saw Theodosia grab something from a shelf before the door closed behind me. I chewed on the inside of my lip as we walked, the metallic taste of my blood flooding my tastebuds. Suddenly, Delmare sighed and he stopped walking, forcing me to stop and turn to him.

"Why did you want to go on this walk?"

"What do you mean? I can't just go on a walk with you?" I inquired, feigning confusion.

"Don't play dumb with me, Anna. There's something bugging you. What is it?"

"Why are you acting like this?" I blurted out. "Why are you so calm and collected? I know your hurting, Delmare. I see it in your eyes! Do you believe you have to be so put together? Do you think that if you show any emotion, you'll be less of a man? Talk to me! I know what it's like to lose a parent. You won't stress me out, and you won't hurt me. You won't be able to heal if you keep pushing down your feelings."

"Anna."

"No, don't change the subject. I'm not done," I snapped. "You aren't a burden, Delmare. You could never be a burden. I know you care about my wellbeing, but you should think about yourself and your needs too. Right now, you need to think about what's best for you."

"I can't."

"Yes, you can!" I exclaimed, my voice loader than I fully intended.

"No, I can't!" he yelled. "I am the future king of this kingdom. I can't think about myself. I have to think about what is best for the *kingdom* and its *people*. If I show weakness, that means I am not strong enough to be king."

"If you don't show emotion, Delmare, what kind of example would that be for our children?" I asked, not waiting for an answer before turning and walking away from him, anger filling me.

Delmare called after me, but never followed.

Shutting my bedroom door, I sunk to the floor, barely realizing there were others in the room. I buried my head in my hands, sobs consuming me.

"My lady, are you hurt? What happened?" Consuela asked.

I stayed put, tears flowing down my face as I tried to get a handle on my emotions.

"Did you see the physician? Is the pup alright?"

"Can you just— Please, I need some time alone," I replied, standing and making my way over to my bed. The covers were made perfect, as if they hadn't been used before.

I didn't look at the maids when they left, staring instead at the covers as my emotions overflowed. Kicking my shoes off, I unraveled the perfectly made bed and jumped in, pulling the covers over my body. I stared at the blue-green ceiling shimmering above me. This was all too much. I knew I loved Delmare, and I knew I should be there for him in his grief. It was probably wrong of me for snapping at him, but I didn't want him to worry about others' wellbeing before his own. Yes, I believed we should care about others, but *only* caring about others would cause heartache. He needed to have a healthy balance of caring for others and himself.

I wasn't sure when I fell asleep, but a soft knock on my door woke me up as someone came inside, apologizing profusely. "I'm sorry, Lady Anna. I know you said you wanted to be left alone, but we brought you some lunch."

"Thank you," I replied as Ondina handed me a plate, her eyes filled with sympathy and something else I couldn't put my finger on.

"Can I sit beside you while you eat?" She paused. "To keep you company?"

I simply nodded as she grinned, taking the spot near my feet as I ate. We sat in silence as I ate, Ondina never once asking me questions about what had happened or if there was anything she could do. She just sat there, hoping her presence would help and I had to admit, it did. Ondina looked over at me as I set my empty plate down, worry and concern evident on her face.

"The baby is fine. I guess you could say *babies*, because we're having twins. I'm upset because Delmare is upset. His father just died, but he refuses to let it out. He says he has to be strong because he's going to be king soon, and believes he should be putting the kingdom before everything else. I don't want our children to think it's okay to hold your emotions in. I believe there should be a healthy balance, yes. Be compassionate and caring for other people, but also to yourself. Do what is best for yourself and others. But it's like he has to follow his duty."

"He's royalty," Ondina replied simply. "It requires specific obligations that require a great deal from those who are in power. They do not have the same freedoms that others do." Then she realized what she said and placed a hand over her mouth, her eyes wide, "I'm sorry, my lady. It isn't my place."

"No, it's alright. And please, call me Anna. I'm not a lady. I am like you."

"No, you are so much more than I am. You are a lady of great importance, even though only a few of us know of your existence. You will be a great queen one day." She smiled knowingly.

"I still can't believe any of this. I didn't expect my life to turn out quite like this. Sometimes I wonder if this is a bizarre dream."

"I suppose for a human who did not know of our world, it can seem daunting. But you have taken it well from what I can tell," she said, looking back at me.

"Thank you for lunch. If Delmare comes back, let him know he can sleep in here tonight if he wants. If he needs to talk about anything, I'm here for him. I'm just tired, so I think I'm going to go back to sleep."

She nodded, hopping off of the bed and grabbing my discarded plate. "Okay, Anna. I'll let him know. Sweet dreams!"

***

Rubbing my eyes, I turned, craning my neck to see who was next to me. Relief washed over me as I realized Delmare was lying beside me. His eyes were closed, but there were wet streaks on his face as if he had been crying. Rolling over so that I was facing him, I pushed a fallen strand of his black hair out of his face, feeling the scruff of his cheek from his stubble. He seemed so at peace then, and it helped as I hugged him, pulling him close to me. He sighed happily in his sleep. No matter what, I would be there for him and I hoped he would let me help him during this hard time in his life. Especially after we'd promised we would be there for each other through the good times and the bad.

TWENTY

I awoke cocooned in the comforter, warmth spreading across my body as my eyes fluttered open. I did not hear any breathing beside me or feel an arm drape protectively around me like usual. Confused, I turned around, craning my neck to look behind me, realizing that Delmare was no longer asleep beside me or in bed.

Suddenly, my door flew open, banging up against the wall as whoever was intruding made their way inside. Whipping my head back around, I quickly stood, ready to take action if I was in trouble. Thankfully, it was just Ondina holding a tray of food and Consuela with a dress bag.

"Good morning," they greeted, curtsying deeply before laying out their items.

"Good morning," I replied. "Where is Delmare?"

"He left earlier this morning. I'm not sure where he went, my lady—I mean, Anna," Ondina said, setting my tray down on the bedside table.

"Oh," I said, picking up the plate of food. "I wonder where he went."

"He probably just went to check on the preparations for this afternoon," Consuela suggested as she placed the dress bag into the wardrobe.

"What's that, Consuela?" I asked after taking a few bites of my breakfast.

She turned around and smiled sweetly at me. "It's your dress for this afternoon. After you eat, we'll get you ready for the day."

"Oh," I replied as the room was filled with silence again. "Have you both eaten yet?"

"Yes, Anna, we have," Ondina said with a smile.

After I finished eating, Consuela handed me the gown she had placed in the wardrobe. The fabric was black, and the dress was simple yet modest. The dress had an empire waist, concealing my baby bump under a layer of flowing fabric. Slipping ballet flats on my feet, I looked at myself in the floor-length mirror as Ondina pinned my hair up and out of my face, using a seashell to hold it in place.

"I don't think it will be a good idea to put makeup on me. My hormones are everywhere and if everyone cries, I might start too," I said, waving Consuela's hand away as she came toward me with something that looked like powder.

"You're probably right," she said, setting it down on the vanity just as someone knocked on the door.

Consuela turned and cracked the door open, letting whoever knocked inside. "Good morning, your Highness."

"Good morning, Consuela, Ondina," Delmare said. "I hope you don't mind, but I would like to borrow Anna."

They giggled, a knowing look spreading across their features. "No, we don't mind at all."

"What?" I asked as Delmare held both of my hands. "What's going on?"

"Well, I realized you had asked *me* to marry *you* and I know this probably isn't the best time to do this. My father's funeral is in just a few hours and our citizens will wonder who you are and where you came from, but I want there to be no mistake about who you are with, so I got you something." His eyes shone their familiar mix of gold and purple as he reached behind him, pulling out a box wrapped in paper—not the frilly kind you found at a jewelry store, but the kid kind that you use when you're wrapping your kids' Christmas presents, covered in cartoon characters you only knew the name of because you've watched the movie five billion times. If you were really feeling stubborn, you wrapped the present twice. "Go on, open it," he said.

"Is that what I think it is?"

He nodded, reaching out his hand.

I took the box, the colorful wrapping paper gleaming against the shine of the tape. I stared at it for a moment, realizing that he was trying to distract himself once again, trying to make this day less of a mournful one. I knew why he did it, but I knew that this wasn't how I wanted to do it.

I shook my head, taking a seat before looking over at Consuela and Ondina who were nearly bursting at the seams. "Consuela, Ondina, could you give us a moment alone, please?"

Once they were gone and the door was securely shut, I looked over at Delmare, still holding the unopened box that I knew held an engagement ring.

"What's wrong? Why aren't you opening it?"

Sighing, I set the box on the side table and reached for Delmare. He sat beside me, confusion etched across his face. "Delmare, you can't keep jumping from one thing to the next. Today is a day to celebrate your father's life, to remember him. I will not open that box and take that away from him. You deserve to mourn properly for his death. I know everyone mourns differently, but I know that this isn't healthy." I paused, placing my hand on his knee. "I will be here for you always, you know that. I don't think now is the best time for us to announce our engagement. The country and your family are in mourning. Let's wait a few days and take it one day at a time."

He said nothing, but looked away, deep in thought. Finally, he looked back at me. "I want to see your face when you open it. We don't have to announce anything, and you don't have to wear it, but I'd like to see the woman I love wearing the ring I made for her."

I sighed. "You're stubborn, you know that?" I sighed before snatching the box up in my hands and carefully and quietly unraveling the wrapping paper, letting the pieces fall to the floor as I stared at the little black box. Popping the lid off, I reached inside to find a closed clam. It opened up to reveal a silver band with tiny diamonds around a pink pearl that was set in the center. It was absolutely beautiful. "Did you get me a pearl because that's my birthstone?" I asked, completely in awe at the beauty of the ring.

"I picked the pearl for a lot of reasons, not just that," he said as I handed him the ring and he slid it onto my finger, his eyes entirely violet now. "The pearl symbolizes integrity and loyalty and protection, while the diamonds symbolize faithfulness and love. I want you to know that by properly asking you to marry me, as I am right now,

I want our marriage and the rest of our lives to be filled with integrity, faithfulness, love, and loyalty. But I also want us to trust and protect one another. I want to grow old together and raise our children together. I want to show you all the secrets the ocean has kept hidden for centuries, and to grow together into the individuals we are meant to be. I know this has been a very stressful summer, but—"

I couldn't help but pull him close, throwing my arms around him and kissing him hard, completely overjoyed, but I also knew that in just a few hours, this feeling of happiness would falter when everyone around me was crying.

Delmare broke away, resting his head against my forehead. "Don't think about the funeral. Let's just enjoy this moment while it lasts."

"Your Highness, I don't mean to impose, but the funeral is about to start in thirty minutes, and you and Anna are needed," Ondina said, bursting through the door.

"Alright, we'll be right down," he said, turning back to me, a hint of sadness playing along his features.

I knew that this would be a hard time for him, and I hoped he would let me help him in his time of need. I followed Delmare into the hallway, our hands entwined. As we were walking, I realized I was still wearing Delmare's engagement ring. So much for keeping it a secret for a few days. Letting go of his hand, I started to take it off but Delmare grabbed my hand, stopping me. "No one will even notice."

"How much do you want to bet that's the first thing your mother mentions when she sees us?" I said, giving him a pointed look as we walked together down the hallway, toward the large group of people gathered in one of the grand rooms.

I felt my heartbeat quicken as we walked toward the group, hoping I wouldn't make a fool of myself. They all turned to us, their rainbow of features staring at Delmare with familiarity, and then moving to me with confused and wondering glances. I bit my cheek, hoping they wouldn't notice the engagement ring or the fact that I wasn't their species. I hoped his cousins liked me.

I watched as a woman who looked to be in her early thirties came towards us, her teal-colored hair in several loose braids that billowed around her face. She greeted Delmare, hugging him quickly before turning to me. "This must be Emilia. My name is Avisa Stowryn. I'm his cousin."

"Actually, my name's Anna," I said, tucking a fallen strand of hair out of my eyes with my left hand, suddenly realizing that she could see my ring. I hid my hand behind me, but it was too late.

She gasped, taking my hand in her hands. "Oh, look at this ring! You're engaged!? How wonderful! Where did you two meet?" she asked, amongst several other questions that I wasn't sure I should answer. Luckily, Theodosia arrived, announcing that we would begin the ceremony now.

The fireplaces were set ablaze, blue fire dancing in the hearth as I sat beside Delmare. He clenched and unclenched his jaw as I held his hand.

Occasionally he would squeeze it as the speaker spoke about the late king's life and his legacy. I could feel the emotions of everyone around me and it hurt to feel their pain.

After an hour, the service was over and we followed the group of guards out into the open sea where the same blue fire that filled the fireplaces was set to the coffin. As it burned, the king's body turned into sea foam, filling the ocean and swirling around us. Sticking close to Delmare, I felt his body shake uncontrollably. I looked up and saw tears flowing feely down his face. I wrapped my arms around him as he clutched me tight, crying into my shoulder as I felt my own tears escape. I hated to see him hurt, but I knew that this needed to be done in order for him to heal.

After twenty minutes of holding each other, his family retired, their emotions swirling around them—anger, sadness, despair. Some hid their emotions while others clutched their partners, emotions consuming them, tears streaming down their faces. I felt for them; I knew what it was like to lose a loved one. Wiping my face, I was secretly glad I had opted out of wearing makeup, not that I usually wore it, anyway. I knew that if I had, I would be a horrid mess by now.

Turning to Delmare, I rested my head on his shoulder, my mind wandering once again when Delmare leaned down and mumbled something in my ear. I couldn't hear him, but he stood, guiding me out of the room, back toward my bedroom. But before I could speak, my world went black and I fell to the castle floor.

TWENTY-ONE

The scratchy sheets that were draped over me clung to my skin when I finally awoke, my head throbbing while I tried to sit up but failed to do so. My limbs felt heavy and sore, and the queasy feeling in my stomach hinted that I hadn't eaten in hours, maybe days. What happened to me?

With a groan, I shifted under the blankets, my mind filling with hundreds of questions as I forced my eyelids open. A white light shown in my face, forcing me to shut my eyes, shielding myself from the blinding light. Cautiously, my eyes fell open again, hoping my eyes would adjust to the surrounding light. Blinking several times, I immediately recognized the room filled with beds and the desk along one wall. Turning over on my side, I caught sight of Delmare curled up in a chair beside me. His facial hair had grown, and his hair was a mess on top of his hair. Dark crescents shadowed his eyes and his skin was an ashen color, as if he had been worrying himself sick. Reaching over, I lightly touched his knee, hoping to comfort him even though I was too weak to get up. Why was I like this? What had happened?

"Good, you're awake!" George said as he hustled across the room toward me. I tensed up at the sharp sound of his voice. "It's alright, dear. I brought you some water. Do you need help to sit up?" he asked as he set the glass down on the side table.

I nodded. "What happened?" I asked, my voice hoarse. George helped me into a sitting position. "Am I sick? Are the babies okay?"

"I will explain everything, but first you need to drink something." He handed me the glass of water and I guzzled it down as if I had just spent the last twenty-four hours in a desert.

"Someone had poisoned your breakfast this morning," George stated firmly. "Thankfully, it was a mild poison, only intending to put the victim in a coma. We have yet to find the traitor, but once we do, they will be punished for their crimes."

"Why would anyone poison me?" I asked, fear filling me. "Only those working in the palace know I exist."

"We believe it might have been a Syren. It must have evaded our guards up until the night of the funeral." He paused. "The heirs are fine, completely healthy. There is no need to worry."

"How long have I been asleep?" I asked, turning to look at Delmare who stirred.

"Four days." He paused as Delmare sprang from the chair, his face filled with relief at the sight of me awake and unharmed.

In an instant, he was by my side, tears flowing down his face as he looked me up and down. Instinctively, I ran my hand through his hair as he sat next to me. He wrapped his arms around me, and I instantly relaxed.

"I'm so glad you're awake," he said, kissing me all over, unable to control himself any longer as his emotions overtook him. "Are you okay? You aren't hurting anywhere, right? Do you want anything? Are you hungry?"

"I think I'm okay," I replied, turning to him. I smiled softly, the soreness in my limbs spreading across my body as my stomach growled. "I'm a little sore and hungry."

"What do you want to eat?" he inquired as he got up, standing near the bed, his eyes filled with a purple hue.

I sat up, trying to think of what I wanted. I was craving a big, fat, juicy hamburger, the kind that clogs your pores but tastes so good you can't resist.

He smiled and nodded, winking at me as he gave me a quick peck on my lips. "Okay, I'll be right back with your pore-clogging hamburger. Do you want any of the fixings?"

I only nodded, pursing my lips as I realized he read my mind once again. "I told you to quit that!" I teased as he laughed.

"I'll be back," he replied with a cheeky grin, before skipping out of the room, whistling as he went.

George chuckled, shaking his head as he shuffled some papers, the sound of the rustling paper bouncing across the room.

"What's so funny?"

"I've never seen him like that before." He looked over at me as my stomach turned, feeling movement. "He stayed beside you for days, Anna, refusing to eat or sleep. I had finally gotten him to sleep a few hours ago. That boy is stubborn, I tell you what."

I smiled to myself as I rested my head against the wall. I could tell I had gotten bigger in the last few day, which seemed nearly impossible. Resting my hand on my stomach, I wondered how our children were, what gender they were, and what traits they would get from Delmare and I. "Yeah, he is pretty stubborn sometimes, but I love him."

George who walked toward me, resting his hand on my arm. "You're good together." He smiled, his eyes sparkling as he spoke, a knowing look written across his face. "I hope it is not overstepping my bounds, Anna, but I believe you will make a fine queen one day. I can tell you will be an exceptional mother. It shines through you every day."

"Thank you." I smiled, looking away sheepishly. "But I think I'm going to need to learn a thing or two about how to run a kingdom before I become queen. I hope I can be as good of a mother as my mother was."

"Alright," Delmare called as he threw the door open, walking toward us. The smell of the burger filled the room and made my mouth water. "I brought you your food."

Taking the plate from his outstretched hand, I grinned, kissing him quickly on his cheek before placing the warm plate onto my lap. I picked up the burger, grease pouring out of the meat and onto the plate. I took a bite and relished the taste of familiar food from home, entirely tired of eating seafood all day. I suppressed a moan, swallowed, and took another bite. Delmare reached for my burger and I moved my hand away from his, protective of my food. I glared at him.

"Hey, I want a bite." He pouted as he crawled into bed beside me.

I chuckled, licking my lips, then wiping the grease from my chin. "You should have gotten your own," I teased as I went for another bite. Before I could get it in my mouth, though, Delmare reached down and stole a bite of my burger, making me gasp. "Hey!"

He chewed, choking back a laugh.

I dropped the burger and playfully slapped his shoulder, feigning outrage.

"Ow, why are you abusing me?"

"Oh, hush, don't give me that. You just stole my food!" I teased, finishing off the burger, then licking my fingers. "Thank you for the burger."

"You're welcome." He grinned and handed me a napkin, then moved my plate to the table. With my stomach full, I curled back into bed, Delmare following suit, wrapping his arms around me.

"You two better not sleep together on that bed," George called from across the room, his voice filled with authority, the kind you might hear from a father scolding his children. "I don't want to see or hear any of that."

Delmare cracked a grin as he turned, wrapping his arm around my waist and making circular motions across my skin, setting my skin ablaze. I closed my eyes, thoroughly enjoying his touch. "I can't make any promises, George."

"What's that human saying again?" he asked, looking up from his papers.

"Get a room?" I offered, as Delmare's hand played with the band of my cotton underwear, making me hold back a gasp. "Delmare, please."

"Yes, get a room," George agreed as I felt my underwear soak. I hoped he wouldn't explore more.

Delmare turned to me, a knowing look in his eyes. I stared back at the color that confirmed how turned on he was. I would not do this with an audience.

George sighed and slammed the stack of paper down. "I, uh. I forgot something in the other room." He looked over at us with a knowing look.

Once the door closed behind him, Delmare turned to me, kissing me fast and deep, leaving a trail of kisses along my jaw and neck, sucking softly on the skin near my collarbone. He caressed my thigh and neck, holding me closer to him. I kissed him back, gaining a sound from deep in his throat before he moved on top of me.

His eyes were shining now as I realized just how much he wanted me. Reaching up, I tugged on his shirt until he pulled it over his head, revealing his naked chest, then he helped me out of my clothes. For a second, we stared, admiring each other before we closed the distance, our arms and legs entwined. He centered himself before easing into me, a breathy moan escaping my lips. My breathing hitched as he went deeper, my body relaxing as he went in and out, in and out, my legs shaking as he continued. He took extra care to tease my nipples and my back arched into him when I climaxed. He let out a moan just as his eyes rolled back into his head, the pleasure overwhelming him before he pulled out. Our breathing was heavy as we held each other close, the sheets barely covering our naked bodies.

Suddenly, tiredness consumed me, my limbs going heavy, falling back against the mattress, the high I had felt only moments before leaving me. Delmare wrapped his arms around me as I rested my head on his chest. His heartbeat thumped hard against his chest, into my ear. I wondered what George would say when he came back to see us naked in one of the hospital beds. Would he scold us for having sex when he had specifically asked us not to? Smiling to myself, I shut my eyes, letting my body relax.

I hoped George and Theodosia were right. I hoped I would be a good queen for this kingdom, but was I cut out for it? Would I find time to care for our children *and* help run a country? I knew that my children and family should come first, but a part of me knew that probably wasn't the case for those lucky enough to be in my position.

As Delmare made circular motions along my stomach, urging me to fall back asleep, I wondered what kind of king Delmare would be.

TWENTY-TWO

It had been two days since I'd been discharged from the medical wing, and a little over a week since the funeral. Delmare had stayed by my side, occasionally being replaced by his mother so he could finish his work.

Currently, I was in the library, indulging in the history of the kingdoms of the sea. A guard stood near the door, his eyes searching the entire room, awaiting any danger that might dare to enter the area. I flashed my pearly whites at him, hoping I could ease the stern look on his face, but he didn't smile back. He reminded me of those guards from Britain with their big black hats that never seemed to move no matter what you did. At least, from what I had seen in movies.

Flipping through the book, the silence filled the room as I read. I rested my cheek on my hand. Suddenly, I heard the familiar sound of something scraping against the wall. I turned toward the sound, realizing it was coming from the hidden passageway at the back of the library. Looking back at the guard, I watched as he walked cautiously toward the sound, motioning for me to stay where I was. My heart pounded against my chest. Had the Syren creatures broken into the castle again? Were they trying to come back to finish what they had started? Why were they so intent on harming the royal members of this kingdom?

"Who's there?" the guard called, his hand on the hilt of his sword. "State your business."

The intruder stepped out of the shadows, shaking as if they feared for their life. "M-my name's Clara, sir. I do not wish to harm you."

I felt my body relax. The guard let go of his sword and he waved the woman over before she sped out of the library, apologizing profusely. My heart ached for her, knowing that the guard was probably intimidating, especially if he thought you weren't who you said you were. Turning back to my book, I tried to concentrate on the chapter I had been reading, but I found my mind wandering to the night Delmare's father had been killed. I remembered seeing the Syren that looked almost exactly like Delmare, but was a monster in disguise. I shuddered then, realizing that the same creature that had tried to go after me, or another member of its race, had successfully poisoned me just a few days after.

With a sigh, I shut the book, rubbing my temple, trying to ease the headache that spread across my forehead, before standing and grabbing the books off the table to put them back where they belonged. With my head pounding, I made my way to the door, the guard following me out of the room and escorting me into the hallway. Quietly, we walked together toward Delmare's room, our room. I had moved in a few days ago, much to Ondina and Consuela's protest. They wouldn't be able to help me get dressed anymore. A part of me was sad they wouldn't be able to do their original jobs, but being able to dress myself made me feel normal. I didn't want to rely on other people for things I could do on my own.

Dismissing the guard, he quickly bowed before leaving me alone. I sat at the edge of the bed. The room still smelled like him, although I wasn't surprised—he had spent most of his childhood and adulthood in this room. Laying down, I rested my hand on my stomach, still amazed that my stomach had grown so much after such a short amount of time. I had been taking etiquette classes with Theodosia, just enough that I would pass in front of our citizens. After a few months, she was fairly certain I would be ready. Delmare's coronation was in two weeks and the palace had been busy with preparations, including Delmare himself. I knew he had a responsibility to his kingdom and its people, but a part of me wanted him to be selfish and spend days with me, picking out furniture for the nursery and painting the walls. The paint was made of shells and was insanely vibrant, probably better than paint on land. I loved the thought of us working on it together, but I also knew that with some things we had to do on our own.

With a sigh, I got up, kicking my shoes off as I entered my old room, now the nursery. I stared at the two cribs resting side by side and smiled, thinking about our children resting soundly in their beds, but I knew that that thought wouldn't be true at all. They would probably cry all night and need to be fed every two hours like clockwork. At least, my robot baby had done that. And if our children were anything like it, I hoped we would be okay.

"Hey, Annie!" Sedna squealed from behind me.

I had met her a few days ago. I hadn't seen her at the funeral, but she had visited me an hour after Delmare and I had had sex in the hospital bed. George had scolded us like children afterward, his face beet red, but he still smiled all the same, as if understanding.

Sedna was a ball of energy and the complete opposite of Delmare personality wise, but you could definitely tell the resemblance in their looks, although Sedna took after her mother more in that department. She had hugged me tight after I offered my hand for a handshake, instantly asking me hundreds of questions as if she wanted to know every aspect of my life. It was refreshing actually; I had always been quite reserved and to have someone outgoing around might make me come out of my shell.

"Hi Sedna." I smiled, looking over my shoulder at her. "What have you been up to?"

"Oh, nothing." She walked further into the room while I looked around, catching her eye. She looked back at me with her golden eyes, ones that didn't change and were constantly that haunting golden color, just like her namesake's. "What have you been up to?"

"I was in the library reading. I was tired of it, so I came in here. I need to decide if I want to paint the walls or leave the sea glass bare," I replied, picking up a stuffed octopus off the dresser and setting it in one of the cribs. "I'm leaning toward keeping it bare, but I don't want to make all the decisions. They're Delmare's children too. He should have a say, as well, but he's been so busy, and I don't want to bother him."

Looking away, I bit the inside of my cheek, hopelessly trying not to cry. *Curse you, hormones!* But hey, at least I wasn't bleeding every month, but of course, I had a plethora of other problems. My feet hurt, my breasts were always sore. I didn't fit into pants anymore, so I always had to wear dresses. I couldn't stand wearing any shoes other than slippers. One day I wanted sea food and the next, a pickle with peanut butter. Never in my wildest dreams had I thought that would ever taste good.

My stomach growled as I realized Sedna had said something. I looked over at her. "What did you say?"

"I'm sure Delmare wouldn't mind helping. Why don't you ask him? The worst he could say is no. Are you hungry? I heard the other day you wanted pickles and peanut butter?"

"Hey, it was amazing," I defended myself. "And yeah, I could eat."

"Cool, I was about to head into the kitchen to make something. Thought you might want to come with me. Also, if you need any help with the nursery, this auntie would be glad to help," she said with a wink, grinning at me before hooking her arm in mine and walking out the door, into the hallway.

A few minutes later, we were in the kitchen as Sedna greeted the cook. She was a plump lady with big rosy cheeks and an accent I couldn't quite pinpoint, but she was as sweet as could be. She smiled at us as she went about her business, while Sedna grabbed some ingredients from the pantry and ate while I munched on a pickle, eying the jar of peanut butter I was shocked they'd smuggled down hundreds of feet under the sea. Sitting down, I tried not to be in the way as I ate in silence, my mind wandering before I felt a movement in my stomach. This movement was distinct though, stronger than usual. I knew by now, I looked as if I was three or four months along. It still amazed me that my body could handle a Symari pregnancy, as I remembered Delmare had once said it was difficult for humans. Suddenly, though, I felt a sharp kick against my stomach, making me gasp, and I dropped the pickle I had been eating. It fell with a plop onto the table.

"Are you alright?" Sedna asked, turning to me, her face filled with concern.

I placed my hand on my stomach, waiting for them to kick me again. Waving over Sedna, I watched her out of the corner of my eye as she came toward me, resting her hand on my shoulder as she asked me what was wrong.

"They kicked me!" I exclaimed. As if on cue, they kicked again, this time near my side. I laughed in pure amazement, just as I heard the familiar voice of the man that I loved. Turning around, I watched as he leaned up against the door frame, smiling at us both. "What's so funny?"

"Del, come here!" I exclaimed, enthusiastically motioning for him to come over, which he did, his face full of amusement. Grabbing his hand, I placed it onto my stomach as they kicked again, watching as his eyes lit up. He stared before looking back up at me, his face showing every emotion imaginable.

"Wow," he breathed as their kicking fit stopped. He got down onto his knees. "That's amazing."

I nodded in agreement as he placed a kiss on my stomach, only touching the fabric of the shirt I had stolen from him. Although, I don't think he minded much as long as I was happy. "Did they just start doing that?"

"Yeah, right before you came in. I was eating a pickle and then they just started kicking." I grinned as he rested his hand on my stomach again, but nothing happened. I watched the disappointment show across his features. "After this snack, I was going to go finish the nursery if you wanted to go with me."

"Sure, I would like that." He grinned as I scarfed down the rest of my food and hopped out of the chair, following Delmare to the nursery that would house our babies until they were a few years older.

"Wait, weren't we supposed to go to George's office?" I asked, turning to Delmare, realizing I needed to go for my weekly check up with him.

"Oh, right. Yeah, let's do that first and then we can work on the nursery. What are you wanting to add in there?" he asked as we turned down the hallway that would lead us to Dr. George's medical wing.

"We just need to decide if we want to paint the room or leave it how it is," I said as Delmare opened the door for me.

"I say let's leave it how it is. That paint is awful to get off," he suggested, and I nodded just as George greeted us from behind his desk.

"Ah, there you are, I was wondering when you two would stop by. Now, are you ready to find out what you're having?" George asked as I laid down on one of the many hospital beds.

"Yes," Delmare and I said together, both grinning as George stood beside the bed.

"Good now, just relax, Anna, dear. Thank you." He paused as I released the breath I had been holding, hoping to ease my nerves as I stared over at Delmare. His eyes fixated on George's hands, how they hovered over my stomach and the warmth that radiated off of him. George chuckled slightly and I looked over at him, a knowing look spreading across his features. "It looks like you've been blessed with two healthy children, one girl and one boy." He beamed as I let the information sink in.

    We were having one of each! I felt Delmare pull me closer as tears brimmed in my eyes. I had always wanted a boy and a girl and now I would have them both at the same time. I would raise them with Delmare to be kind, loyal, and to protect all living things. Just like my parents did.

TWENTY-THREE

The rocking chair where I sat in the nursery moved back and forth as I rocked, humming softly while I crocheted. I was determined to make a blanket, though the string of knots was not as straight a line as I had hoped and looked more like a circle than I would care to admit. With a frustrated groan, I threw it on the ground, watching as the ball of yarn rolled across the floor and ran into a pair of men's boots. Delmare walked further into the room. Looking up, I watched the amusing look play across his features as he leaned down to pick up the ball of yarn. Chuckling, he wound the yarn back up as he walked toward me, his eyes never leaving my face.

"Why are you abusing your scarf?" he asked, picking it up off the floor and setting it on the table beside me.

"It's supposed to be a blanket," I groaned, getting up. Delmare tried to help me up, but I waved him off. I was just pregnant, not helpless. "I'm fine, thanks. How are the preparations for tomorrow coming? Is there anything I can do to help?"

"Everything's going fine. You don't need to do anything," he replied with a smile.

"Oh," I said, trying not to show my disappointment. "I guess I could sit here and fail at crocheting."

"I think I have a better idea."

"What's your better idea?" I asked as I followed him into our room. He pulled out two sets of clothing, the fabric taught and dirty, completely the opposite of the clothing we were both currently wearing.

"I want to show you our kingdom through the eyes of our citizens," he said, handing me a pair of clothes. Thankfully he handed me a pair of pants, the band made of a stretchy material, reminding me of the maternity pants I had seen in stores. "I'd like to give you the tour without anyone recognizing us."

"You're going to have to do a lot more to disguise that handsome face of yours," I replied, peeling my dress off and getting dressed in the clothes he'd handed me. "No one has seen me yet, so you don't have to worry about anyone recognizing me. But how are you going to disguise your face and hair? Haven't your people grown up with you? Wouldn't they know every inch of your face? What are we going to do if they ask us who we are?"

"I have everything covered. If someone asks us who we are, we are Mr. and Mrs. Waters." He smiled as he unbuttoned his shirt. "And if my face is a little dirty, it will hide some of my features, so hopefully no one will recognize us."

"Oh, we're married, are we?" I asked, picking up the dress off the floor and hanging it back in the closet.

"Yes, because no one will question our relationship, especially with you carrying our children as you are." He smiled, now fully clothed. He reached down to hold my stomach just as one of them kicked. "They're pretty active today, aren't they?"

"Yes, very." I paused. "So, how are we going to get out of the castle with no one noticing?"

His eyes sparkled with excitement and he took my hand, leading me toward one wall of his room. He placed his hand on it. Suddenly, the wall moved on its own, opening up to reveal a secret passageway. Following him into the passageway, we walked quietly and cautiously as I clung to his arm. After a few minutes, we made it to another door. Watching quietly beside him, he opened the door to reveal the expanse of the ocean ahead of us. Strangely enough, no water escaped through the opening, instead stopping as if there was a barrier and falling down the opening like a waterfall.

"Wow," I breathed, staring at the water and then back at Delmare. "Why isn't the water coming through the doorway?"

"Because my mom took the water away from the palace. No water will enter the palace walls. Once we come back, the water will leave our skin and hair as if we hadn't spent the afternoon in the ocean." He motioned me to go through the opening before him. "Ladies first."

Taking a step toward the opening, I let go of Delmare's arm before I jumped out of the castle. The water flowed around me as I jumped into the ocean. Letting out my breath, I watched as the air escaped my lungs and floated above me. I turned to watch Delmare jump after me, shifting into his fish form a few seconds after.

"Are you ready for an adventure you will never forget?" he asked, his eyes sparking orange, further confirming his excitement.

"Yes, I'd love to see the kingdom we will rule one day," I said, grinning. I took his hand, letting him lead me away from the castle grounds and into the underwater city below.

The sound of the busy streets filled the surrounding ocean. Symari of different sizes and shapes swam around us, some even with different appendages. They didn't seem to notice the two newcomers that had just entered the city from the direction of the palace. Looking back at Delmare, I smiled, unsure of where I should go or what I should say.

 Instinctively, he took my hand, guiding me toward one of the many booths in town. Some were selling food, while others held various dresses and clothes made of ship's sails. We stopped in front of one and I watched as he greeted the woman behind the counter. The booth seemed to be overflowing with food labeled in a language I didn't recognize. Delmare gestured to me and nervously I hovered beside him, watching as the woman's green eyes sparkled as she stared at my stomach.

 "It's lovely to meet you, Mrs. Waters," she said in English now, and swam around the booth to the outside, stopping in front of us. As she halted, her dress swished, revealing toes. Excitement rose in me to see a Symari with feet rather than a tail. "I never learned much English myself, but it's good to meet a Kamrik who looks like myself. There are so few of us it would seem."

 "It's nice to meet you too." I smiled at her genuinely, looking over at Delmare slightly confused. He had never mentioned there were other classifications of his race, especially ones who only had legs rather than changing forms. "So, do you have a farm?"

"Oh yes, I have my son help me every morning." She smiled, her face filling with pride.

"He sounds like a great help for you," I said as she nodded. "What's that smell?"

"Oh, that's just some Odabech I cooked up." Sensing my confusion, she handed me a small treat that looked suspiciously like a strange taffy. Hesitating, I looked back at Delmare, who wasn't the least bit concerned. I plopped it into my mouth and chewed, the taste exploding in my mouth, making my eyebrows raise in surprise. Never had I eaten taffy that tasted so good.

"That was fantastic. Thank you!" Suddenly, I realized I didn't bring any money and wasn't sure how would we pay her back. Just as I was about to ask her how much, Delmare handed her a single coin that looked like old pirate treasure.

"Oh, you don't have to, and besides, I'm glad I am the first one to meet the princess," she said with a hushed tone. I panicked, realizing that our disguises weren't working. "Oh, calm down, child. There is no need to worry. I can tell a human when I see one, but those of us around here have never seen one before. You should be just fine."

With a worried glance at Delmare, he thanked the shopkeeper and guided me away. We visited the shops, and I watched Delmare play a game of Token Ball, as the children called it, with a group of young children who all decided it would be a great idea to jump on top of him after he won. Smiling as I watched him play, I enjoyed the vibrancy of this city and the citizens who lived here. I knew without a doubt that I would learn everything I could about these people, the people I would serve and protect.

I watched as Delmare grinned at me just as a Symari girl with bright blue eyes and an orange tail clung to his side, forgetting the pufferfish they were using as a ball as it swam away scared. "Alright, now, I want all of you off me or else," he said, slightly stern but still lighthearted all the same.

The children laughed before jumping off of him and swam toward the pufferfish that was trying to escape. I held back a laugh of my own as Delmare swam toward me, his silver tail glistening against the sunlight that streamed in from the surface. He reached down and wrapped his arms around my waist, caressing the side of my bump as he kissed me quickly on my cheek.

Reluctantly, I pulled away as my hair floated around us. "We should probably get back. Everyone might be worried something had happened to us."

"We've only been gone for three hours," he said, taking my hand as I swam in the direction of the castle.

"Anything can happen in three hours," I said matter-of-factly as we swam. "I had a good time. Thank you for sneaking us out and letting me meet some of them."

"I'm glad you had a good time. Maybe we could do it again sometime, Mrs. Waters." He grinned, his eyes shining with the purple hue of love and orange of excitement.

Sneaking past the guards, we made it back to the castle's secret entrance as we dove through the entrance together, Delmare making sure we wouldn't harm the children when we landed. Our skin and hair were dry once we hit the floor and the disappointed sound of Theodosia's voice rang throughout the tunnel.

"Delmare Triton Stormborn, what we're you thinking?" Theodosia exclaimed as she came toward us, her silver eyes filled with worry and disappointment. "You both could have gotten hurt!"

"Mom, we're fine. I wanted Anna to see the city without feeling like a title. She may never have another opportunity like this, and I wanted to give it to her. Don't be mad at her. Tt was my idea."

"You can't take all the blame yourself," I said to defend him. "I went with you. So, it's partially my fault as well. We are sorry we worried you, Theodosia. He just thought it would be good for me to get out of the castle and meet the people we will protect and serve until our children are ready to take over."

I watched as her eyes softened. She walked towards us, embracing us both before kissing us on our cheeks. "Don't scare me like that! Next time you decide to go on an adventure through town, leave a note."

We just nodded, following her through the tunnel and back into our bedroom. I suddenly didn't feel nervous about being queen. I guess it wasn't too different from my job on land. I was protecting the ocean and all the living beings in it. It wasn't the entire expanse of the sea, no. It was just a little paradise tucked away in the icy waters off the coast of the north pole. I loved it and the people who lived here, and I knew I would die caring for them and the ocean we lived in. I just hoped I wouldn't disappoint any of them, and be the woman they needed to continue to thrive.

TWENTY-FOUR

The next morning, I awoke to someone poking me several times on my shoulder, and feet kicking my stomach. The annoying prodding wouldn't stop. I swatted whoever was poking me. He groaned in protest as I shuffled farther away from him. With a huff, he stopped poking me, but the kicking persisted as I tried to fall back asleep. I felt something wet against my cheek and immediately opened my eyes. Delmare's face was inches away from my own as he grinned mischievously back at me.

"Ew, why is my face wet? Did you lick me?" I asked as I wiped my face with the comforter. His face showed what I said was true, making me scrunch up my nose in disgust. "You're disgusting."

"I love you too." He laughed and reached down for a kiss just as I moved away from his reach. "Hey! I want to kiss you good morning!"

"Well, now you can't," I said with a huff, shimmying out of my nightgown, which nowadays only meant one of Delmare's T-shirts, and changed into the dress that I was expected to wear during Delmare's coronation that day. The fabric was soft and comfortable and flowed over my baby bump with ease.

"You're no fun," Delmare complained from bed.

I turned around, a cheeky grin on my face. "I know." I laughed, slipping on some sandals and hoping no one would see my swollen ankles.

"I love your swollen ankles," Delmare said, walking toward me and hugging me from behind just as the children kicked. "I love your baby bump and the children it holds."

"You mean my uterus?" I said with a giggle, craning my neck to look behind me. "You need to get dressed. Your coronation is in two hours and I don't want you to be late."

I heard him huff in protest, moving my hair away from my neck as I felt his lips brush against the base of my neck. He spun me around to face him, his eyes burning gold now. I shook my head, knowing we didn't have any time for his horny outbursts. "Delmare, you need to get dressed."

"I will, later," he mumbled, his thumb rubbing softly against my cheek as he leaned in for a kiss, pulling me closer to him. I felt him grab the zipper of my dress, pulling it down slowly. Instinctively, I ran my fingers through his hair, completely forgetting what we were supposed to be doing as I tugged on his shirt. My hormones were everywhere—one minute I hated him for licking me and the next, I wanted him so badly I couldn't stand it.

I kissed him back and he lifted me up, carrying me over to the bed as I kissed his neck. Effortlessly, he set me down while I closed my eyes. I heard a rustle and opened them again, reaching up to touch his bare chest. His eyes were a mix of gold and purple as he crawled into the bed, holding me close and spooning me from behind. I found myself closing my eyes again, feeling his fingers play with my bra as he teased me, leaving a trail of soft kisses along my shoulder before I turned onto my back. I stared at him as he rested his head on his hand, leaning up against the pillows. He smiled as I reached behind me, unclasping my bra before flinging it in the direction of my discarded dress. Within seconds, we were all over each other, kissing each other long and hard as we breathed in each other's familiar scent. My breathing hitched as he kissed down my neck before sucking on my breasts. A moan escaped my lips.

"Delmare," I moaned as he kissed my stomach twice just as someone knocked on the door, interrupting the moment. Delmare lifted his head and stared at me, his face falling with disappointment.

"Your highness, my lady, you are needed downstairs in the throne room," a guard said through the cracked door. Delmare groaned in protest, kissing me again on the lips.

Breathless, I called, "We'll be right down!"

Delmare's eyes were entirely gold now as he looked at me mischievously, his hands playing with the band on my underwear before he pulled them off effortlessly. "Delmare, we can't do this right now." He began to play with my soft spot as pleasure spread throughout my body, forcing me to close my eyes, enjoying every second of it. "You're stubborn."

"So are you," he said as he climbed on top of me, resting his knees on the bed. He looked down at me, a knowing look on his face as he smiled cheekily at me.

"If we aren't down there in twenty minutes, they're going to send the cavalry," I said, beginning to get up before Delmare rested his hand on my knee.

"Just stay with me for a few more minutes. We'll be down there on time," he replied, kissing my cheek and chuckling softly. "And don't worry, we don't have land horses. We have seahorses and they can't get in here."

I sighed, watching as he rubbed the inside of my thigh, his fingers grazing softly up and down my leg as I gave in, pulling him closer to me. "Fine. But if we get yelled at, I'm blaming you."

***

The sound of our shoes bounced against the walls of the hallway as we sprinted, laughing, knowing we would be scolded by his mother once we made it to the throne room. Within minutes, we made it to the double doors, taking a second to catch our breath. I ran my fingers through my hair, knowing I looked like a complete mess despite the beautiful gown I wore. We were lucky we had an hour and half before the ceremony started.

I tried to hold back a giggle as I looked at Delmare. His hair was sticking up in odd places and it looked like he had just rolled out of bed, which was sort of true. But before I could fix his hair, someone threw open the doors ahead of us, yelling at us to come inside.

"Sorry, Mom," Delmare called, wrapping his arm around my waist and kissing me softly on my left cheek.

"What happened?" she asked, her hands on her hips as she stared the both of us down. "I asked for you two nearly forty minutes ago!"

"We slept in," I replied, feeling my cheeks burn as I lied, hoping she wouldn't press any further.

"You can't do that anymore. If you are expected at a certain time, you should be there on time, if not early." She looked between the both of us before turning to Ondina. "Dear, would you make Anna look presentable, please? And Delmare, comb your hair back. You look like a mess."

I held back a laugh as I kissed Delmare before turning to Ondina, who looked at me with a knowing look. She guided me over to a chair where she ran a brush through my hair. As I fumbled with the fabric of my dress, I found my mind wandering to this morning and bit my lip. "It's alright, Anna. You don't have to be nervous. Everything will go as planned." She paused, grinning cheekily as she clipped my hair back and grabbed some makeup from a bag. "So, how was it?"

"I don't know what you're talking about," I replied, but knew my face betrayed me as she applied powder to my face to hide the red blush creeping up my skin.

"Hmm," Ondina hummed, setting the sponge down and applying another fine powder over my eyes, which I could only guess was their version of eyeshadow. "Well, I'm not judging or anything. You two are cute together, but I think I'm biased because we're friends."

"You consider me a friend?" I asked.

She smiled. "Of course. As Consuela is my friend. I see you as an equal. Although, as far as title goes, we may never be equal. Maybe, with the future kings and your reign, we can finally get rid of those monsters."

"The Syrens?" I asked as she stepped away and gave me a nod.

"They killed my mother, but there is nothing I can do to stop them. So maybe, with a new ruler, we can stop their tyranny and the kingdoms can finally have a true peace they haven't had in years."

"I'm sorry about your mother," I replied, hugging her softly.

"It's okay," she said, dismissing it with a wave of her hand.

"No, it's not." I shook my head. "I swear I will do anything I can to help stop those monsters. To protect you, your family, and the rest of our citizens."

She smiled at me before lightly touching my stomach. "Also for future generations. They should be able to live in a world of peace."

I nodded before turning to Delmare who was staring back at us, his eyes back to their silver color. I walked toward him, looking him up and down as I did. He looked handsome in a suit, but even more handsome with it off. I bit my lip, trying not to look like I was as horny as I was, before Theodosia directed everyone to leave as people would be arriving soon.

"Later," Delmare whispered so only I could hear. In that moment, I was sure he would continue to read my mind until the day we died.

Theodosia waved me over. "Now, Anna, you'll sit here next to Avisa and her daughter Alana. You remember Avisa, right?" Theodosia asked. I nodded. "Del, you're going to walk down as soon as the music starts and stand here, where I will say a few words and place the crown on your head. Once you are crowned, you may choose to announce your engagement to Anna, or we can wait until you are both ready."

Delmare looked to me. I chewed on my lip before saying, "I actually don't mind announcing our engagement, but what do you think the citizens will say about me being human?"

"Well, I can't tell you everyone will love you, but it will take time. You just need to prove to them you are worthy of their respect and loyalty."

I nodded, feeling my nerves form in the pit of my stomach. "I'm sure it will be just fine."

An hour later, everyone began filing in, filling the seats. Most of them I recognized from the funeral, but some I didn't recognize at all. Avisa smiled at me after she sat down, hugging me quickly as a woman, I believed to be her daughter, Alana, sat next to her, smiling at me shyly.

"Oh, you're practically glowing!" Avisa grinned, her eyes shining bright. "Have you found out the sex yet?"

"I—yes, we have, but we kind of aren't sure when to make the announcement yet. Everything has happened so quickly that it's hard to keep up," I said, looking away nervously. "I'm still just trying to get used to everything."

"You're human right?" Alana whispered, her brown eyes searching mine with a knowing look.

I nodded.

"What's it like up there? I've heard stories, but my mother won't let me go."

"Alana, please, you know it's dangerous," Avisa reminded her before turning to me. "No offense, Anna, but our kind isn't safe mingling with yours.

I'm just glad you weren't one of those evil marine biologists who test you until you find your demise."

"I am a marine biologist, or at least I was until Delmare brought me here. Now everything I had planned for in my life will no longer happen. I wanted to get married and start a family, but I always thought it would be on land near the sea, not *in* it."

"Sometimes what we think we want isn't what we are meant to have, or where we are meant to be," Avisa said simply as the music began to play.

We turned around to see Delmare walking confidently toward his mother, who stood beside a podium that held a single crown.

I couldn't help but hold my breath as I stared. He seemed so different from the man I had fallen in love with. He seemed so regal, like this was what he was meant to do. I barely heard what Theodosia said as Delmare stopped before her, staring ahead of him. Everyone repeated something in a language I hadn't yet mastered. I watched silently as Theodosia placed the crown on Delmare's head. He bowed low and everyone else did the same. Not quite catching on fast enough, I bowed a second later than everyone else, jumping a little when the room was filled with hoots and hollers as everyone cheered.

When I looked back up, he was staring directly at me. I smiled at him as he grinned, motioning for everyone to quiet down as he began to speak. He looked at me for a moment longer than he probably should have, then swept his gaze around the room, "I have an announcement to make. I am engaged to a wonderful woman who is as crazy about me as I am about her. We haven't set the date yet, but know that Lady Anna Jane Lisle will be the new queen of Arcania. And she is the love of my life." He paused, looking me in the eyes as he smiled. "I can't think of anyone better to rule beside me and raise our children together."

Suddenly, I found everyone's eyes on me as I whispered, "Hello." Everyone stood again, turning to me and placing their fists over their chests and bowing. I couldn't help but smile, not knowing what to do as everyone's eyes sparking with joy, admiration, and curiosity. Before I knew it, everyone was leaving, heading toward the reception hall, but I stayed, as did Delmare.

"Well, that was fun," I said as he came toward me, smiling from ear to ear. "What were they thinking?"

"They think you're nice. You have an air of respect around you." He paused, laughing as he grabbed my hand and began to follow everyone out. "They are also wondering how you managed to fall in love with a weirdo like me."

"You aren't that weird. You're cute," I said, grinning as I grabbed his crown from him, laughing as I began to run, but only managing to get a few feet before he pinned me to the floor, careful not to hurt me or the children as he grabbed his crown from my hand. "We're going to get dirty and then your mother will kill us."

"Now who's fault was that?" He grinned, setting the crown down as he kissed me before helping me up off the ground.

By the time we entered the reception hall, I could tell Delmare was giddy with excitement. No doubt this was an event he had been looking forward to since he was a child. Everyone greeted us, asking us all sorts of questions about the wedding and congratulating us on our engagement. I learned that Avisa was the granddaughter of Oshun, Sedna's brother, and the Queen of Stowryn. Her husband Matthew had died a few years back and their daughter Alana would take over a few years from now.

Looking up from my glass of water, I watched as a couple came toward me, their smiles bright as they approached. "Hi, you must be Lady Anna, right? I am King James Whittaker of Terenia. This is my wife, Semarah, and our son, Lorkan, is around here somewhere." The man had dark midnight blue hair and the woman was something. He pointed to a couple talking and laughing. "Ah, see him there? He's talking to that woman there in the green. That's Elizabeth, another one of our many cousins."

"You have a big family," I breathed as James turned back around. Semarah squeezed my arm reassuringly.

"Yes, I suppose we do," James replied. "Sometimes it's hard to keep track of everyone. I guess for someone outside the family, it can be confusing, but I'm sure after a few months, you should be able to tell us apart."

"I hope so," I mumbled, taking a sip of my glass.

"Are you well from your fall from a week ago?" Semarah asked, her dark gray eyes looking over at me with concern before flickering down to my stomach and back again. "You seem fine now. We were worried about you."

"I'm fine now. A Syren poisoned my food, but I've recovered."

"Oh goodness, I hope the baby is alright!" she exclaimed in a hushed tone, trying not to make a spectacle. I knew that there was no hiding my baby bump now.

"We are fine, healthy as can be. Although, I'm still getting used to how fast this pregnancy has been. Usually, for a human, it lasts nine months, but I now look as if I'm five months along. It's honestly daunting to me," I confessed as Semarah gave me a sympathetic look.

"I know how you feel, dear. My mother was human. She said the same thing when she spoke of her pregnancy. Unfortunately, she passed away nearly two hundred years ago."

I couldn't help but gasp. "Oh, I'm sorry for your loss!"

"It's alright. It's a part of life. But don't worry about being unable to see your children grow up. Lately, we haven't been able to age as well as our ancestors have. It's a shame, though. I would like to see 2,400," she said with a wink.

"I think I would just like to see 100," I replied with a smile.

"I'm sure you will. I can sense a resilience in you, a strong heart," she commented, taking a sip of her water.

"What are we discussing today?" I heard Delmare ask as he came toward us, wrapping his arm around my waist.

"We were just discussing how long I would live," I replied casually, as I turned toward him. "I'd like to see 100. What age would you like to see?"

"I'd say any age that can let me spend every waking moment with you and our children. We can die together, old and gray in our beds," he said, kissing me softly on my cheek.

"Why are we talking about death? This is a celebration! Ol' Delmare here has found himself a pretty human girl *and* just became king of his own kingdom! Congratulations, bud!" I heard a man say. I recognized him as James and Semarah's son, Lorkan, as he gave Delmare a big pat on his back. "What I would like to know is what you did with that fancy wine you had in that cellar of yours. So where's the alcohol?"

Semarah grimaced before scolding her son. James bowed slightly and left with his wife and son, leaving Delmare and I alone, wrapped in each other's embrace. I was starting to feel a little overwhelmed and I knew Delmare could tell. But I also knew I probably shouldn't leave the party. I'd have to get used to large social events.

"When this is done, we can just relax in our room. Maybe celebrate if you want to," he said, turning to me.

"Celebrate, as in—" I cut myself off, seeing his eyes turn gold, which only confirmed my suspicions. I smiled at him. "We'll have to see. It's been a long day. Maybe a nap and *then* some fun. How does that sound?"

"Perfect," he said, staring at me as I quickly kissed him, a small peck, barely noticeable if you weren't paying attention.

But Delmare wasn't having any of that. He pulled me closer, kissing me properly in front of his entire family as the world fell away and it was just us in a moment of simple bliss.

TWENTY-FIVE

I awoke from my nap, wrapped snuggly against Delmare. His breathing was slow and deep, confirming he was still fast asleep. I wasn't sure how long we had been asleep, but I silently wished I could fall back into the dreamless rest I had grown so fond of. Shifting in my spot, I tried to move my arm, hoping I could ease the numbness and let the blood flow freely again. Instinctively, Delmare wrapped his arms around me again, pulling me closer to him in his sleep.

"Delmare," I mumbled, trying to unravel myself from him.

He groaned in protest.

"Delmare, get up."

"Go back to sleep," he said, whispering in my ear as he snuggled closer to me. Something hard pressed against my butt and I could only guess what that was.

"Delmare, we have to get up. We can't stay in bed all day," I replied, louder this time as I turned onto my side to face him, resting my head on my hand.

His eyes were still closed, but I could tell he wasn't asleep. Grinning mischievously, I gasped, grasping his hand as I enthusiastically lied that the children were kicking. Immediately, his eyes opened, bright with excitement. He placed a hand on my stomach hoping to feel a successful kick, but the disappointment was clear on his face when there wasn't one.

"Why would you lie like that?" he asked as I pulled him out of bed.

"It was the only way I'd get you out of bed." I grinned, ruffling his hair before turning to go take a shower.

I still wasn't sure how they had plumbing down here, but I was thankful I could take a decent shower instead of never taking one at all. Stretching, I heard and felt the satisfying pop of my back as I padded into the bathroom, closing the door behind me with a click. Absentmindedly, I twirled my hair, a habit I thought I had gotten rid of years ago. I turned the faucet on, feeling the warm water flow from the waterfall-like showerhead. Letting my clothes fall to the floor, I quietly stepped into the shower. Over the sound of the water, I heard the door open and close. I peeked through the shower curtain to find Delmare smiling at me, then pointing at the toilet. With a nod, I turned my attention to the bar of soap that rested on the shelf made of driftwood. As I lathered my body with soap, I tried to ignore the sound of Delmare using the restroom beside the shower. I rinsed myself, attempting to ease the grogginess that threatened to make me crawl back into bed with Delmare.

Suddenly, though, the water turned icy. I jumped from the stream of water just as Delmare apologized, cursing under his breath as he quickly washed his hands and turned the sink off. Immediately, the water turned warm again, and I rinsed.

"Are you okay?"

"Yeah, I'm fine." I paused before shutting the water off and grabbing a towel from its hook. I dabbed myself dry, looking over at him as his eyes wandered. "If you want to take a shower, you can. I was going to go downstairs to read some more, *your Highness*." I grinned, wrapping the towel around myself as I walked back out of the bathroom and padded toward the dresser.

"Okay, but wait for me to be done before you go," he called as I grabbed an outfit from the dresser and changed.

"Okay!" I called back, walking into the nursery. I stared at the tiny mobiles that were made to look like different sea creatures. Smiling to myself, making my way over to the rocking chair, staring at the still-discarded ball of yarn and the disgrace I hoped would magically turn into a blanket. Easing down, I rested my head on the back of the rocking chair, and began rocking softly as I rested my hand on my stomach. My mind wandered to South Carolina as I wondered how Claire was doing and if my coworkers thought about where I went. Would they send a search party for me? Would I become a missing person and end up being one of the many cases that would never be solved?

I felt homesickness hit me all at once. I missed home. Not the sea I escaped to, or the beach cottage I had purchased not too long ago, but I missed the countryside of Kansas. I missed my family, and I wished I could see my mother again, ask her what I should do as I started this new chapter with Delmare. What were we going to do about the Syren creatures? How many were there? Was it an impossible request to kill them all?

I hadn't noticed Delmare had finished showering or getting dressed until I saw him out of the corner of my eye. His face was calm and collected, the complete opposite of how I was feeling now.

"Stop worrying. Everything will be fine. I plan to talk with my cousins and see what we can do about the Syrens." He paused, walking toward me with confident strides. "The only thing you should be worried about is what you'll be wearing at our wedding."

"It doesn't have to be in front of the entire country, right?" I asked, turning to him as he smiled at me knowingly. "We could just have it in front of a few friends."

"You will be queen, Anna. A part of that means you will be in the public eye." He said, kissing me on my forehead as I relaxed. "And we'll only have it in front of my cousins and a few of the nobles. After, we'll take a carriage out and greet our citizens."

"What if we did a small ceremony, just us, something that embodies both of us before having the overwhelming wedding the kingdom expects."

"Is that what you want to do?" he asked, already knowing my answer. His eyes flashed purple filled with complete understanding.

I nodded. "We could run it by your mom, see what she thinks. I want our wedding to be special, something that isn't expected of us. Something the both of us can do together, just like we will continue to do as husband and wife."

"Let's do it."

"What?" I asked, not expecting that answer, fully expecting him to say no.

"Yeah, let's do it. I've been thinking about doing something different, especially with our wedding. When do you want to do it?"

I paused, but I already knew my answer. I wanted it now. "Is it bad if I say today?"

He grinned, helping me up as he did. "Well, if it is bad to want to marry me right here and now, what does that say about me if I want the same thing?"

Quickly, I kissed him, smiling so big my cheeks hurt as he pulled me along, away from the nursery. We ran through the hallways and into the study, where Theodosia sat, reading.

"Well, hello, what has gotten you two in a rush?" she asked with a laugh as she set her book down, her attention fully on us.

"Mom, we have something to ask you," Delmare started, looking from his mother, to me, and then back again. "We were wondering if you would give us your blessing."

"My blessing? For your wedding? Of course. You know you have that already," she said, her face contorted with surprise and concern.

"No, I know. It's just, we were wondering if we could get married *before* the wedding. Where it's just us, no expectations from the kingdom or anything. We will still get married under the public eye but," he paused, looking over at me as he smiled, "we want the first wedding to be for us only."

"When were you wanting to do this? The wedding is in three weeks. We'll be busy with the preparations, so I don't think there will be enough time for another wedding." She looked between both of us with understanding, a look that seemed to say she knew exactly where we were coming from.

"We were wondering if we could do it today," I said, as Delmare reached for my hand. "That is, if you don't disagree with our idea of marrying quicker than planned."

We held our breath as Theodosia stood, staring at both of us, her expression never changing before she breathed the one word that would change everything "Okay."

"Wait, what?" Delmare asked, looking at his mother with disbelief.

"Okay. I will marry you two, but you aren't wearing those things. Change into something worthy of a wedding and meet me in the throne room in ten," she said, trying to hide her smile as she walked past us, letting the door fall shut behind her.

"What just happened?" I asked, turning to Delmare as he grinned, his eyes still the same violet shade as earlier.

"We're getting married!" he exclaimed, his overwhelming joy spilling out of him as he hugged me tight.

Within minutes, we were making our way to the throne room, both wearing nicer clothes that were still somewhat casual, so as to not bring too much attention to ourselves. Delmare pushed open the doors. There, in front of the podium, Theodosia gushed as we walked toward her, hand in hand.

"Now, I grabbed the rings while you two were changing. This ceremony should only take a few minutes and I asked no one to bother us. Now, I want you both to stand right here. Anna, please stand to my right, and Delmare, across from her," she said.

We did as we were told.

"Take each other's hands and look at each other while I start."

I couldn't help but giggle as Delmare took my hands, rubbing his thumb over the back of my hand. He stared at me, his eyes entirely purple. I loved how his eyes changed. I loved everything about him. I couldn't believe we were doing this.

"Anna and Delmare, you have chosen to become husband and wife. I am here not only to witness your commitment to each other, but to wish you every happiness in your future life together." She smiled. "Marriage is founded on sincerity and understanding, which leads to tolerance, confidence, and trust. I believe that these qualities, which have attracted you to each other, can be best developed during a life spent together. A happy marriage will enable you to establish a home with love and stability, where your family and friends will always be welcome." She handed Delmare a piece of paper.

He took it, then looked over at me. "I, Delmare Triton Stormborn, affirm my love to you, Anna Jane Lisle, as I invite you to share my life with me. I promise always to respect your needs. I will endeavor through kindness, unselfishness, and trust to achieve the warm, rich life we now look forward to." He paused, looking into my eyes as he smiled. "I take you to be my lawful wife, to have and to hold, from this day forward, for better or for worse, for richer or for poorer, in sickness and in health, as long as we both shall live."

I couldn't help myself as I pulled him to me, my emotions overtaking me as I kissed him much to Theodosia's protest.

"Hey, we aren't there yet. Now, Anna, repeat the words to Delmare, and then we can do the rings."

Grinning like a fool, I took a step away. "Me too. I, Anna Jane or whatever, take you, Delmare."

Delmare laughed. "I don't think it counts if you don't say it all the same."

"Like hell it doesn't!" I laughed as Theodosia scolded me. I grabbed the piece of paper from Delmare's hand, reading it aloud. "I, Anna Jane Lisle, affirm my love to you, Delmare Triton Stormborn, as I invite you to share my life with me. I promise always to respect your needs. I will endeavor through kindness, unselfishness, and trust to achieve the warm, rich life we now look forward to. I take you to be my lawfully wife, to have and to hold, from this day forward, for better or for worse, for richer or for poorer, in sickness and in health, as long as we both shall live."

"*Wife?*" He grinned, eyes sparkling with excitement.

"I meant husband." I paused. "Great, I ruined it!"

I heard Theodosia sigh as she handed us our rings. We placed them on our ring fingers, pulling each other close and kissing passionately as we heard Theodosia walk away with a defeated sigh.

Pulling away, I watched Delmare's eyes flicker to gold as I held on to him.

"I love you, Mrs. Stormborn," he breathed, barely inches away from my face as we held each other, the paper with our vows resting near our feet.

"I love you, too, Mr. Stormborn." I grinned, kissing him again as I ran my fingers through his hair, wondering if we could make it to our room or consummate the marriage right here in the throne room. A part of me knew the last option probably wasn't the best thing to do, and as we pulled apart and walked together toward the double doors, I was glad we were starting this new chapter of our lives together—our own way.

TWENTY-SIX

The room we were in was insanely loud, louder than what I was used to as Sedna and Delmare fought over who would be the car as we set up Monopoly that I had introduced Delmare to a month ago. I shook my head, placing the steamship—which I liked to call the Titanic—on the Go square at the corner of the board before sorting through the money. Shuffling the cards a few times, I waited patiently for them to stop bickering, but unfortunately, I didn't think they would stop until one of them gave up. I knew that would never happen.

With a sigh, I grabbed the car out of Delmare's hand, looking at both of them with a stern expression, hoping they would know I meant what I said, "Neither of you are going to be the car if you two don't stop bickering like children. It doesn't matter what piece you are, just pick one and be done with it." With a huff, I threw the car back into the box and grabbed the dice. "Youngest goes first. Sedna, roll please."

"Sorry," they both mumbled as Sedna grabbed the dice from my hand and rolled.

After a few minutes of playing, I was getting hungry, but I didn't want to leave my stuff laying there and risk my money being stolen by the two cheaters I was playing with. I grabbed the dice to roll and let them fall onto the board. Moving my piece, I bit my lip as I realized I would immediately be sent to jail.

"Damn," I cursed, pouting a little as I set the Titanic in the jail.

"Aww, you went to jail," she said, her golden eyes gleaming with laughter. "Well, I'll be sure to visit you, sis!"

I couldn't help but smile at her as my disappointment ceased. Sedna and Theodosia were the only ones who knew that Delmare and I had eloped. She had been more than thrilled when we told her, but a little upset that she hadn't been there.

I could tell that she wanted to plan me a party still, even if I was already married to her brother.

"So, I was thinking, I haven't been on land in a while and you must miss it up there…" Sedna trailed off as she purchased one of the yellow properties. "Maybe we could take a trip to that beach town where you're from. What was it again? Myrtle Beach?"

"Well, I've been missing for a few months, so we probably shouldn't go to Myrtle Beach," I said, grabbing the die from the board and rolling, hoping I could get out of jail. "Not unless we want to be questioned by the police about where I've been for the past two months. And I don't think we should say I ran away with a merman king who is now my husband, and now that I'm married, I'm supposed to help rule an underwater kingdom that only a few humans in the entire world know about. Yeah, that'll go over well." I laughed, handing the dice over to Delmare, who looked over at me knowingly.

"Is there a city you've always wanted to visit?" Delmare asked, setting the dice down and turning his full attention on me.

"I've always wanted to visit the Gold Coast in Australia," I replied automatically. "There's the Sea World aquarium and the beaches are absolutely beautiful."

"Sounds nice. We'll definitely go there. We can have the girls come along as well," Sedna said excitedly, clapping her hands together.

"What?"

"Your old maids, Ondina and Consuela. They're your friends, right? We can even ask Avisa, Alana, Elizabeth, and her mother to come along as well! Oh, it'll be so much fun!"

"Elizabeth Caudill? The future queen to Waverly, right?" I asked.

"Yeah, our second cousin once removed, but there's so many of us, we just call them our cousins." She laughed.

"That seems like a lot of people," I commented nervously. "Can't we just spend a day at the beach or something? It really doesn't have to be a big deal."

"But that's no fun," Sedna pouted. "This is a celebration of your marriage to my brother!"

"I had enough celebration the night I married your brother." I grinned, making her grimace as I kissed Delmare on his cheek.

"That was not a visual I wanted, Anna," she groaned, looking away as her face turned red.

"I didn't say anything. What did you think I meant?" I asked, laughing as Delmare chuckled beside me, wrapping his arms around my waist and kissing me back.

She shook her head, not looking either of us in the eye. "Forget it. Avisa was wondering when you will have your baby shower. Are you going to announce that you're having a boy and a girl, or are you going to wait till they're born? Have you thought of names yet?"

"Well, we haven't really discussed it," I replied, biting my lip.

"But you're due in two months. You don't have much time now! Oh, can I plan it? Oh, please!" she exclaimed, jumping up. "Oh, we could do streamers and balloons. It will be so much fun!"

"I guess you can," I replied as Delmare shook his head.

"Great! We'll do it a few days after your wedding and coronation on the seventh! This is going to be so much fun! I have to go get the invitations ready!" she squealed, running out of the room, leaving her full set of properties vulnerable.

"Well, that was fun." Delmare laughed.

"I'm still surprised she's your sister." I grinned. "She's the complete opposite of you."

"Yes, but I think having a sister who is enthusiastic about socializing helps the quiet and reserved ones get out of their shell." He paused, looking over at me thoughtfully. "She is right though. We'll need to pick out names "

"Hmm," I hummed. "What about Gilbert?" I asked jokingly.

"Gilbert?" he asked, his face contorted as if he hated the name. Poor Gilbert.

"Yeah, Gilbert. I *love* that name!"

"I'm going to have to disagree with you," he said, his eyes saying he knew I was playing with him. He shuffled on the couch so we could cuddle together. "I was thinking maybe naming our son after both of our fathers."

"Paul Ronan?" I asked, "Or Ronan Paul?"

"Ronan Paul Stormborn." He paused, his voice filling with pride. "What do you think?"

"I love it." I grinned, then sighed as I leaned into him. "So, what about our daughter?"

"What about Chelsea? I've always wanted to name my daughter that."

"That's a beautiful name." I commented, staring at the blue fire dancing in the fireplace, cracking and sparking. "What about Marie for the middle name?"

"Chelsea Marie," he whispered. "I like it."

"I don't think we'll be finishing this game anytime soon," I sighed, motioning toward the half-finished game of Monopoly. "And I'm getting hungry."

"You're probably right. How about you go get some food and I'll put the game up and meet you in the dining hall for dinner?" he suggested, hopping off the couch while I watched him put the pieces away and my stomach growled.

"Okay, I'll see you over there," I replied, pulling myself up before kissing him swiftly on his cheek and making a dash toward the hallway.

As I walked through the hall, the guards watched me as I passed. I fought the urge to wave or greet them, as my newfound knowledge told me I wasn't supposed to acknowledge that they were there. It still seemed wrong to me as I rounded the corner and made my way into the kitchen, instead greeting one of the many chefs who was peeling something I didn't recognize.

"Oh, your Highness—I mean, my lady. I'm sorry. I didn't see you there." The woman stumbled, curtsying quickly as she brought her full attention to me. "What can I do for you?"

"Oh, it's fine. Don't worry about it. I was just wondering if I could make myself something to eat."

"Oh, if you're hungry, I believe there're some leftovers in the icebox." She paused, setting her knife down and started toward it, but I motioned for her to stay.

"That sounds perfect, and there's no need for you to fix it for me, I think I can manage." I smiled, walking over to the icebox and grabbing whatever looked good.

After everything was heated, I plated it before cleaning up my mess and taking my plate of goodness into the dining room. Just as I was about to sit down and eat, Delmare strode into the dining room, catching my eye as I turned and smiled at him.

"That smells good!" Delmare exclaimed as I looked down at my plate and then back to him. "Can I have some?"

"Do you only want it because it's mine?" I asked with a knowing look as I took a bite and pointed my fork at him. "No, you can't have my food. I'm feeding your children!"

"But I'm hungry!" he whined, completely ignoring my question as he grinned mischievously at me.

"You have two hands. Go make it yourself," I replied, stabbing the food with my fork before stuffing it in my mouth just as Delmare reached over and grabbed my plate, running across the room with it.

"Hey!" I exclaimed, jumping up from my chair to chase after my husband and my food. "Delmare, give me back my food right now!"

"Why? Are you going to make me?" He chuckled as I took long strides after him.

"Delmare Triton Stormborn, you give me my food right now! I'm hungry and I'm tired and everything hurts and I just want to eat a plate of whatever the hell that is in peace without having to chase after it!" I felt my blood boil as I stopped crossed-armed behind him until he turned around, guilt written all over his face.

"I'm sorry. Here." He handed me my plate and I turned to sit down and eat, while he went to grab some food of his own.

"Thank you." I said, taking a bite as he sat down next to me.

"You're welcome, now you can't be mad at me." he smiled over at me, feigning innocence as I shook my head.

We ate in silence. That was, until Sedna burst through the door carrying all kinds of papers, balloons, and swatches. Her excitement was radiating off her in waves, and I could only imagine what she was thinking. She threw the stuff on the table with a sigh of relief.

"What's all this?" I asked, picking up a streamer that had hit my plate when it rolled.

"It's the decorations for the baby shower, obviously," she replied, her tone teasing as she thrust an invitation into my hands. "I just sent these out. We should receive notification from the kingdoms in a few days, or we'll find out at the wedding. Wither way, I know everyone will show up."

"That sounds good, sis." Delmare smiled. "So we're going to have it on the thirtieth?" he asked, looking over at me and then back at his sister.

"Yes, five days from now. I will do more of the set up and we'll be using the north hall for the party. The only thing you both need to do is show up." She paused. "Oh, also, I'm bringing my girlfriend."

"You have a girlfriend?" I asked, a little surprised.

"Yes, Emilia, Delmare's former fiancée." Sedna commented, as Delmare smiled knowingly as if he already knew the information Sedna was telling us. "We actually have been seeing each other for a year, but our parents don't approve of same-sex couples." She paused, disappointment in her voice. "But I'm planning to tell Mom tomorrow. I'm hoping she won't hate me."

"She loves you. She'll come around," I said, standing to give her a hug.

342

"I hope so, because I plan to spend the rest of my life with Emilia," she said, a mystified look across her features as she hugged me back. She let go and looked between the two of us. "It's too bad we don't have a law that makes it legal to marry someone of the same sex."

"That can be arranged," Delmare replied with a smile. "I never liked that law anyway, and I'm happy both of you are happy."

Sedna beamed. "Thank you, Del! I can't wait for you to meet her, Anna! You will get along, swimmingly!" she said with a wink before picking up all of her supplies and skipping out of the hall, her excitement trailing after her.

TWENTY-SEVEN

The morning of the wedding came faster than expected. I wanted to stay in bed, wrapped in the warmth of the covers and Delmare, but unfortunately, I couldn't. We were both expected to get ready for the ceremony three hours ahead of it, and I was not happy about it.

"We have to get up," Delmare whispered in my ear, brushing my hair out of my face, his fingers grazing against my temple as I groaned in protest. "I know, babe, but we have to."

"No, I don't want to go!" I groaned, pulling the covers tighter around me as I snuggled closer to Delmare. Sighing, I shuffled onto my back, staring up at the ceiling as Delmare lay beside me. "Fine, I'll get up."

"I can't wait to see that dress of yours, Mrs. Stormborn," he said, winking at me with a cheeky grin. "I can't wait to take it off too."

"I think that will have to wait for later." I laughed. "We can at least have breakfast together, right?"

"Of course," he said, crawling out of bed wearing nothing but his blue boxers. I watched as he stretched, my mind falling away from me as I crawled out of bed myself.

"I think I'm going to take a shower," I called, looking back at him before padding into the bathroom, letting my clothes fall to the floor before turning the faucet on.

Stepping into the tub, I closed the sheer curtain, listening to the sound of the water as it sprayed over my head, down my face, and off my shoulders. Sighing deeply, I tried to relax until I heard the curtain slide open and someone step inside. Through watery eyes, I stared at my husband, who was standing in front of me, grinning like a fool.

"Do you mind if I join you?" he inquired, taking a step toward me as I moved out of the water.

"No, I don't mind at all," I replied, reaching down to grab the shampoo to run it through my hair, but Delmare grabbed it before I could.

He took another step toward me, his eyes never leaving mine as my breathing quickened. He poured the shampoo into his palm, then massaged it into my scalp, the sensation forcing me to close my eyes and sigh happily. Grabbing the soap from his hand, I carefully poured a small amount into my palm and lathered the soap all over his chest, feeling his heart thump fast against my palm. I didn't think this was what he had in mind when he asked to join me, but I didn't think we had enough time for a quickie in the shower.

As if he read my mind, he placed his hands under the waterfall of steaming liquid and pulled me toward him, kissing me fast and hard, shocking my system as we stepped under the water. The soap streamed off us, escaping down the drain while we wrapped our arms around each other, our need overwhelming. We finally pulled apart, completely breathless. I breathed in his familiar sent before reaching up and resting my lips against the base of his neck, kissing him softly as I made circular motions along his hip. Within moments we were all over each other again, wanting to finish what we had started, ignoring the insistent knocking from the hallway as we positioned ourselves for a simple moment of fun between husband and wife.

***

The scolding we received from Theodosia was almost comical. My hair was still damp, but I was wearing something almost presentable. I couldn't say the same for Delmare. After breakfast, we were expected to leave each other and not see each other again until the ceremony this afternoon. That part, of course, disappointed me, but I was more excited to see his face when he saw me in my dress. A part of me was glad we were already married; we had had a ceremony just for us, with no expectations from anyone else, and I knew we wouldn't regret that. Taking a seat in front of the mirror, I stared at my reflection while Consuela did my hair. I hadn't seen Ondina in days and was worried something might have happened to her.

"Consuela?" I asked, staring at her face through the mirror as she concentrated on making my hair curl, even though I knew it never would.

"Yes, ma'am?" she replied, looking up for a moment.

"Have you seen Ondina lately? Is she doing alright?"

She hesitated, looking around her nervously before looking back at me. "I haven't, ma'am. She said she wasn't feeling good a few days ago, so she hasn't been at work since then."

"Is she in the medical wing or at home? Does she need any help?"

"There's no need to worry, ma'am. She should be better in a few days. She would have loved to see your wedding." Consuela grinned, but her smile didn't reach her eyes. I wondered if she was telling me the full truth.

"Consuela, you know that lying to your future queen is a punishable offense, right?" I replied, my voice no longer cheery as it once was. I sounded more regal than I'd intended. "What are you hiding?"

"It's nothing, your Highness," she dismissed, her voice on edge. "I don't mean to worry you."

"Well, you *are* worrying me," I said, turning to look her in the eye, "What is it that has you so on edge?"

"Ondina is missing," she said before looking away.

"What do you mean she's missing?"

"Ondina has been acting strange lately," she confessed. "She's usually very energetic, but lately she's been reclusive, and she wouldn't open up with me. Then she said she was sick and when I went by her home that afternoon, she was gone. I don't know where she is and I've had my family search for her, but she isn't here. I'm afraid that—"

"What are you afraid of?"

"I'm afraid that the Syrens have taken her," she replied, looking at me, her face and tone entirely serious as she fought back the tears threatening to fall down her face. "There have been more attacks lately than there have been in years prior, and I fear something horrible is about to happen. I don't want our people to suffer because of those monsters. Promise me you will get rid of those horrible creatures and you will find Ondina."

"I promise." I nodded. "We want the same thing."

"Good," she said before quickly wiping her face. She turned me around so she could finish my hair. "We're running out of time. We have to get you ready for wedding number two."

"You know?" I asked, shocked as I looked up at her.

"You can't really hide anything here." She shrugged, then smiled. "It was quite obvious that you had eloped. My fiancé noticed you were wearing a second band a few days ago."

I felt my cheeks burn for a moment before I rose my eyebrow at her. "Fiancé?"

"Yeah," she said, a whimsical look on her face.

"Do they work in the palace?"

"He does. Trench is one of the guards. He usually stands guard around your room."

"Oh, I've met him!" I exclaimed. "He seems nice."

"He is," Consuela gushed. "His family loves me, but—" She paused, her demeanor changing suddenly.

"But what?" I asked as she finished messing with my hair before applying something that looked like makeup on my face.

"My father doesn't approve of him." She frowned. "He thinks I could do better. But I don't think there is anyone else I could spend the rest of my life with."

"Sometimes our parents just want the best for us and are concerned for our wellbeing. He just wants to make sure you aren't making a decision that you'll regret," I said, as she looked me over.

"Maybe." She sighed, before motioning for me to stand. She walked over to grab my dress that was hanging along the wall. "Anyway, enough about me. Let's get you in your gown."

I let Consuela help me into the white chiffon gown, giddy excitement consuming me as she fastened the buttons that ran the length of my back. I wasn't sure if I would have the patience to do the same, but Consuela didn't seem to mind. Looking back at my reflection, I smiled, noticing the modest and whimsical look the dress seemed to give off. It insinuated my curves and my baby bump, but didn't make me feel beautiful.

"I look amazing!" I exclaimed, looking back at Consuela who smiled over at me. I wrapped my arms around her, unable to stop myself. "Thank you!"

"Oh!" She paused, before cautiously hugging me back. "You're welcome, your Highness."

"It's Anna." I winked. "In public, it's your Highness."

She smiled and nodded. "Are you ready to marry the king?"

I nodded. "Of course. I can't wait to see his face when he sees me in this."

"You look cute." She winked. "Oh, don't forget your flowers! Don't ask me how they got them down here because I do not know."

I couldn't help but laugh as Theodosia poked her head through the door. "Anna, are you ready?"

"Yes, I'm coming!" I exclaimed, hugging Consuela once more before following Theodosia out of the room and down the hall.

I felt my nerves well up inside me as we walked, the soft sound of whispers and music escaping the slightly open door of the throne room. My heartbeat quickened as the music grew louder and the whispers ceased, pulling me to the task at hand. Theodosia looked at me. Her smile grew as she cupped my cheek, a thoughtful look on her face, and she led me into the room that would start my new life.

Everyone stood, their faces turned to me as Theodosia and I walked toward the two thrones, and where Delmare stood, wearing a suit I hadn't seen before. We caught each other's eyes then, his changing colors, flickering from gold to purple as we walked toward him. I couldn't describe the sheer amount of adoration and amazement written all over his face, and I knew he was trying to hold it in. Theodosia kissed my cheek before making her way onto the stage. I turned to Delmare and he grabbed my hands, staring at me as I smiled, fighting the urge to wipe the tears that escaped his eyes.

"Hi," he mouthed, making me giggle as I fought the nerves in the pit of my stomach.

As Theodosia spoke, I couldn't think of anything else but sheer amazement that I was here, marrying the man that I loved for the second time, about to become the queen of a kingdom I hadn't known existed until three months ago. And as we said I do, Theodosia grabbed the crown off her own head and gently placed it on mine, motioning for me to turn toward the family I was officially a part of now.

"May I present Anna Jane Stormborn, Queen of Arcania. May she reign forevermore!" Theodosia called as everyone in the room shouted in a language I had yet to learn.

I looked at Delmare and he smiled, linking his hand in mine as everyone stood, throwing something that looked like petals into the air, signaling their excitement as we exited the room. And as we walked, I couldn't help but feel excited for this new chapter, but I wondered what we would do about our Syren problem.

***

The wedding reception seemed to go on forever—so long, in fact, that I lost track of how many times Delmare's cousins asked me when I was due, what I was having, or if we were planning to have a honeymoon. Avisa was the last one to ask me, of course, her eyes shining bright with excitement.

"Sedna is planning to host our baby shower, actually." I smiled. "It's going to be on the thirteenth. And to answer your other questions, we're having twins, a boy and a girl, and we aren't having a honeymoon. We'll be lucky if we get a few moments of peace."

"Oh, how wonderful!" Avisa squealed. "Alana and I will definitely be there!"

"Great." I grinned just as I saw Sedna holding hands with a woman I didn't recognize. "Excuse me for a moment, please."

I walked across the room toward Sedna and the woman I could only guess was Emilia, and greeted them warmly, hoping I could stop answering questions. I noticed nervousness coming off them in waves as they looked around them, silently hiding their hand holding through the fabric of their dresses.

"Sedna! Hi! Oh, this must be Emilia."

I watched as Sedna's eyes shone brighter as she saw me, but Emilia still seemed nervous. "Hey, Anna! Yes, this is Emilia."

"Hi, it's nice to meet you," I greeted. Emilia smiled, her midnight blue hair pulled up in several braids as her eyes shined a familiar gray, like Theodosia's silver eyes.

"Have you told your mom yet?" I asked, as Sedna looked at Emilia nervously. I stiffened as I felt a presence behind me.

"Told me what?" I heard Theodosia ask, and I silently hoped this would go well. "Why are you hiding the fact that you're holding this woman's hand? Emilia VanCoup, what are you doing here?"

"Mom," Sedna started. I saw Delmare turn toward us from across the room. I motioned him over, silently watching as the mess unfolded. "Here's the thing, I—well, Emilia and I—we're romantically involved."

"Romantically?"

"Yes, romantically. As in, I'm dating Emilia. She is my girlfriend and I love her. I want to spend the rest of my life with her." Sedna paused. "I thought you should know."

"How long has this been going on?" Theodosia asked, disbelief filling her tone.

"A year. Please don't be mad."

"Mad?" Theodosia scoffed. "Why would I be mad?"

"Well, I just thought…" Sedna trailed off. She looked over at Emilia, who smiled nervously back at her.

"I love you no matter who you love, baby. I can't believe you'd think I'd hate you. This isn't how I expected Emilia to join our family but I'm so happy nonetheless." Theodosia paused, opening up her arms for a hug. "Come here, you two!"

I couldn't help but smile as I watched them hug each other. Feeling happy, I turned and embraced Delmare. I couldn't think of a better moment as everyone around us celebrated, blissfully unaware of the danger that would soon befall our family.

TWENTY-EIGHT

The familiar smell of the sandy seaside town of Garden City, South Carolina greeted us as Delmare and I came ashore. Our clothes and hair were soaked. I coughed up the last of the saltwater from my lungs, taking in a deep breath of crisp, clean oxygen. Looking over at Delmare, I smiled as he brushed the sand off of his pants. It had been two days since my coronation and things were going well, but I had begun to get homesick and we thought it would be good for us to take a day to spend for ourselves.

"Anna, is that you?" a familiar woman's voice called. We both turned to see who it was. There, in the sand, stood Claire, a white dress gracing her features, an enormous hat on her head. Her arm was pressed firmly on top, as if she was trying to keep it on as the wind blew around us. Her smile was big as she ran toward us, her eyes sparkling in disbelief and excitement. She ran to us, wrapping her arms around us both. "Oh, it's so good to see you! Look how big you've gotten! Have you found out what you're having? I assumed you went home to Arcania, but it was confirmed when Adam came back home a few weeks ago."

"It's good to see you, too, Claire. A lot has happened since we've been gone, and we'd like to tell you all about it if we can visit." I smiled as she enthusiastically nodded.

"Sure, I'd love for you two to visit. Come inside before someone sees you two." She grabbed my hand and guided us across the sand, toward a home that looked similar to the one I had owned.

Once inside, she handed us each a towel to dry ourselves. Wrapped in the warm cloth, we sat together at the dining room table, silence filling the room except for the distant sounds of waves crashing onto shore.

"You're married?" Claire asked, an eyebrow raised as she sipped from her glass of wine, eyeing my ring finger with an air of expectation.

"Um, yes, we are. Technically, we've been married for a month, but the public ceremony was a few days ago." I paused, looking over at Delmare, who lightly placed his hand on my knee. "To answer your earlier question, we're having twins, a boy and a girl. We wanted to name our son Ronan Paul after both of our fathers, and our daughter Chelsea Marie because we like that name."

"Oh, those are very fitting names." Claire smiled, but seemed sad. "John and Adam are both in Stowryn on business, so now I'm home alone."

"I'm sorry to hear that. Did they say when they'll be back?" I asked.

She shook her head. "No, it's alright. I'm used to it by now. Oh, I hope you don't mind. I grabbed a few pictures from your photo album before they put your stuff away for evidence of your disappearance. I thought you might want to have these to show the children when they're older," she said, grabbing a plastic bag filled with pictures and handing it to me.

"Oh, thank you!" I exclaimed, hugging her as she kissed my cheek.

"It's no problem, dear."

"Claire, have you been seeing anything odd wash up on shore lately?" I asked, turning to her as I set the pictures down. "Do you know what a Syren is?"

"I've heard stories. They take the form of the ones you love and then murder you. They were created by Sedna, right? I thought they were all destroyed." She paused. "They weren't destroyed, were they?"

"No," Delmare said. "The original Syrens are all dead, but their children live on. They killed my father and poisoned Anna. We aren't sure what their agenda is, but plan to put a stop to their tyranny."

"Oh, dear." Claire gasped, but she wasn't looking at us. "Adam, you're home early."

As I turned, I felt my heart stop. Adam stood before us, only it wasn't Adam. It was a Syren. Silently, I went to stand, but Delmare pulled me down, keeping me behind him so he could keep me safe.

"Hello, my king," the Syren greeted, his voice a mix of Adam's and a scratchy gargle. He cocked his

364

head to look at me. "My, my, how time flies. You are already having children? You royals work fast."

"Why are you here?" Delmare asked, standing with so much force that the chair fell, falling to the floor with a load *thwack*. "What do you want?"

I felt a hand on my shoulder. I turned and saw Claire, who silently motioned toward the other room. The Syren was focused on Delmare. His mother had told me he could hold his own, but what if he got hurt? Not knowing what else to do, we quietly backed away from the pair, hoping they would be distracted enough that we could hide in the other room. As we shut the door of the bedroom and Claire locked it, a crash sounded as something broke.

"What are we going to do?" I whispered, turning to Claire who sat at the edge of the bed before patting the space beside her.

"John should be home in twenty minutes. As long as Delmare can hold him off that long, we'll be fine."

"How do you know?" I asked as she wrapped her arms around me as if to comfort me, but it didn't help.

"He always comes home around this time, but just in case, I know a thing or two about fighting." She paused before grabbing a case out from under the bed and setting it on top of the covers. I watched as she unbuckled the case to reveal a shotgun. Quietly, I watched her load it before cocking the gun, motioning for me to stay here, but I wasn't about to let her go out there by herself. She swung the door open, and we cautiously walked around the corner to see Delmare and the creature sprawled on the floor, kicking and clawing at each other. The creature above him was now gray and bald and had claws for hands, no longer taking Adam's form.

"Get out of my house!" Claire screamed, pulling the trigger. The bullet went through the creature's shoulder and it looked up.

I watched as it stood, forgetting all about Delmare. It began to walk toward us as Claire cocked the gun again, shooting again and again and again. Each time, the shells hit their target, but didn't weaken it. I slowly backed away, tugging on Claire to follow me as the creature smiled. In one fell swoop, he lunged forward and stabbed her in the chest with his own claws. Not caring to watch as her body crumbled to the floor, the monster turned its sights on me.

Without a second thought, I turned, running out the front door and making a dash down the driveway, but I stopped short when I heard the gurgled scream and a thud. My heart beating against my chest, I turned around, hoping it hadn't been Delmare screaming. I stood there, frozen, as the front door flew open and a figure covered in black blood staggered toward me. His eyes were filled with worry as I ran toward him, not caring that I would be covered in that monster's blood. I hugged Delmare, so relieved that he was safe. In horror, I realized that Claire was still inside. I ran through the front door and fell to the ground beside Claire, her crumpled body lying in her own blood. As I took her hand, the back door flew open, making us tense up.

"Mom!? What happened!" John exclaimed, running over to us and falling to his knees. His hands shook as he watched his mother gasp for life. "Mom?"

He caressed his mother's cheek and she opened her eyes. Her breathing was shaky as she grabbed his arm, reaching up to ruffle his hair. She smiled softly before turning to us.

"Is it dead?" she asked, her voice barely above a whisper. We nodded before she turned back to her son, who was absolutely distraught. "Honey, I love you so much."

"No, don't say your goodbyes! You're going to be just fine. We—We just have to—" A sob escaped him before he could finish.

I knelt down beside him, wrapping my arms around him as Claire's arm dropped, and her chest stopped rising.

It only took him a second before he realized she was gone, and then his walls crumbled. He hugged his mother's lifeless body to him, begging her over and over to not leave him.

"John," I mumbled, cautiously placing my hand on his shoulder as he gently set her down. "I'm so, so sorry."

"You should be!" The force in his tone shocked me, making me stand and back away as he turned to me, a fire in his eyes. "Why are you here? Did you lead that thing here? Why would you do that? She was going to meet Asherah tomorrow. She was going to attend our wedding and meet our children if we had any and I—" He paused, looking away as his anger was turned to sadness. "I think you should leave."

"John," I said, taking a step toward him, Delmare following.

"Just go, please."

"Anna." It was Delmare this time, his voice calm and collected as I turned to look back at him.

"No, I won't leave!" I exclaimed, shaking Delmare's hand off me as I knelt beside John. "Claire was my friend, practically a mother to me, and I won't leave him here alone. I'm sorry this happened, but your mother put up a fight." I paused, knowing I couldn't say anything to help the pain he was going through. I wrapped my arms around him as my emotions overcame me. After a minute of hugging, he finally let his guard down, hugging me back as we cried over the loss of our loved one.

"We'll give her a proper burial," Delmare said, placing his hand on John's shoulder as he looked up. "Grab your mother and I'll take care of the Syren. Anna, go with John."

"What are you going to do?" I asked, looking at Delmare as he stood, helping me up as John cradled his mother in his arms.

"I'm going to get rid of the evidence."

"Delmare, be careful," I called after him, grabbing the bag of pictures off the floor, barely disturbed by the ruckus it had just endured, before I followed John outside as the house began smoking and the home was engulfed in flames.

I felt Delmare's presence then as we walked together into the water, none of us looking back, grief overtaking us. All I knew then was that we would get rid of those monstrous creatures and they would harm no one ever again. I just hoped in doing so, no one else would die because I wasn't sure how much heartache I could take.

 Once our bodies were submerged in the warm Atlantic Ocean, we made our way to the Indian Ocean to bury a friend, a wife, and a mother.

TWENTY-NINE

The swim to the Stowryn kingdom was quiet, and by the time we made it to the Saltheir homestead, hours had gone by. It was a quaint home covered in vibrant coral, and the door looked as if it were made of a ship's hull. We followed John inside, Delmare's hand entwined with mine as John explained what happened on shore. We watched silently as Adam grieved for his wife's death, shock being replaced with an overwhelming sadness. Within minutes, the men went into action, all three of them setting up the pyre as I sat next to Claire's body.

My lip quivered, my mind on the many moments I had spent with the woman now lying beside me. I missed her, and I wanted her here. I wanted to show her the kingdoms, to introduce her to my babies once they were born. I wanted her to meet the woman her son was in love with and watch them get married. Why had it attacked her? Why couldn't it have been me?

I wondered if she was happy in heaven or wherever she had gone. Would she be able to meet my parents? Maybe she and my mom could catch up. Looking down, I felt Ronan and Chelsea kick my stomach, although I wasn't sure which of them it was. Closing my eyes, I rubbed my stomach and tried to smile, but a sob escaped instead.

God, I was such a mess. Why was my life so up and down? It was just one thing after another. I just wanted a day that had no events whatsoever, where I could spend the day relaxing. But I didn't think I would get that until our Syren problem was solved and I knew stress wasn't good for the babies.

Suddenly, the water felt warm around me. I was shocked as a white glow shone along Claire's wounds. Within seconds, her wounds were healed and I stared in disbelief as her chest rose and fell before me. *Oh my God, this can't be happening.*

"Delmare!"

"What is it, Annie?" Delmare called as I looked over at him. "What's wrong? You look like you just saw a ghost."

"Delmare, she's breathing!" I exclaimed, checking her pulse. I realized I wasn't seeing things when I felt her steady pulse against my fingers. "Get over here! We have to take her to a doctor. How is this possible?"

"What's going on?" Adam called as the men came toward me and I shifted Claire's head to rest on my legs.

"She's alive! I don't know how this is possible, but she is! We need to take her to a doctor. Isn't there a doctor at Avisa's castle? Let's take her there."

I couldn't keep the excitement from overwhelming me as Delmare's confusion was replaced with understanding. "There's only one being I know who can bring someone back from the dead, and that's Kyanen."

"Who's Kyanen?"

"He's the God of Life, the brother of Keilani. I haven't met him personally because he lives in the Otherworld," Delmare explained as Daniel took his wife in his arms, kissing her softly on her forehead.

"Let's go," I said motioning for them to follow me as I swam in the castle's direction, determined to save Claire even if I had to barge into the castle unannounced.

***

The sound of the shower running pulled me out of my dreamless sleep. I wasn't sure when I had fallen asleep, and a part of me wasn't sure where I was. Sitting up in bed, I looked around the room, suddenly remembering that we were staying in Avisa's palace until Claire got better. The doctor had said she was in some kind of coma, but her wounds had healed completely, as if she hadn't been hurt at all.

Shuffling out of bed, I grabbed some clothes that Avisa had let me borrow and padded into the bathroom, plopping the clothes down on the toilet just as Delmare stepped into the tub that was filled with warm liquid.

"Good morning." He smiled. "How are you feeling?"

I shrugged. "I'm okay. Can I join you?" I asked, tugging off Delmare's shirt before taking a step toward the tub where Delmare now lounged.

"There's no need to ask." He smiled, grabbing my hand to help me in. I eased down, resting my back against his chest as the warm liquid relaxed my muscles.

Closing my eyes, Delmare held me close, kissing the back of my head as we sat in in silence. I knew he could tell I was worried, but I didn't want to worry him because I knew we had a lot on our plates. But a part of me knew he could easily just read my mind to get the answers he sought anyway.

Sighing, I opened my eyes, craning my neck to look behind me. "I'm worried about everyone. About those Syren creatures. They've attacked our citizens and what's worse is we now know they can go on land. What's stopping them from attacking other humans? We need to come up with a plan to get rid of them. Ondina is missing, and Claire is now in a coma. I know I need to stop worrying and stressing out because it's not good for the babies, but I can't help it." I paused. "It's just one thing after another. Are we ever going to have a day of peace?"

"I'm not sure, babe." Delmare sighed, rubbing my shoulders as if trying to comfort me. "We can't do everything all at once. We have to do one thing at a time, and I believe that once the Syrens are gone, our world can have peace again. I know it's hard not to worry but, can you try? Not just for me, but for the children. I plan to discuss what can be done tomorrow."

"I'll try." I nodded as Delmare grabbed the soap and lathered it on my back, massaging the knots that I hadn't known were there.

With a sigh of relief, I let him clean my body before I dunked under the water and worked on him, even though he insisted he wash his own face, because the last time I'd done it, I'd gotten soap in his eyes. After our bath, I threw a towel at him, giggling when he threw it back at me. As I pulled the maternity pants on, I tried not to watch Delmare as he got dressed himself. With my hair still damp, I pulled the shirt on over my prominent belly and wondered if it would be okay if I just wore sandals today.

"What do you want to do today?" Delmare asked as he pulled his shirt on, his eyes a vibrant purple.

"I want to stay in bed with you all day," I replied, grinning up at him.

He chuckled knowingly. "That sounds tempting. I do have to speak with my cousin about the recent Syren attacks. Alana said she wanted to speak with you about something as well. Don't we have our baby shower in a few days?"

I nodded. "Let me know what you come up with. I would like to be there when you talk to all the kingdoms."

"Of course. A king is nothing without his queen by his side." He smiled, kissing me on my cheek as he led me out the door and into the unfamiliar castle.

***

Alana was in the library when I finally went to meet her. She was huddled in the corner, stretched out on a blanket, and seemed to be absorbed in the book she was reading. She giggled and turned the page as I watched her devour the written words.

"Um, Alana?" I asked, making her jump. "Oh, I'm sorry. I didn't mean to scare you."

"It's okay," she said, marking the spot in her book before standing and grabbing my hand, "I'm glad you're here. I wanted to show you something. Come on."

"What? Where are we going?"

"You'll see!" she said excitedly, pulling me out of the library, down the halls, and out into the open sea. "You've always wanted to visit Australia, right?"

"Um, yes. I don't understand what that has to do with anything."

"You'll see, Anna!" She grinned, swimming gracefully as she pulled me along, and in minutes, the sandy seafloor rose as we swam toward the surface.

I wasn't sure where we were when we walked onto the shore. The sun was brutal, but the sight of two familiar faces was the biggest shock. Delmare and Avisa stood in the sand a few feet away, smiles filling half of their faces as we walked further onto shore.

"I don't understand."

"This is your wedding present!" Alana exclaimed. "Mom thought it would be better than getting you something you wouldn't use."

"I thought you said you weren't allowed on land," I said, looking at Alana as excitement radiated off of her.

"Not without a guide of course," Avisa piped in. "We can only stay near the coast, though, but I know you've been worried, so I think it would be best if you spend time not worrying with your husband. Anna Stormborn, welcome to Australia."

"I don't know what to say," I stammered, looking over at Delmare, who smiled calmly at me.

"I hope you enjoy yourselves," Avisa called before wrapping her arm around her daughter and walking down the beach, leaving Delmare and I alone.

"What do you want to do now?" he asked as I walked up to him, kissing him and wrapped my arms around him, not knowing what to say as the joy overtook me.

"I want to spend the rest of the afternoon with you, having a peaceful day with the man that I love." I grinned as he nodded, entwining his hand in mine and we began walking down the coast.

"I think I can handle that."

And as we walked, I was glad we could be ourselves in a country we had never visited before, with no expectations other than spending the day in peace. With the sound of the waves crashing onto shore and the sun high in the sky, I wished every day could be like this, but I knew peace like this could only last so long. I felt a storm brewing, one that no one could prepare for.

THIRTY

The news we received the morning of the baby shower overwhelmed me. Thankfully, it wasn't bad news when I forced Delmare to get out of bed and run with me to the medical wing where Claire had spent the last three days. When we arrived, Claire was upright in bed, flowers sitting on her bedside table, and her husband and son standing beside her.

"Hi, dear."

I couldn't control myself as I ran toward her, pulling her into a tight hug as I cried. "I'm so happy you're alright!"

She laughed, pulling away from me before handing me a box of tissues, which I gladly took. "I'm better than alright." She paused. "Don't you have a baby shower this afternoon?"

"Yes." I nodded, taking a seat in the armchair near her bed, as I wiped the tears from my eyes and looking over at her expectantly. "What did the doctor say?"

"Well, they have to run a few tests, but I should be cleared to go home." She smiled. "I may not make it to your baby shower, but I would like to visit sometime soon."

"Of course." I grinned, looking back at Delmare who smiled. "We'd love to have you and your family come visit."

"Great." Claire smiled before grabbing Adam's hand. "Now, run along before you miss your party!"

With a nod, I stood, grabbing Delmare's hand as we made our way out of the castle doors and toward our home in Arcania.

***

By the time we arrived home, I was exhausted; it had taken us nearly three hours to get there. As soon as we entered the castle, we were overwhelmed with pink, blue, and purple balloons and streamers lining the castle's walls. I let go of Delmare's arm and made my way through the halls and toward our room, hoping I could get some sleep before the guests arrived.

Shutting our bedroom door behind me, I kicked my shoes off, practically ripping my clothes off before I crawled into bed. Just as I was about to close my eyes to fall asleep, our door opened again as Delmare walked into the room, before he crawled in beside me. Rolling onto my back, I couldn't help but run my fingers through his hair, smiling to myself as he fell swiftly asleep. Once he did, the exhaustion overtook me, pulling me into my dreamscape.

The sound of the waves crashing onto the shore pulled me along as I walked barefoot across the white powdery sand of the beach. The world seemed so real to me, as if I wasn't dreaming at all. I continued towards the approaching waves, breathing in the salty air, enjoying the lull of the sea as I walked. When my toes finally touched the water, the world around me seemed to slow as someone rose from the water before me. I stared in disbelief as the blue-skinned woman rose above the water, the waves brushing against her toes while her midnight blue hair floated around her as if she was still underwater. Her eyes shone a bright silver when she smiled at me, the waves clinging to her skin, barely covering her naked body. I looked away, a blush creeping across my skin, and I heard the mysterious woman laugh. She seemed so familiar, as if I had seen her before.

"There is no need to be embarrassed, Anna," she said, her voice sounding so beautiful I couldn't help but gasp. I turned to look at her, wondering if I was imagining things. "My, I see what my great-grandson sees in you."

"How do you—" I paused, taking a step toward her before thinking better of it, and jumping back. "You're Keilani, Delmare's great-grandmother, right? Why am I here? Where am I?"

"You're in Achera, my daughter. You were here before, with your mother. I didn't want to visit you then, as I wasn't sure if you were ready," she explained, taking a step toward me as the waves still danced slowly around her, "You are here because I want to warn you about a danger that should have been taken care of a long time ago."

"Do you mean the Syrens?"

"There are far worse dangers than those creatures, and far more secrets my people have yet to uncover. You see, Anna, I had two daughters." She smiled, though it was somewhat sad as she looked off into the distance. "Sedna looked like me, but unlike her siblings, she did not possess a tail, and because of this, she was taunted by her younger sister, Avisa. Although, I didn't know my youngest daughter was so full of hate until the War, and by then, she was too far gone."

"What happened?" I asked as she looked over at me.

"I killed her," she said simply, a hint of sadness in her tone as her eyes changed to a shade of blue. She had the same ability Delmare had. "She was a threat to the safety of the world I had created. My children believed she was the last of her line, but they are wrong."

"Wait, Avisa had a child?" I asked, bewildered.

She nodded. "Find my granddaughter, or else I fear more harm will come to our family and the Symari."

With that last sentence, the waves engulfed her, leaving me alone as the waves pulled me under, forcing me awake. Clawing at the bedsheets as I awoke, drenched in sweat, I screamed.

"Hey, hey, what's wrong?" Delmare asked, suddenly awake beside me, his face contorted in worry as he tried to calm me.

"It was just a dream," I mumbled. "I was on the beach, talking to your great-grandmother, Keilani."

"You talked to Keilani in your dream?" he asked, sitting up in bed.

"Yes, and she was talking about the War and about Sedna and Avisa. She said that we—" I paused, trying to think. "She said that Avisa had a child, a daughter, and that we need to find her. She says the ocean and its people are in danger, and if we don't find her, more death will follow."

He shot out of bed, getting dressed quickly as a determined look played across his features "The party will have to wait, Anna. If what you say is true, there is something much bigger and more pressing going on here. Here, get dressed. We're going to speak to my cousins about what we can do to find our long-lost aunt."

"What if she's as dangerous as Avisa was?" I asked as I got dressed.

"Let's hope not. I want our children to grow up in a world of peace, not one of fear," he said, his voice serious as he took my hand and walked with me out of our bedroom, making our way toward the loudest room in the palace.

***

I sat at one of the large tables at the front of the entertainment room, next to a large cake that would reveal to our family what we were having. We had told them a few days ago that we were having twins, but had yet to tell them about the genders. Sedna seemed to enjoy party planning, and from what I could tell, was the complete opposite of her girlfriend, Emilia.

"Queen Anna, how are you enjoying married life?" Emilia asked as she came up to me.

"I'm enjoying it very much, and please, you don't have to call me by my title. Anna is just fine." I smiled. "How are things with you and Sedna?"

"Things are going great! Apart from the fact that my parents hate the idea of us being together, but I am glad your family has welcomed me with open arms. I'm also glad Delmare didn't marry me after all. No offense, your grace, but I believe we would have been miserable together."

"I'm sorry your family isn't as accepting as ours, but I think I can consider you a member of this family, if you would like to be. I know you and Sedna are happy together, and I just want you both to be happy. There is no offense taken. I am *also* glad you and Delmare didn't marry, then I wouldn't have met the greatest man on earth."

"What are you two talking about?" Delmare asked as he came toward us, two plates in his hands that were overflowing with food.

"Oh, nothing you need to worry about." I grinned, taking the plate from his outstretched hand, and set it down in front of me as Delmare sat down beside me.

"Ah, I see." He cocked an eyebrow at me as he popped a cherry into his mouth. "It's nice to see you again, Emilia. Have you seen my sister?"

"Oh, I think she's around here somewhere."

"When you find her, let her know I have an announcement before we start with the celebrations."

"Of course." She nodded, curtseying quickly before disappearing into the crowd.

"What are we going to do about your cousin and the Syrens?" I asked, not touching my food. "Ondina is still missing."

"We will send a party out to find them both. I plan to go with them."

"What? No, Delmare, it's too dangerous. You don't even know how many of those things exist!"

"Anna," he said, his tone serious. "There is a threat to this kingdom. They have already killed my father. I will not let our children live in a world with those creatures, and I cannot sit idly by when I know they're still out there. You will stay here with the children, where it's safe."

I shook my head. "No."

"Anna, this is not up for discussion."

Biting my lip, I looked away. "When are you planning to leave?"

"Two weeks," he said. "I'm not sure how long I'll be gone. We will send scouts out and all the able-bodied men will go with us. We will defeat the Syrens, and find Ondina and my cousin before any more harm can befall the kingdoms."

"And what will you do if you find your cousin and *she's* behind the Syren attacks?"

"We will imprison her, and she will stand before us to receive judgment for her crimes."

"But what happens if—" I paused, unable to say the words, but I noticed the sad blue color spread across his irises as he read my mind.

"If, somehow, I find my death, my mother will help raise our children," he said, touching my cheek as I touched his.

"Try not to die, okay?"

"Okay," he said, kissing my forehead.

With a shaky sigh, everyone stood, placing their fists on their hearts and bowed low, a signal I knew meant they would fight by our side in the coming war. And I only hoped there would be no bloodshed and that our world could find peace again. It seemed forever ago that I had started my new life as a marine biologist, and now I was a queen to a kingdom that was threatened. I missed Ondina and wondered where she was. If she had known the Syrens were so dangerous, why had she disappeared, or did she have an agenda greater than what we knew? After all, she said her mother was killed by one, so maybe she wanted to avenge her death.

I felt a hand lightly graze my wrist, pulling me from my thoughts. Delmare's eyes swirled, changing colors so many times I couldn't comprehend what it meant.

"Anna, are you okay?"

"Yeah, um, I'm fine." I smiled, but I knew he could tell I was lying.

No, I'm not okay, I wanted to say.

Delmare would leave in two weeks and he didn't know how long he would be gone. Even if it took him two weeks to find Ondina, his cousin, and kill all the Syrens, it would take him two weeks to come back. He would be gone for a month—minimum—and he would miss the birth of his children. I wanted him there. I wanted him to see our children coming into the world, and to help me through the pain I would be feeling. I wanted my mom and dad. I wished my life differed from the reality, but it didn't, and I needed to come to terms with it.

"I love you," I whispered, looking over at him as everyone waited for us to cut the cake.

I watched him smile, a knowing look on his face as if he had just read my mind. "I will love you forever. And I will try to be there for their birth," he promised, but a part of me knew he probably wouldn't make it in time.

THIRTY-ONE

Delmare strapped his sword across his waist, his face focused on the task at hand, but I could tell he was sad he had to leave. I had been worrying about this day ever since he told me he was leaving two weeks ago at the baby shower, and now the day had finally arrived. With a sigh, I crawled out of bed, my gigantic belly making me feel as if I was a whale, rather than a pregnant mother. With my bare feet padding against the crystal flooring, I watched him turn around, staring at me, trying to smile, but failing as the saddened look never left his face.

"Delmare, don't feel bad," I said, as I wrapped my arms around him, my belly keeping me from accomplishing it entirely. "You have to do this. Just focus on staying alive, okay? I don't think I can handle raising our children alone."

"You won't be alone," he replied, his jaw clenched at the mention of the possibility of this being the last time we see each other.

"That's not what I meant," I whispered. "Ronan and Chelsea deserve to know their father."

He closed his eyes and nodded, "That reminds me." He paused, walking over to rummage through a drawer before handing me a heavy envelope. "If I don't make it, I want you to read this to them. I want them to know me, and know that I—" His voice broke as I took the envelope from him, cupping my hand to his cheek as he stared down at me.

"I will. They will know you." My eyes watered and my breathing shook before I hugged him again, desperately wanting him to stay, but knowing he had to leave for the good of everyone we served and cared for. "They will know that you love them."

He hugged me back, holding me close as a sob escaped both our lips. I didn't want him to leave sad, but I couldn't keep my emotions from overwhelming me. Kissing him on his cheek, I rested my forehead against his, running my fingers through his hair as I tried to comfort him, tried to make him forget he would leave me to defend the ocean.

"I love you, Delmare Stormborn," I whispered, kissing him as he grabbed my waist, drawing circles across my skin underneath his T-shirt that I had insisted on wearing.

He kissed me back, needy as he kissed along my jaw and down my neck, making me forget why we were saying goodbye. He stopped to catch his breath. His eyes were a mix of blue and purple, but the sadness written on his face was replaced with a cocky grin.

"Don't go falling in love with anyone else, Mrs. Stormborn." He grinned, trying to change the mood.

I couldn't help but laugh. "I'll try not to, Mr. Stormborn." I grinned as he leaned into me, placing another kiss against my lips just as someone knocked on our door.

"I have to go." He sighed, sounding defeated as he pulled away, but I stopped him, grabbing his hand and gently placing it on my stomach as the children kicked against his palm.

He leaned down, exposing the skin of my belly and kissing it softly, whispering to them before looking up at me, his eyes brimming with tears as he kissed me again. Turning away, Delmare walked out the door, looking back once before shutting the door behind him. I fell to my knees, my emotions overwhelming me as someone ran into the room, wrapping their arms around me, but to my disappointment, it wasn't the Symari I wanted.

"Come on, Anna," Consuela cooed, helping me up and into bed as my sobs continued. "Let's get you to bed."

"I'm sorry I'm a mess," I mumbled, hiccupping as my salty tears stained the pillow.

"It's okay," she said, pulling the covers over me. "I know how you feel. My fiancé is also going with the king. We'll get through this together, alright?"

I nodded, wiping my face as she gave me a soft smile. "Thank you, Connie."

"You're welcome, Annie." She smiled, then walked toward the door as sleep overtook me.

***

The familiar sound of waves filled my ears as I blinked back the brightness of the sun. The sand burned against my feet as I ran, being chased by a being I did not recognize, but knew was dangerous. Suddenly, I fell to the sandy floor and I felt something wet between my legs. Looking down, I gasped as I saw the red blood gush from where I knew my unborn children were housed. I heard the creature laugh, the sound a mix of Delmare's and something else entirely, as I looked up, meeting Delmare's face. His eyes were consumed in a black haze. It was a Syren, and it was here to kill me. And before it could pounce to finish me off, I awoke, screaming at the top of my lungs as the effects of the dream overtook me.

Guards ran in, searching the room for any dangers as they assessed my condition. "Are you alright, my queen?"

"I—" I paused, taking a deep breath as I sat up in bed. "I'm fine, it was just a nightmare."

"Would you like us to get the doctor or the queen mother?" One of them asked as I stood, shaking my head.

"No, don't wake them. I just need some water," I replied.

They nodded, one of them motioning for me to go ahead as he intended to escort me to the kitchen.

Once there, I filled a glass, guzzling the glass in seconds before filling it up again. As I was placing the cup in the sink to clean it, I accidentally dropped the glass, which shattered into hundreds of pieces at my feet. Cursing under my breath, I went to lean down to pick up the pieces, but someone rested a hand on my shoulder, stopping me from going any further.

"It's okay, Anna. I got it," Theodosia whispered, helping me not to step on the broken glass. "Go back to bed, dear. You're going to need the sleep."

With a shaky breath, I followed the guard out of the kitchen, walking in a quiet haze as he led me back to my room. He bowed to me before leaving me in the room alone. Suddenly the door opened as someone padded into the room.

"Hi, Anna," Sedna whispered. "I was wondering if I could stay in here with you tonight, or if you wanted my company."

I nodded, unable to speak as I crawled back into bed. She crawled onto the other side. My mind was everywhere, swirling with hundreds of questions as I tried to fall back asleep, but couldn't. I couldn't help but worry about Delmare. What would happen if he found his aunt, and she was behind the attacks, or if Ondina was dead? What would happen if Delmare came back, but he, too, was dead? Would I be able to raise our children with Theodosia and Sedna's help? What if something were wrong?

"Don't worry, Anna," Sedna whispered beside me. "Delmare is an exceptional fighter. He will come back alive. My niece and nephew will meet their father and you *both* will raise them together."

I sighed, knowing she'd know what I was thinking as I pulled the covers closer to me. "I know. I'm just scared."

"I am too," she said, her voice echoing in the room's darkness as I fell back to sleep.

Happily, no nightmares plagued my dreams, but I hoped my nightmares would stay in my dreams and not fill my reality. I could only hope my fears didn't come true and Delmare would come home, alive, and our world could be at peace again.

THIRTY-TWO

The game of Connect Four Sedna was trying to distract me with wasn't helping, much to her disappointment. This was the seventh game she had played with me that day, hoping I would stop worrying. Unfortunately, it only made me worry more. It had been three weeks since Delmare had left, and I had been on bed rest since then, my back pain getting worse as I got nearer and nearer to my due date. Claire had written to me a week ago, wanting to come visit, and would arrive today. I was glad she wanted to visit, but I felt like I was being watched, as if I would break down any moment.

"Anna, are you listening?"

"What?" I asked, looking up as Sedna placed her final token, making four in a row.

"I was asking if you were hungry."

"Oh, I'm not hungry," I replied, flipping the bottom lever to make all the pieces fall to the table.

"Are you sure?" she asked, an eyebrow raised as she threw the red and yellow pieces back into the box just as my stomach growled, betraying me.

"I just—" I paused, looking away, feeling a little guilty that I had lied. "I don't feel like eating."

Sedna sighed, shaking her head at me as she put the game back into its cubby. "Well, you're going to have to eat something. You can't just *not* eat because you don't feel like it."

"I know," I replied just as the door opened and Theodosia strode in, her violet-colored hair up in perfect braids, unlike my hair, which I knew was a total mess.

I had noticed that the children hadn't been as active as they had been in weeks prior, and I wondered if it was because we were so close to the due date. I was due in a week, and not only was I stressed about giving birth, I was also worrying about how Delmare was and if he was okay. I haven't heard from him since he left, and I did not know if he was alive. As if Theodosia could read my thoughts, she came over to me, wrapping her arms around me tight and whispering soothing words into my ear.

"How about we have brunch in the dining room?" Theodosia suggested with a smile.

"That sounds great!" Sedna smiled as she turned to me. "That sounds great, doesn't it, Anna?"

"Mmm," I hummed, as my stomach growled again, urging me to get out of bed and eat. "It sounds fine. Are you sure I should get up and everything?"

"Of course! A walk will do you good," Theodosia replied, helping me out of bed so I could stand after weeks of not doing anything.

Linking their arms in mine, we slowly made our way toward the dining room. What I expected when we opened the doors to the dining room was a delicious breakfast. What I didn't expect was to see Claire eating quietly at the table.

"Claire!" I exclaimed, rushing over to her to give her a quick hug.

"Hi, dear. How are you?"

"I'm okay," I breathed, taking a seat next to her as Sedna and Theodosia sat across from us.

"George says he's planning to come by later today to check on the condition of the twins," Theodosia said, stabbing something that looked suspiciously like seaweed and placed it onto her plate. "Are you still having back pain?"

I nodded, slapping a few pancakes onto my plate. "Yeah, my feet have been killing me and I've noticed the children aren't as active as they were before. I've also been getting some pelvic pain, but it doesn't last very long. I thought it was because I slept wrong."

I watched as Theodosia and Claire shared a knowing look before looking over at me. Claire touched my arm. "How long have these symptoms been going on?"

I shrugged, swallowing the piece of pancake. "Just a few days. Why? Is there something wrong?"

"No, honey, nothing's wrong. It's just that usually cramping is a sign of labor."

"What? But I have a week. I can't have them early, can I?" I felt the panic squeeze my heart as Claire tried to calm me down.

"Everything's going to be fine. Don't stress yourself out," Sedna chipped in. She took a bite of a strawberry before feeding Emilia another one.

I hadn't noticed Emilia had arrived until just now. Sighing, I nodded. "Okay, I'll try to remain calm. It's hard because I'm worried about giving birth, about the state of our kingdoms, and I'm also scared something's happened to Delmare. I know I need to be calm and collected and not worry about anything, but I have a responsibility. I can't just lay in bed all day. I can't—"

Suddenly I felt liquid pool in my chair as I sat there, immediately making me stop talking mid-rant. I looked down at my lap. "I think I just peed myself."

Standing up, I expected the distinct smell of urine, but it didn't smell like it at all. Everyone stood around me, worried glances filling their faces as realization took hold long. I couldn't go into labor now! I still had a week left!

"We have to get you to the medical wing now!" Theodosia exclaimed as she ran around the table, completely forgetting about her breakfast and entirely focused on me.

Within seconds, they were rushing me to the other side of the palace, our food left on the table, and the trail of liquid behind us. They pushed open the doors, Theodosia screaming at the top of her lungs for George to help me. Claire squeezed my hand as she and Sedna helped me onto the bed. George ran over, strapping the stirrups onto the bed I was lying on. Just as he strapped them on, a wave of pain ran along my pelvis and back, making me gasp. Sedna handed Claire another pillow as she whispered something I couldn't hear through the pain of my contractions. This went on for a few seconds, the pain disappearing, but then coming back just as quickly.

"This sucks," I moaned, laying against the pillows, trying not to think about the pain or the fact that Delmare wasn't here with me.

"I know it sucks, but you're going to be just fine." Theodosia smiled, cupping my cheek in her hand. "We'll be with you through it all. You won't have to do this alone."

I nodded, clenching my teeth as another contraction ran through my body. I thought they were supposed to be every three minutes, but they were happening every three seconds. Maybe I couldn't tell time while the pain went through me, but the calm and collected faces of the surrounding woman reassured me that this was normal. I would be fine, and the children would be fine. I sighed, my breathing shaky as I closed my eyes, taking a small sip of the water from the glass Sedna help.

"Thank you, all of you, for being here," I whispered, my voice hoarse.

"Of course, dear," Claire smiled beside me, running her hands through my hair as if to soothe me. "Just try to relax."

I nodded, closing my eyes as I leaned my head on my pillow. Sedna and Emilia helped George get everything he needed. I took in slow breaths, each contraction getting closer and closer until I was having one every minute. Every once in a while, George would check how far I had dilated. I wouldn't be able to give birth until I was at ten centimeters, which was honestly a little terrifying. I would be giving birth to two watermelon-sized children.

"Alright, Anna, are you ready?" George asked, a confident grin on his face as I set my feet securely on each stirrup.

"No," I whispered, shaking my head, desperately wishing he would just cut me open and I can give birth that way.

"Well, you should be, because I'm going to need you to push now, for ten seconds and then you can rest, and we'll try again, alright?" he said.
"Now, Mrs. Saltheir, I want you to hold her hand now and Anna, give me a great big push."

Claire did as he asked, squeezing my hand as I held on to it for dear life, pushing and wishing for this to be over as quickly as it had started. Minutes passed, and I felt one of them leave my body, the pain escaping me as I heard the most beautiful sound on Earth as they cried. I didn't have time to look up as George handed them over to another servant, who cut the umbilical cord and washed them clean.

"What is it?" I asked, breathless.

"You had a beautiful baby boy. Now, stay with me Anna. You still have a daughter to deliver." George beamed as I laughed.

I wanted nothing more than to hold them both, kissing every inch of their chubby little faces. Within minutes, Chelsea was born. The twins were both healthy, and I was a total mess. Emilia held Chelsea, a beaming smile on her face as she came over to me, placing her in my arms as Theodosia grabbed her grandson and smiled at me, a proud look written across her face.

"Can I hold him?" I asked, tears already falling freely down my face. Theodosia handed Ronan to me.

They were so beautiful. Their eyes were shut and their faces looked so serene, as if they loved where they were. That was, until someone burst through the door, an exasperated look in his eyes.

"I'm here!" a familiar voice called as he strode in.

I looked up, unsure if I was imagining things, but it was real. Delmare was home, he was home, and he was safe.

"Anna, are you alright?" he asked as tears fell from my face.

"Delmare come here," I said, partly mad that he hadn't been here for the twins' birth, but overjoyed that he was here now. "Do you want to meet our babies?"

"How am I supposed to hold them?" he asked, concern and joy written across his face as he stood next to me, kissing me several times before leaning his head against mine.

"Just mind his head," I whispered, successfully handing Ronan to Delmare, who cradled him. Sheer amazement was written across his features as he looked down. I watched silently as Ronan grabbed ahold of Delmare's finger, smiling as Chelsea cooed in my arms. This was the happiest day of my life.

"Anna, can I hold Chelsea?" Theodosia asked, a knowing look on her face as she came toward me. "I think you need to rest now."

I nodded, falling back into the pillows as my adrenaline left me. I watched as Delmare sat down in an armchair, holding his son silently, but looking around the room, his eyes meeting mine. He beamed before worry overtook his features.

I fell fast asleep, the events of the day consuming me. As I fell, I wondered if our world would finally be at peace, if Ondina and his aunt had been found, and what it would be like to raise our two beautiful children together. I was ready for this new chapter in my life, even if everything had happened quicker than I expected.

THIRTY-THREE

I awoke with a start. Beautiful white and pink lilies sat in a crystal vase on the bedside table, the sight of the beautiful flowers making me smile. Turning over on my side, I met Delmare's violet eyes as he grinned at me. Reaching over, I ruffled his hair, laughing as he swatted my hand away just as Ronan and Chelsea cried. It had only been a few days since giving birth to the twins, and during time had been exciting and exhausting. Every two hours I fed them, then they would fall back to sleep, and then at night, Delmare and I would bathe them. Theodosia helped, of course, as we did not know what we were doing.

"I got it, babe." Delmare smiled, springing from the bed as he escaped into the nursery.

With a sigh, I sat up, swinging my legs over the side of the bed before standing and following after him. Leaning against the door frame, I watched as

Delmare changed Ronan's diaper, throwing the old one into the bin before cradling him in his arms.

"Now, don't make so much noise or you'll wake up your sister," he cooed at him, grinning as Ronan smiled a toothless smile, his silver eyes stark against the black hair that had sprouted from his head.

I giggled at them both, shaking my head as I checked on Chelsea, picking her up and shushed her softly, kissing her sweetly on her little forehead as she calmed down. Her sea green eyes shined bright against her ginger red hair. "I think we got a pair of ornery twins, don't you?"

He laughed. "Yes, they are a little ornery. But I wonder where they got that from."

"Well, they didn't get it from me!" I grinned, walking over to the rocking chair so I could feed Chelsea.

Easing down, I pulled my bra off, helping Chelsea nurse. "And besides, we both know we're stubborn, so I wouldn't be surprised if one of them got that trait."

"True," Delmare commented, looking up from his son to look over at me.

"We still haven't talked about your trip," I said as Chelsea finished nursing. I stood, handing Chelsea and a spit rag to Delmare as he handed Ronan to me so I could feed him as well. "Did you solve our Syren problem? Did you find Ondina and your aunt?"

"Well, we found Ondina and my aunt. She's in the dungeon. But unfortunately, we weren't able to get rid of all the Syrens. Some of them escaped."

"Wait, if you found Ondina, why hasn't she come to see me? Is she okay?" I asked, patting Ronan on his back as he burped up his remaining milk before setting him back down in his crib.

"Well." He paused, walking over to me to set Chelsea back down. "Ondina *is* my cousin."

"What?"

"The only thing about her that was true was her name. Her mother wasn't killed by Syrens; she was killed by Keilani. She has been living under our roof for years and we had no idea who she really was!"

"I want to talk to her," I said firmly, meeting Delmare's gaze.

He shook his head. "No/ I know she's your friend, but she isn't who she says she is." He paused, grabbing hold of my hands. "She's dangerous."

"I'll be careful. You can come with me, but I'm sure she's secure in the dungeon. She can't hurt me," I reassured him, getting dressed in one of my many dresses and combing my hair with a brush before placing a crown on my head. "She will realize that she has not only committed treason, but she has jeopardized the safety of our people and my family. She will be judged to the full extent of the law, but I want to hear her say it. I want to meet the real Ondina."

Turning on my heel, I left the room just as Consuela passed me. "Can you watch the children for me? Delmare and I have something we must do."

"Of course, your Highness." She smiled, nodding her head to both of us as she walked into the nursery.

Without a second thought, I followed Delmare toward the dungeon. Our steps were sure and true as we descended the stairs that would lead us into the dark. The guards bowed to us as he approached, opening the doors for us as we walked inside. A single spotlight shone on a woman with aqua hair. Her clothes were torn, and she was covered in a silver substance I knew was her own blood. I watched as she looked up, grinning from ear to ear, but it wasn't a friendly grin. It was kind you might see on any villain. The normal bubbly attitude that had come off her in waves had been replaced with so much hatred, it threatened to choke me. I took a step toward her as she stood, chains clanking, echoing across the room. She sauntered toward the edge of her cell.

"Hello, *Queen Anna*. Isn't this a lovely surprise?" she asked, tilting her head as her eyes sparked with a fierce fire. She was nothing like the Ondina I knew.

"What happened to you?" I asked, feigning concern as I tried to play it like I didn't feel the pure evil radiating off of her skin. "What did those awful creatures do to you? Why are you here?"

"Oh, dear cousin, you didn't tell her?" she asked, ignoring my questions as she looked behind me. "Well, it would seem that my cover has been blown. You see, Anna, I am not who you think I am. My name is Ondina, yes, but my mother wasn't killed by Syrens. My mother, Queen Avisa, was killed by her bitch of a mother you call a goddess. She killed her because she knew she should rule over more than just the Southern kingdom. My mother was a force to be reckoned with." She paused before glaring at Delmare. "And your grandmother had no right to the Arcanian throne Keilani gave her. I suppose she was good for one thing, but I am a better Syren queen than she ever was. You can't keep me in here forever."

"What did you do?"

"Be specific, dear," she purred. "I've done a lot of things in my time."

"Did you order the Syren attack on my kingdom?" Delmare asked, running up to the cell before I could stop him.

Her grin told us she had, and I knew she was probably responsible for poisoning me as well. "Even better, I killed your father."

Within seconds, Delmare was yelling, banging on the cell. I grabbed his arm, pulling him back just as guards came in, surrounding us. "You will pay for this!"

She threw her head back and laughed, unbothered by Delmare's threats as he clenched and unclenched his fists. "Delmare, let's go."

"Yes, run back to your precious babies. It's too bad they didn't die when I poisoned you," she huffed, before looking up at the both of us. "But I suppose there are other means of ruining your lives."

I gasped, turning to run from the room, moving as fast as my legs could carry me toward the

425

nursery. Why had we left them alone with Consuela? What if she was behind the attacks as well? I couldn't believe Ondina was Delmare's cousin, that she had poisoned me, and that she had killed Ronan. Throwing open the nursery door, I was relieved to see Consuela rocking Chelsea to sleep, her soft humming filling the room as she looked up, concern filling her face.

"Anna, what's wrong?" She paused. "Did something happen?"

"Did you know?" I asked, walking over to Consuela, beckoning her to hand over my daughter. She stood, handing Chelsea over without a second thought.

"Know what? Anna, what has happened?"

"Ondina! She's Delmare's cousin, and she's been behind the Syren attacks. She killed King Ronan and poisoned me! Did you know who she was?"

"What? That's impossible. No, of course I didn't know. I would never have had her around you had I known."

"Apparently, she's Avisa's daughter, and she's in the dungeon."

"What? She's here? Maybe I could reason with her. We can change her mind and she can be happy again," Consuela offered.

"No." I shook my head. "She is evil, Consuela. There is no changing her mind. She will pay for her crimes against the kingdom and our world will finally be at peace."

"Are they okay?" Delmare asked, bursting through the nursery door.

"Yes, they're fine," I replied, nodding as he came toward me, anger and relief evident on his face as I set Chelsea back down in her crib.

"I swear, she will pay for everything she has done to our family," Delmare vowed, looking at me with a fierce look in his eye.

"She'll go through a fair trial. We can't just punish her for her crimes," I said thoughtfully, before turning to Consuela. "Thank you for your help, Consuela. You can go."

She nodded, curtsying swiftly before walking to the door, glancing behind her before shutting the door with a soft click. Just as she left, the sounds of shouting rang through the castle. As we peered into the hallway, chaos was unfolding around us, guards shouting and fighting as Ondina walked casually down the halls. She turned to us, a knowing look on her face, before she disappeared in a cloud of black smoke.

What just happened? Did Ondina just escape her prison? Suddenly, everything stopped as I looked back at Delmare. I knew then that I wanted my children to live in a world of peace, where they could rule with confidence and compassion, alongside a loving family. I didn't want revenge to consume them as it had Ondina, and I wished she would see the error of her ways. She wanted to bring harm to me and my family, and for that, I would never forgive her. She had successfully escaped our prison, but it wouldn't take long for us to find her and she would pay for her crimes.

"Anna, what do you think we should do?" Delmare asked, looking at me, determination on his face.

"I think that should be your decision, but I hope she rots wherever she ends up." I paused before looking back at Delmare. "I think I need to take a shower."

I knew we would rule with compassion and love, but as we did this, we would do everything in our power to protect the ocean we served, even if it meant we would have to conduct a trial against a member of our family for crimes she had committed. I no longer wanted our world to be filled with hurt, and I definitely didn't want Ondina to harm my family any longer. I was certain that when we found her, she would pay for everything she had done, even if she thought she was the new Syren queen. I was a real queen, and as Queen of Arcania, I would rule with my husband, till death do us part.

EPILOGUE

Ondina looked up into the darkness, sneering at the guards who unlocked her cell. The heavy chains bound her thin wrists. Weeks of forcing herself to not eat had made her body a thin frame, her skin clinging to the bones in her body. The men grabbed ahold of her, pulling her to her feet with such a force that a bone might have broken, though, she wasn't sure which nor did she care. She was being sent to her death after all.

Ondina didn't resist as the two men dragged her up the stairs to the main floor of the palace, down the long hallways she had spent years cleaning, and into the throne room. There, in the grand hall, nine members of the royal family stood, their heads held high as they stared at Ondina walking toward them. Suddenly, the guards stopped, halting her steps. She stumbled before they pushed her to the floor.

"Ondina Oceane, daughter of Queen Avisa and Kai Waters, how do you plead?" the Queen of

Arcania asked, her voice ringing loud in clear in the ancient mer-language she had spent the last year mastering while Ondina had been missing. Her skin glowed under the fire light, hinting at her condition. If you were paying attention, you could see the small baby bump that had already begun to form.

"Guilty," Ondina replied, grinning. "And I would do it again."

"Very well," Anna said, no sympathy in her tone as she stared at her former confidante.

Once she said this, a blue-skinned figure stood before Ondina. There was no mistaking who the Symari was. Everyone knew their creator and family, even Ondina. And before she could even begin to realize the grave mistakes she had made, her grandmother touched her forehead and a searing pain shot through her body, turning her body to ash. Ondina Oceane would no longer harm those of the sea, and the Syrens would no longer continue to wreak havoc on the world. But these enemies were just the beginning, for there was a greater danger our world is facing — humans and their waste that would soon turn the world into a wasteland.

ACKNOWLEDGMENTS

There is so much I wish to say or do to thank those who helped me along this journey. First, of course, I wish to thank my editor, Jessica, you are amazing, and I could not have finished this book without you. Next, I would like to thank all my fellow author friends who have given me advice along the way. Know that your friendship and advice is greatly appreciated. Thank you to my beta readers, who decided they wanted to start this journey with me and see this book to its end: you are awesome! Finally, to the one who is reading this book right now: thank you for taking the chance to read my book. I hope you enjoy reading Anna and Delmare's story just as much as I enjoyed writing it.

ABOUT THE AUTHOR

Mikayla Whitaker is a Fantasy and Romance author whose dream is to share the wonderful oceanic world she has grown so fond of. She is currently studying Marine Biology at Unity College in Maine and hopes to fulfill her lifelong dream to care for the world's oceans and the creatures who inhabit it. Mikayla lives in Missouri and hopes to someday live in a coastal town, living a peaceful existence.

CPSIA information can be obtained
at www.ICGtesting.com
Printed in the USA
LVHW010426090621
689683LV00016B/2024